DIVIDED LOYALTY

DIVIDED LOYALTY

ROBERTA GRIEVE

ISIS
LARGE PRINT
Oxford

First published in Great Britain 2013
by
Robert Hale Limited

Published in Large Print 2014 by ISIS Publishing Ltd.,
7 Centremead, Osney Mead, Oxford OX2 0ES
by arrangement with
Robert Hale Limited

CIP data is available for this title from the British Library

ISBN 978–0–7531–5388–8 (hb)
ISBN 978–0–7531–5389–5 (pb)

Printed and bound in Great Britain by
T. J. International Ltd., Padstow, Cornwall

CHAPTER
ONE

The hens clucked round Celia's feet as she shook the tablecloth free of crumbs. She watched them for a moment and was about to go indoors when she heard the sound of a motorcycle in the lane. She shaded her eyes against the glare from the sun as her heart began to beat a little faster. She knew of only one person who had a motorbike — her brother's friend, Flight Lieutenant Matthew Dangerfield.

But what was he doing at the farm? For a brief moment she wondered if something had happened to Edgar. No, she said to herself. That kind of news would merit an official notification. Still, she couldn't help being a bit apprehensive. The Battle of Britain had been over for more than a year, but her brother and his fellow airmen still took their lives in their hands every time they flew.

The motorcycle crested the hill and roared down the track into the farmyard. In a flurry of dirt, it roared to a stop, leaving a smell of exhaust in the air and a silence broken only by the sound of the hens clucking around the yard.

To Celia's relief she saw that the motorcycle carried a pillion passenger — her brother. Edgar rushed towards her, throwing his arms round her. "Great to be home, sis," he said, swinging her round.

"Ed, it's wonderful to see you."

Despite his being stationed only a few miles away she hadn't seen her brother for ages and she was surprised he'd come home. Usually he asked her to meet him in town. It saddened her that he avoided seeing their father. But he was here now. Perhaps he'd decided it was time to heal the rift between them. She hoped so.

"Just a flying visit, I'm afraid," he said. "Dad around?"

"He's gone to get the cows in for milking," Celia said. "What are you doing here?"

"We've been posted to Suffolk. Had to pop in and say cheerio before we left. But it's you I came to see, sis." He frowned. "Has he come round yet?"

Celia bit her lip and shook her head. If only the two people she loved most in all the world would settle their differences and agree to disagree. As usual, she could see both sides of the question. "Just talk to him, Ed," she said.

The man who'd accompanied her brother was still standing beside the motorbike and now he stepped tentatively forward. "Aren't you going to say hello?" he said, holding out his hand. "You do remember me, don't you?"

Celia nodded, suddenly feeling a little shy. She had met Matthew Dangerfield several times over the past year, but it had usually been in a crowd. She and her friends sometimes went to the Unicorn pub in

Chichester on market days. It was a favourite haunt of Ed and his fellow airmen from Tangmere.

Now Matthew shook her hand, a warm firm grasp and said, "I couldn't miss the chance of seeing you again before we go off to Suffolk. Giving Ed a lift was the perfect excuse. I'm just glad we found you at home."

He gave a cheeky grin and Celia felt herself blushing. She was used to such comments from her brother's friends and usually turned them aside with a tart rejoinder. But this man with his blue eyes and mop of curly black hair evoked a different response and she couldn't deny that she was pleased to see him again. It wasn't just his looks. There was a hint of seriousness behind the banter and a warmth in his voice that hinted he wasn't just flirting with her.

Flustered, she turned away. "You'd better come in. I bet you're both hungry. We've just finished tea, but I expect I can rustle something up."

"I don't want to impose," said Matt.

"Don't take any notice of him," said Ed. "We're starving."

"You're always starving. Hollow legs," Celia said with a laugh, the tension broken. "Anyway, food may be rationed but we've got plenty of eggs."

They followed her into the farmhouse kitchen — a large, warm, beamed room which smelled of baking.

"Sit down, mate," Ed said, pulling out a chair.

The two men sprawled at the kitchen table while Celia whisked eggs in a bowl and put two rashers of bacon in a pan. "It's all we've got left, I'm afraid," she said.

Within minutes she had placed steaming platefuls of scrambled eggs and bacon and large mugs of tea in front of the men. She sat down opposite them and watched as they wolfed the food down.

"Better than camp grub," Edgar said through a mouthful of egg. He pushed his chair back. "I s'pose I'd better go and have a word with the old man."

Matt made to get up, but Edgar told him to stay and chat to Celia. "I need to do this alone," he said. He went out slamming the door behind him.

Celia stood up with a sigh and began clearing the table.

"I know Ed had a bit of a barney with your father, but he wouldn't say what it was about," Matt said tentatively.

"It was nothing really. I'm sure they'll sort things out," she replied.

"I hope so." Matt hesitated. "I probably shouldn't tell you this. Ed won't say anything I know, but this posting — well, it's likely to be dangerous."

"More dangerous than Tangmere?" Celia scoffed. The airfield at the foot of the Downs had been bombed many times over the past year and she knew that often planes did not return from their missions. Every day she heard them taking off and at night she lay awake listening to the heavy bombers going over.

"We've been posted to a bomber squadron," Matt told her. "They'll be getting the new Lancasters soon and we'll be training on them before they go into operation."

"Now I see why Ed needs to talk to Dad. I just hope he'll listen this time."

"What's the problem between them?"

"Dad needs Ed on the farm. He doesn't understand why he had to join the RAF. But Ed's always been mad about planes, couldn't keep away from the local flying club. It was all right until we knew there was going to be a war."

"I can understand Mr Raines wanting his son to follow him. My Dad was the same. But I didn't fancy being a barrister." Matt laughed. "Can you see me in one of those silly wigs?"

Celia laughed too. "So you and Ed — both rebels then?"

"I was lucky. Dad saw my point of view."

"It's nice you get on well with him. So why come here instead of going home?" Celia asked.

"Too far — they live in Exeter." Matt paused. He carried the dirty plates over to the sink, then turned to Celia. "This problem with Ed and your father — it's serious, isn't it?"

"Dad's taken it hard. He always dreamt of Ed taking over the farm one day."

"I'm sure he'll come back and take his place here after the war," said Matt.

Celia picked up the kettle which was simmering on the range and poured hot water onto the used crockery. The unspoken thought that Edgar might not come back at all hung between them.

"Ed tells me you work in an office in town," Matt said.

"I'd rather be farming, but Dad says it's not a woman's job."

"How is he managing?"

"Not very well. Two of the younger hands joined up at the beginning of the war and then our cowman left a few months ago. Now there's only old Len Robson."

"I thought farming was a reserved occupation."

"It is — but they volunteered." Celia sighed. "I wish Dad would agree to me leaving my job and working with him. But he won't hear of it."

Matt picked up a tea towel. "Might as well make myself useful while I wait for Ed."

"Thanks." She didn't try to deter him and they worked in silence for a few minutes. When the last cup was dried and hung on its hook below the dresser shelf, she glanced towards the back door. "He's been gone a long time," she said.

"We ought to be getting on," Matt said, looking at his watch.

Celia took off her apron and opened the door. "Here he is now."

Edgar was alone, no sign of her father.

"Everything all right?" she asked.

He shrugged. "Come on, Matt, let's be off."

He gave Celia a hug and, after promising to write, climbed onto the pillion.

Matt kick-started the motorcycle and, as it roared to life, he turned to Celia. "I'll write too — if I may?"

They disappeared down the lane in a cloud of chalky dust and Celia stood for a few moments until the sound of the bike had faded. She sighed. The rift between her father and brother hurt her deeply. She loved them both and understood how they both felt. But she couldn't help feeling that, by showing his disapproval so strongly, her Dad was only reinforcing Edgar's determination to go his own way. "They're both so stubborn," she muttered, striding across the yard towards the milking shed.

Her father was washing down the floor and he looked up, his expression grim, "He's gone then?" He gave a final swipe with the mop and picked up the bucket, pushing past her into the yard. "I s'pose he told you he was off to Suffolk? All the way up there on that damned motorbike. Well, if the Germans don't get him, that contraption will."

Celia shivered as much from the truth of his words as from the chill wind that had sprung up, the first sign of approaching autumn after the long hot summer. She watched in silence as he rinsed the bucket and mop under the pump and slammed them down angrily. When he turned to her his face was bleak and she could swear there were tears in his eyes. "Why did he do it, love? He'd be safe here on the farm, reserved occupation. And he'd still be doing his bit, wouldn't he?"

What words of comfort could she offer? It was too late now. Edgar had joined up at the outbreak of war. She wanted to tell him that he still had her. She loved the farm and would have worked alongside her father willingly, but he wouldn't hear of it. He'd insisted on her doing secretarial training and getting a job.

Ever since she was old enough to toddle around after him she'd tried to help — feeding the motherless lambs, working as hard as any of the men at haymaking time and going with him to the market in Chichester every week.

She had always imagined herself taking over from Dad one day. After all, Edgar had never had any interest in farming. And there was no one else, was there? She'd always thought Dad felt the same. It was when her mother had died that he'd changed his tune; he convinced himself it was his fault that she had become ill, worn out with doing the work of two men during the slump in agriculture when they couldn't afford to employ farmhands.

"I don't want you ending up a drudge like your mother," he'd said. "She was always on the go — hardly ever sat down. And when she did it was mending, or knitting."

When Celia was about to leave school he had re-stated his view. "I'm not having that happen to you, love," he said. "Farming's no job for a woman. Helping out in the holidays is one thing, but not full time. No. I mean it," he said, when Celia tried to protest.

So, she'd given in and gone to college while still helping on the farm during weekends and holidays, determined that when the course was finished she would persuade Dad to let her join him full time. She'd passed the book-keeping and shorthand and typing exams with top marks.

"Well done, Cee. I knew you were cut out for better things than milking cows," said Larry. "So, have you thought where you'll apply for a job?"

"Plenty of time for that," she said.

But when he pointed out the vacancy at the Downland Press, she applied for the job without arguing. She had not inherited her brother's stubborn streak. Besides, she told herself, she wouldn't get it. There were probably far more experienced applicants.

She'd been wrong. The owner of the printing works, Dennis Allen, had been impressed by her exam results and had taken her on straight away. After two years she had to admit that she enjoyed her work. And she still had the long summer evenings and weekends free to work on the farm.

The Downland Press was a small printing works in Sullingford about three miles from High Trees Farm. They specialized in printing posters for the livestock market, auction sales, posters and flyers as well as a small weekly newspaper, the *Downland Weekly Advertiser*, which was produced almost single-handedly by Dennis Allen while his son, Russell, ran the printing side of things.

The day after Edgar's visit, Celia cycled into town, still worried about the rift between her Dad and brother. She wheeled her bicycle down the alley beside the printing office, leaned her bike against the wall and opened the door to the big shed which housed the printing machines. The noise was deafening and she could only smile in response to the mouthed greeting from old Barney who manned the big flatbed press.

She picked up some proofs from the table by the door and crossed the yard to the newspaper office which consisted of the two downstairs rooms of an old cottage in the High Street. Dennis Allen still lived above the shop, alone now since his wife had died and his son Russell had married.

The front room, where Celia worked, housed the main office where customers could come and place advertisements or order their posters and stationery. The back room was the editor's domain where he typed his editorials and the main stories of the week at a scarred old oak desk which took up most of the room. His son Russell worked at a smaller desk in the corner, although he mostly supervised the printing works these days. The rest of the space was dominated by a bench along one wall where Mr Allen did the page layouts for the paper.

He was already there, hunched over the typewriter, ash from the ever-present cigarette falling between the keys. Celia wondered if he ever retired upstairs to his living quarters. He looked as if he hadn't moved since she'd left to go home last night.

"Good morning, Mr Allen, lovely day," she said cheerfully, trying to put her family worries behind her.

He grunted a reply, then glanced up and said, "It may be a lovely day out here in the country. Not so elsewhere. Haven't you heard the news?" He proceeded to tell her about the bombs that had dropped on

London that night, as well as along the coast at Portsmouth and Southampton.

Celia had been trying not to think about the war, especially her brother's part in it. The mention of bombing brought it to the fore again and she bit back a sob at the memory of her father's bleak expression after Edgar had left.

She brought her attention back to what her boss was saying. "Well at least our boys are giving them a pasting now. No more flying over there and dropping leaflets."

A laugh from the open door caused Celia to turn round. Russell Allen stood there, a bunch of flyers in his hand. "You trying to do us out of a job, Dad? We've just printed another batch for the Ministry, you know."

Dennis looked up from his typewriter. "Can't you take anything seriously? It's no laughing matter, people being bombed out of their homes."

Russell looked chastened. "Sorry, Dad. Just trying to lighten the mood. It's all doom and gloom these days."

For once Celia agreed with her boss. Usually Russell's little jokes cheered up the working day and she knew he was popular with the boys in the printing shed. But she wasn't in the mood today.

Her face must have showed it as Russell immediately became businesslike. "Actually, I only came over to see if there were any new jobs in."

"I've only just got here," Celia said. "I'll go and look."

She went through to the front office and picked up the post. "Nothing here," she said, going through the envelopes.

He perched on the edge of the desk and watched her. "Why so glum today?" he asked. "Boyfriend let you down?"

"You know very well I haven't got a boyfriend," she said, blushing a little at the thought of her brother's friend and his promise to write.

He grinned. "Pity I'm spoken for, then."

Celia didn't reply. She never knew if he was being serious. They got on well at work, but there was no way she'd get involved with a married man, especially one whose wife was an old friend of hers.

Marion was a little older than Celia, but they'd become friends travelling to school on the bus. They'd gone to the pictures and to young farmers' dances together, which is where they'd met Russell. Marion, more sophisticated than Celia, had caught his eye straight away. And he'd caught hers, drawn by his slicked back dark hair and Ronald Colman moustache. "Not my type," Celia had told her friend.

He still wasn't and she didn't like his flirting with her. She concentrated on opening the post, sorting the letters into piles, and hoping he'd go away and let her get on with her work.

To her relief he stood up, but he paused before opening the door. "Dad hasn't been getting at you, has he? I know he can be a bit of a slave driver."

She shook her head.

"Good. I don't like to see you upset," he said.

"It's just that Edgar turned up yesterday evening — just a flying visit. He's been posted, came to say goodbye."

12

"They have to go where they're sent, I suppose." He sighed. "Wish I could get away from this dump."

The morning passed quickly as Celia sorted out invoices and typed up the reports sent in by local organizations and village correspondents. The *Advertiser's* only staff reporter had joined up a few months ago. Celia knew Russell would like to enlist as well, but his father had persuaded him to wait until he was called up.

She got the invoices ready for the post and took the typed reports through to Mr Allen's office. He was still hunched over his typewriter, the cigarette drooping from his lip, the cup of tea she'd taken in to him earlier untouched by his side.

"I'm just popping out, Mr Allen," she said.

He nodded without looking up and she picked up her handbag and her packet of sandwiches and went out into the High Street. Sometimes she cycled home at dinner time, but she couldn't face her father today. He would just go over the same old thing again: Edgar's place was at home on the farm. Why couldn't he understand that his stubborn attitude would only drive her brother further away?

Celia walked down to the river and sat on one of the benches facing the water. Although the trees were changing colour, the sun was still warm and she was glad she'd come out instead of eating her lunch indoors. She loved being outside and, although she enjoyed her job, she sometimes felt stifled being cooped up in the office all day. The thought brought her back to her father and brother.

It was her father she was most frustrated by. He had a ready-made heir to the farm, she mused, someone who loved the place and wanted nothing more than to spend the rest of her life there. Why did it have to be a son?

She sighed and stood up. Feeling slightly guilty at the waste of food, she threw the rest of her lunch to the swans hovering expectantly at the water's edge. She'd better get back to work and make sure Mr Allen had stopped for something to eat. He'd sit at that desk all day if no one interrupted him.

As she walked back through the town she thought about the men in her life. There was Dad wanting Edgar to follow in his footsteps and Mr Allen was the same with Russell. And Matthew had told her his father wanted him to join the family law firm. Lucky Matt — his parents understood his desire to make his own way. She smiled, remembering the easy camaraderie that had sprung up between them as they worked together in the farmhouse kitchen. Would he write to her? She hoped so.

She reached the office just as Marion stormed out, almost knocking her over.

"What's wrong?" Celia asked, putting out a hand to steady her friend.

"Bloody Russell — that's what."

"What's he done?" Celia couldn't imagine how he could have upset her. Despite his well-known reputation for casual flirtation, he adored Marion, indulged her every whim. Her expensive shoes and handbag, bought from a top London shop were only some of the gifts he showered on her. He never complained when she went up to town to meet her friends and he was left to get his own meals.

"I've had a fantastic offer from the agency, but he won't hear of my taking it up. I have to stay here in mouldy old Sullingford and be a good little housewife." Marion tossed her golden curls. "Me — a housewife? Did you know that before we married I was on the way to being one of the top models for Vogue?"

Celia smiled and nodded. She did know. Marion had told her often enough. Her constant gloating had put a strain on their friendship for a while. But when she'd got married, to Celia's surprise, she had seemed to settle down, content to put her glamorous life behind her.

Marion pouted. "Well, I don't care what he or his stick-in-the-mud old father say, I'm going — for the interview anyway. I'm off to London on the early train tomorrow."

Celia was about to say that perhaps Russell didn't want her to go to London because of the bombing; he'd be worried about her. But, without waiting for a reply, Marion flounced off.

Good luck to her, Celia thought with a bemused smile. She returned to work wondering if her friend really would defy her husband. Still, she'd always been a bit wayward which had been part of her attraction when they were at school. It had been fun going to dances with her, flirting, staying out late and pretending they'd missed the last bus home. But when Marion went to London to try her luck as a model, urging Celia to go with her, she had realized that wasn't the sort of life she wanted. It had been fun for a while, but she was a country girl at heart. If she had her way, she would never leave the farm.

CHAPTER
TWO

It was a wet and windy morning. Leaves swirled in the air and Celia wished she didn't have to cycle to work. No use asking Dad for a lift, she thought. He's too busy. I should learn to drive myself, but with the petrol rationing there's no chance of that.

As she turned to go indoors she saw the postman on his bike.

"Not a very good morning, is it?" he said with a grin, dismounting and handing her a batch of letters.

"Thanks, Bill." She flicked through them, frowning at the official looking brown envelopes. They seemed to be getting more of those these days as the Ministry of Agriculture dreamed up more and more rules and regulations to harass poor farmers like Larry Raines.

She waved goodbye to Bill and took the post indoors. Her father had finished the milking and was in the kitchen eating the breakfast she'd cooked. She handed him the envelopes and said, "I'm off, Dad."

He'd opened one of the letters and looked up with a grimace. "Listen to this — they want me to take on a couple of land girls. What do I want with girls on my farm? We're managing all right with Len and there's young Mickey to help out at harvest time."

Len's grandson was always ready to earn a bit of pocket money.

"But, Dad, he'll be leaving school soon. He might want to work elsewhere," Celia said. "Besides, they say we've got to produce more. How can we now Fred's gone? And what about poor old Len? Winter's coming on and his arthritis isn't getting any better." She paused, tying her scarf over her head. "Well, Dad, if you'd only let me work here instead of sending me to college, they wouldn't be telling you to take on land girls, would they?"

His reply was predictable. "I tell you, a farm's no place for young girls. How can you expect them to do the heavy work?"

It was the same old argument and Celia sighed. "I'm off. Mustn't be late."

She got her bike out and set off with the wind in her face. Pushing hard on the pedals left her out of breath, but it did help her to work off the frustration caused by her father's stubbornness. By the time she reached the printing works she'd made up her mind. She would hand in her notice today. Dad must be made to understand that if she was working on the farm he wouldn't have to put up with "flibbertigibbet girls who didn't know one end of a cow from the other" as he put it.

When she reached the office she found several official-looking envelopes on her desk and she took them in to Dennis Allen's office without opening them. He thanked her absent-mindedly and went back to checking the page proof on his desk.

To her relief there was no sign of Russell today. He was probably out at a meeting or the magistrates' court. Since their only reporter had joined the army he covered most of the main stories for the paper. Their other news came mostly from freelance writers who sent in stories from the surrounding villages. It was part of Celia's job to take them down over the telephone and type them up for the printer.

The phone stayed silent and no one came into the front office either so she was able to get through everything in record time. It was press day — the day before the paper came out — so it was too late for anyone wanting advertisements or announcements to go in that week. When Mr Allen had finished checking the pages he would cross the yard to the printing shed and give Barney the all clear to start up the big flatbed press.

From then on it would be a flurry of activity. Celia loved press day even if it did mean working late. She decided to eat her sandwiches before the rush and went through to the kitchen to put the kettle on. As she passed Mr Allen's office he looked up and beckoned her in.

"Sit down, Celia," he said. He looked serious, his eyes lacking their usual good-humoured twinkle.

Celia felt a little apprehensive. Although she had decided to hand in her notice today, she still hoped that she hadn't done anything wrong, perhaps made a silly mistake that warranted a reprimand. Did he blame her for the amount of time Russell spent sitting on the edge of her desk flirting? Well, she'd tell him that she had never encouraged him. But what could she about it? He was the boss's son after all.

As she sat down, Mr Allen smiled and her heart rate returned to normal. "Do you like working here?" he asked.

"Oh, yes. It's much more interesting than I thought office work would be." It was true, even though she'd far rather be working on the farm.

Mr Allen nodded. "Good, good." He picked up one of the official-looking letters that had come that morning. "This is from the Ministry of Information. A contract for printing leaflets advising people of various new rules. You know the sort of thing — 'waste not, want not', 'careless talk' etcetera."

"That's good, isn't it, Mr Allen?"

"Oh, yes. We'll be busier than ever. And they'll guarantee paper supplies too."

Celia wondered why he wasn't looking pleased. They'd had to cut the number of pages in the *Downland Weekly Advertiser* due to paper shortages and there were fewer calls for auction posters, letterheads and other small printing jobs these days.

"Are you worried we won't be able to fulfil the contract with only Barney and the other three?" Before the war they had employed fifteen men. Now, besides Barney who was nearing retirement, there was only Ray, the linotype operator, who was waiting for his call-up, and the two apprentices who were too young for the army.

"We'll manage." Dennis Allen shook his head. "It's you I was worried about. Russell let slip that you'd rather be working on the farm than stuck in an office all day. I wondered if you might be thinking of leaving to work with your Dad."

"Would that matter — me leaving, I mean?" Celia didn't want to let Mr Allen down.

"It would now," he said, to her dismay. "You see, it's not just information leaflets we'd be printing. Some of this is pretty sensitive stuff. All my staff would have to sign the Official Secrets Act and pledge to stay with the firm for the duration."

Celia read the letter with growing dismay. How could she let her boss down now? "Must I decide straight away?" she asked.

"They want a quick decision, I'm afraid."

It didn't take long for her to change her mind about resigning and she nodded. "All right — where do I sign?"

"I'm not sure what the procedure is. The lads in the works will have to be told too. I'll sort it all out and call a staff meeting once the paper's out." He leaned across the desk and patted her hand. "Thank you, Celia. I'm pleased you want to stay with us." He lit a cigarette and said through a cloud of smoke, "Now, where's that tea?"

As she went through to the kitchen, she could hear the thump of the big printing press from across the yard. The men usually brought their own flasks, but when they were especially busy she often took a tray of tea across to them.

Today, after handing round the mugs, she lingered, watching the paper slide off the press and onto the folding machine. She always found it fascinating. Soon Mrs Jones, the office cleaner, who came in to help out on press day, would arrive and start bundling up the papers and tying them with string. One of the apprentices would then load the van for delivery to the surrounding villages next morning. Since most of the workers had joined the forces, Mr Allen or Russell did the deliveries these days.

Celia took the tray back to the kitchen and tidied her desk before going back to the works to give Mrs Jones a hand. She never minded staying late on press day. The only job she didn't like was making up the posters, one for each of the newsagents they supplied. Mr Allen would hand her a slip of paper with the main story headlines and she would take large sheets of brown paper, an artist's brush and a bottle of Indian ink. Celia enjoyed drawing and in her limited leisure time had done a little watercolour painting, but she didn't like doing the posters. It was hard to keep the lines straight and as they had to be done in a hurry, the ink was sometimes still damp and smudged easily.

Once, she had asked Mr Allen, rather cheekily, why they didn't print the posters. He had replied that the men were too busy on press nights and besides, the headlines could not be done in advance. Celia had to admit it made sense when they were so short-staffed, but she knew that even when they'd had a full work force the system had been the same.

She was just writing the last poster when Russell stuck his head round the door. "Nearly done?" he asked, making her jump and splash ink across the paper. "Look what you've made me do," she exclaimed. "Now I'll have to start again."

"Don't worry about it. No one will notice."

"Your father will. You know what a perfectionist he is."

Russell blew on the sheet of paper to make sure the ink was dry and slipped it under the top poster. "I'll take these out to the van," he said.

"I really ought to do another one," Celia protested.

"He won't know. I'm doing the deliveries tomorrow. Besides, we've been told not to waste paper." Russell laughed and rolled up the bundle of posters, snapping an elastic band round them. "Come on. Dad wants to talk to everyone over in the shed."

Celia followed him over to works which seemed almost ghostly now that the machines had stopped. The "lads" as Mr Allen called them, were gathered round the "stone", which was actually a large metal table where the type was made up into pages before being loaded on to the press.

When Russell and Celia entered Mr Allen looked up from the sheet of paper he was studying. "Good — everyone's here," he said. When he had their attention he went through the instructions he'd received from the Ministry and outlined what he expected from his workers. "I need to know now if you're prepared to sign on for the duration of the war," he said. "This mainly applies to you, Ray."

The linotype operator nodded. He had been expecting his call-up papers any day and Celia knew he wasn't keen to leave his wife and young baby. "It's not that I don't want to do my bit," he'd confided to her once when she'd stopped by his machine with a batch of copy. "I just don't think Joan's cut out to cope on her own."

Now she could see the relief on his face. "Does this count as a reserved occupation then?" he asked.

Mr Allen nodded. "If we take on this work, yes. And of course, I do intend to take it on. It will mean the firm can keep going however long the war lasts and that means the boys who've joined up will have jobs to come home to." He turned to the two apprentices.

"Danny, I know you're itching to do your bit. But you're far too young, lad. And you've got a couple of years of your indentures yet."

"But what about when I finish my apprenticeship?"

"Let's hope the war doesn't last that long." He turned to the other apprentice. "As for you, Jimmy — only a few months to go for you. If you're determined to join up I can release you now. It's up to you."

Jimmy squirmed a bit, his face reddening. "I'd made up me mind, sir. I want to join the navy, like me brother. I've already applied actually."

"Well lad. We'll just have to manage without you, won't we?"

When the staff meeting broke up they all, with the exception of Jimmy, had signed up for the duration and were pledged to say nothing of the work they were doing. As far as anyone in the town was concerned, the Downland Printing Works were printing the usual agricultural and church notices, as well as the weekly paper.

It was almost dark when Celia wheeled her bicycle out of the works' shed that evening. No lights showed in the town since the introduction of the blackout but living out in the country she was used to that and had no fear of cycling home in the dark. She still jumped when a voice spoke of out the gloom.

"You can't bike home this late," Russell said. "I've got the van. Let me give you a lift."

"What about my bike?" She felt uncomfortable being alone with him and wanted an excuse to refuse.

"We'll put it in the back."

"I thought you'd loaded up with the papers."

"Plenty of room." Without giving her a chance to reply he pulled the bicycle away from her and wheeled it to where he had parked the van. "Come on," he urged.

She got in, edging as close to the door as possible. She didn't think he'd make a pass at her, but his flirty ways at work had left her in no doubt that he found her attractive. She had to admit that he was attractive too in his way; even if he weren't married to her friend, she would not have wanted a relationship with him.

To her surprise though, the flirtatiousness was absent tonight and he began to talk about Marion. "I just don't know what she's thinking these days. We used to have fun together, but now she seems discontented and says I'm boring." He took his eyes off the road and turned to her. "You don't think I'm boring, do you, Cee?"

Celia laughed. "That's not how I would describe you."

Russell sighed. "Perhaps we shouldn't have married. I don't think she was really ready to settle down. Did you know she's gone up to London to see about a modelling job?"

"She did tell me about it," Celia admitted.

"She should realize she's a married woman now. She can't just go swanning off, doing whatever she wants. Besides, I don't want a working wife."

"Russell, you'll have to talk to her about it. I can't take sides, you know. Anyway, if what I hear is true, all the women will be called up for war work soon — even married ones. She might have to go and work in a factory somewhere."

"Bloody war. It's messing up everyone's lives."

Celia didn't reply. She thought he was being selfish. His life was hardly being messed up with his place in his father's business protected by their war work. What about Edgar, she thought. He was thrilled to have been promoted from ground crew to navigator. But that meant that soon he'd be flying over enemy territory. Her thoughts turned to Matthew Dangerfield, who would be sharing the danger. They'd really only talked for a few minutes. Already, though she felt she'd known him forever.

The van turned into the lane, bumping over the ruts and, as it jerked to a stop, she got out quickly, thanking Russell for the lift.

She hurried indoors to find her father in the kitchen heating up the stew that she'd prepared earlier. He gestured to her to sit down. "You must be hungry after working late."

Celia didn't comment. After all, she worked late at least one evening a week and he'd never had a meal ready for her before. And, although she knew he worked hard all day on the farm, she sometimes felt a little resentful when she came in to find him sitting in his armchair by the range reading the paper.

She hung up her coat and put her bag on the dresser. "I'm starving," she said pulling her chair up to the table.

Larry filled two plates and came to sit opposite. "I've been thinking," he said, pausing to take a mouthful of stew. ". . . About those land girls."

Celia smiled. So, he'd changed his mind. Just as well if she was to continue working at Allen's. His next words made her sit up straighter.

"We don't need them, do we? Mickey's leaving school soon and he knows there's a job for him here." He wagged a finger at her. "And you're always on about farming. Well, that's two new farmhands. I won't need the land girls, will I?"

Before she could recover, he said, "I'll write to the Ministry tonight. Tell them not to send anyone. Besides, I heard they're taking on girls with no experience whatever, even from the towns. I don't want townees on my farm."

"But, Dad —"

"I know, you'll have to give your notice in, but Mr Allen will soon find someone else. Besides, it'll only be for the duration. You can have your job back when the war's over."

Forgetting for a moment that she was committed to staying at the printing works, Celia said, "Do you mean you still wouldn't let me work with you permanently?"

Larry waved his fork at her. "You know how I feel about that — and I haven't changed my mind. But this is an unusual situation. We all have to do our bit. Besides, you already help out, feeding the hens and collecting the eggs and doing some of the milking."

"But, Dad, I'm already doing my bit as you call it. And Mr Allen says —"

Once more he interrupted. "Printing a few leaflets and posters is hardly going to help us win the war is it? I'm talking about producing more food. They say we've got to try to feed ourselves instead of relying on foreign imports. Do you know how many ships have been sunk in the past few months?"

"I listen to the news too, Dad. You don't have to tell me how important farming is. If we'd had this discussion before today I would have jumped at the chance of leaving my job and staying on the farm. But it's too late, Dad."

"What do you mean, too late?"

Celia explained what had happened that morning and how her boss had impressed on her the importance of the work they'd be doing. "I've signed up, Dad. I can't go into details but it's official; I can't back out now."

Larry pushed his plate away, the stew now cold and congealed. "What a turn up for the books. I suppose I can't do anything about it now. Just have to put up with whoever they send." He ran his hands through his sparse hair. "Suppose I write to this Ministry of Information — tell them working with me would be vital war work."

"I don't think it would do any good, Dad. They have their rules."

Larry banged his hand on the table making the cutlery rattle. "It's all damned rules and regulations nowadays. Not content with taking my son away, now they want my daughter too."

Celia refrained from pointing out that Edgar had volunteered and that she had more or less been forced into this position because of his stubbornness. She got up and began to clear away the half-eaten food.

Larry switched on the wireless for the evening news but she only half-listened as she washed the dishes and tidied up. If only that letter had arrived a day later.

She made a cup of cocoa for each of them and sat down, resting her aching feet on the fender in front of the range. It had been a long day. Dad looked tired too. He'd been finding it hard since losing his best and fittest farmhands to the army. Farming was a reserved occupation but that hadn't stopped the younger men from wanting to enlist as soon as war broke out. Len was a good worker but he was nearing retirement and couldn't do as much these days due to bad arthritis in his hip.

Even with two extra pairs of hands — albeit girls who might never have been near a cow or sheep — they would find it hard to cope, especially at harvest time next year. Celia sighed. Life wasn't going to get any easier in the coming months. She stood up and stretched. "I'm for bed, Dad," she said.

Larry jerked awake. "I'd better go up too." He opened the back door and stood for a moment looking up at the sky. "Clear night. Might get an early frost."

Celia shivered. "Shut the door, Dad." She took the cups over to the sink. "I've been thinking about these girls. Will they be staying here? I'll have to sort out rooms, beds and so on."

"Don't worry about it now. Let's get some sleep."

As she prepared for bed, Celia wondered what the new farmhands would be like. She hoped they would fit in with the household and not be too demanding of home comforts. At least the farm had electricity, installed when Larry had bought the milking machine after increasing his herd. But the plumbing still left a lot to be desired. Oh well, they'd just have to muck in and make the best of it, she thought as she turned out the light and climbed into bed.

As she fell asleep her last thoughts were a bitter reflection on the fate that had prevented her from doing what she'd always wanted ever since she had been a small child. Oh well, I'll just have to marry a farmer, she thought. But someone else's farm wouldn't be the same as High Trees and going by the farmers she already knew she couldn't imagine being married to any of them. What a pity Matthew Dangerfield wasn't a farmer in civilian life, she thought, laughing a little at her foolishness.

CHAPTER
THREE

Matt and Edgar had arrived at Metworth aerodrome the previous evening too late to meet any of their fellow crew members. They had been shown into a hut containing two empty bunk beds and fallen on them with sighs of relief. In moments both were asleep.

Even the drone of a squadron of bombers landing after a night raid didn't disturb them and it took the sound of running feet and shouting from outside the hut to rouse them.

Matt sat up rubbing his eyes and taking in his new surroundings. He got out of bed, still stiff from the long motorcycle ride of the day before. He was shaking Edgar awake when someone put their head round the door.

"Shake a leg, lads. Briefing in fifteen minutes."

After hastily straightening their uniforms and combing their hair, the two young men went outside to see groups of airmen walking towards a large nissen hut. Inside were rows of chairs with a platform at one end.

The briefing didn't take long and the meeting broke up, leaving Matt and Edgar to introduce themselves to their new crew.

Their pilot, Flying Officer Clive Mitchell, shook hands with both of them and offered to show them round the station. "We'll go via the mess," he said. "You chaps haven't had breakfast yet, have you?"

They grabbed trays and loaded them with scrambled eggs on toast. As they sat down Matt was reminded of the meal Edgar's sister had cooked for them the day before. He hoped his friend would invite him to High Trees Farm on their next leave. In the meantime, he'd write to Celia. He hoped fervently that she would write back.

He came out of his daydream to hear Flying Officer Mitchell saying, "We'll be getting the new Lancasters soon. Meanwhile we're carrying on with the Stirlings. You're both familiar with them, aren't you?"

Both men nodded. "I hear these Avro Lancasters are supposed to be pretty good," said Matt. "The lads at Tangmere mentioned them."

Mitchell scoffed. "Thought those chaps only knew about Spits and Hurricanes."

Matt grinned at Edgar. They had come up against the rivalry between fighter and bomber pilots before. Did it matter who flew what so long as they got the job done, he thought. And the bombers had done their bit in what was now being called the Battle of Britain. The country might still be worrying about an invasion if it hadn't been for their raids on the German fleet.

Still, Matt knew that fighter pilots had a far more glamorous image than flight engineers such as himself and he hoped that Celia wouldn't meet one of these glamorous heroes while he was so far away.

Edgar punched his arm, rousing him from his thoughts. "We're as good as that lot, aren't we?" he said.

Matt pushed back his chair. "Well, we'd better start proving it then. Come on, let's go and look at the plane."

The day after the paper came out was usually quiet and was Celia's usual day off. She was glad of the time at home to sort out the accommodation for the expected land girls. She had planned to vacate her own room and move into Edgar's old room which was the smaller of the two. But she had no idea what the girls would be like or if they would object to sharing a room so she decided to go over to Len Robson's cottage and speak to his wife, Jean. Perhaps she would agree to let one of the girls stay there.

"Oh, I don't know," Jean said, shaking her head. She was a thin frail-looking woman, although Celia knew she was stronger than she looked. When she helped out at hay-making time her wiry arms flailed like windmills as she tossed the hay up on to the wagon.

"I know it's a liberty," Celia said. "But, as you know, we've had these people sent to us and we've got no say in the matter. The poor girls have got to sleep somewhere."

"Well, I do have a room, but Mickey will want it when he comes to work here after leaving school in the summer," Jean said.

"Could the girl stay here till then?" Celia asked.

"I suppose so. Who knows what will happen in the next few months? It wouldn't hurt young Mickey to cycle over from home or get the bus. Besides, I don't really want to be running around after youngsters now. I had all that when mine were young — can't tell you how relieved I was when the last one left home."

Celia smiled. The Robsons had brought up six children in this tiny cottage. All had left the district except for Mickey's father who lived and worked in Chichester. She hastened to reassure the other woman. "You might have to run around after Mickey but a land girl won't expect it, Jean. She'll have her meals at the farmhouse with the other one and see to her own washing and cleaning her room."

"Oh well, then, I suppose that'll be all right. I'll give the room a good going over before they arrive. And I'll come up and give you a hand later on."

Pleased that she wouldn't have to give up her own room, Celia returned to the farmhouse. By the time her father came in from the fields, she had cleaned Edgar's room and put most of his personal belongings in the attic. When Jean turned up after getting her own spare room ready, she helped Celia to make up the bed with fresh linen.

"This is pretty," Jean said, unfolding the patchwork quilt and spreading it over the bed.

"Mum made it," Celia said with a wistful smile.

"Mrs Raines was always good with her hands," Jean said.

"I'd better go down and see to Dad's supper. Thanks for your help."

"Len will be wanting his, too. Cheerio then. I'll be up on Monday to see to the wash."

"I'll see you before then. I'll bring your new lodger along after supper." They went downstairs and Celia glanced at the kitchen clock. "I thought they'd be here by now," she said. "I wonder if they'll want feeding too."

"You're not to go mollycoddling them," Larry said, taking off his boots and sitting down in his usual chair by the kitchen range. "Anyway it's getting late. They'll probably turn up tomorrow."

Celia glanced out of the window. "No, I think this is them."

A shooting brake had turned into the farmyard and three women got out. She opened the door to see a large officious-looking woman holding a clipboard with two very nervous-looking young women standing behind her. The older woman stepped forward holding out her hand. "I'm Marjorie Clifton, Area Land Army Adviser. This is High Trees Farm isn't it? We had a job finding the place."

Celia nodded. "I'm Celia Raines. This is my father's farm."

Mrs Clifton looked her up and down. "I didn't realize there was a daughter. In that case you only need one of these girls."

"No. I don't work here. I have a job in town — a reserved occupation. And we really do need two more workers." Celia smiled reassuringly at the girls who were clutching each other's arms.

The smaller one spoke up. "So we can both stay?" She spoke with a strong London accent and Celia knew she'd have her work cut out convincing her father that such an obvious townee was suitable for farm work.

She invited them in and introduced them to her father. While he and Mrs Clifton discussed the girls' working terms and signed forms, Celia tried to make them welcome. She could tell her father wasn't impressed even when Mrs Clifton said that both had been on a training course and had passed all their tests with flying colours.

"Miss Wilson has proved she has a way with cows," she said, her stern face softening in a smile. "And as for Miss Gray, she may look frail but she has also proved herself more than capable."

Joyce Gray did look as if a puff of wind would knock her over, Celia thought. She was tiny with short dark hair in a thin face which made her brown eyes look enormous. As for Stella Wilson, she was a tall blonde with shiny hair in a pageboy bob. She reminded Celia of Marion's model looks and wondered what on earth had made her join the land army. She could see her father wasn't impressed with either of them.

"We'll see," he muttered.

Mrs Clifton stood up. "I'd better be off. Come on, girls. Get your things from the car." She turned to Larry. "If you have any queries don't hesitate to contact me. But I'm sure everything will be fine."

Joyce Gray, the cockney girl, had elected to stay with Len and Jean, leaving Stella Wilson to occupy Edgar's old room. On their way down the lane to the cottage, Joyce confided in Celia that Stella wasn't keen on walking back on her own after work each day. "She doesn't like the dark see."

"It doesn't bother you then?" Celia asked.

"Not really. We've been getting used to the blackout in London. It's different out in the country though, innit?"

"What made you join the land army?"

"I used to go hopping down in Kent with me mum. I loved it. We slept in huts and used to have singsongs round the fire after we'd finished work."

"Well, we don't grow hops here. And I'm not sure about the singsongs," Celia said with a laugh. "But it's a good farm, mixed dairy and arable."

"I can't wait to get started."

Celia introduced her to Jean and said good night. When she got back to the farmhouse, Stella and her father had already gone to bed. She tidied up the kitchen and laid the table for breakfast to save time in the morning and went upstairs.

A light shone under Stella's door and Celia knocked tentatively.

"Come in."

Stella was sitting on the bed, an unlit cigarette in her hand. "Is it all right if I smoke?" she asked with a nervous smile.

Celia didn't smoke herself and hadn't thought about providing an ashtray for her guest. "Go ahead," she said, picking up a small dish from the window sill and placing it on the bedside table. "My Dad smokes his pipe in the evenings but he's not keen on cigarettes. Don't smoke outside. He worries about the hayricks and the animals."

"I hope I can do this job," Stella said suddenly.

"Mrs Clifton seems to think you can — she said you had a way with cows."

"Not sure about your Dad though."

"He'll come round." Celia gave a short laugh. "He'll have to now, won't he? I have to see the funny side — he didn't want me to work on the farm — no job for a woman he says. And now he's been more or less forced to take on two."

Stella asked what Celia's job was, giving a rather superior smile when she was told. "Not exactly war work is it?"

Celia didn't enlighten her. "I enjoy it — and I do my bit around the farm too. Well, early start tomorrow so I'll say goodnight."

She left the room abruptly, not sure if she was going to like Stella Wilson. She wished that Joyce was staying in the house instead. She had seemed more open and friendly. Not that it really mattered. They were here to work and she herself would be away from the farm most of the time.

As she undressed she wondered how her father would get on with them. Time would tell, she thought.

CHAPTER
FOUR

The next morning Celia got up earlier than usual intending to show the new girls round the farm. Last night it had been too dark by the time they'd eaten and been shown to their quarters.

To her surprise Joyce was already in the kitchen wearing her fawn breeches and green Land Army jumper. The range was alight and a kettle simmered on the hob.

"Morning, Miss Raines. Hope you don't mind me making myself at home. Your Dad told me to come in and get myself some breakfast. Stella's just finishing off in the milking parlour."

"I was going to let you both have a lie-in before starting work. It's a lot to take in, coming to a strange place." Celia got bread and eggs out of the larder and began to prepare breakfast. She'd have to do some shopping in her dinner hour. Thank goodness Mrs Clifton had given her Joyce and Stella's ration books before leaving last night.

"Mrs Robson called me early with a cuppa," Joyce said. "Then she walked down the lane with me — showed me the tractor shed, where the cows were and everything. Stella was already up and started on the milking so I joined her."

"What about Dad?"

"He was out in the yard. Didn't say much but I think he was pleased we were getting on with the work." She grinned. "I get the feeling he doesn't think much of girl farmers."

"You can say that again. He was totally against me working with him when I left school. He made me get a job in an office."

"Yeah — Stella told me." Joyce filled the teapot and set it on the table. "Must be boring, Miss."

"Please, call me Celia." She started laying the table and smiled at Joyce, wondering what she'd say if she knew what sort of work she was now committed to. But of course she couldn't tell her the details. Instead she said, "It's quite interesting actually. Besides, I still get to do some farm work and I'd better get on with it otherwise I'll be late for work."

"What about breakfast?"

"Could you finish off for me? I'll call Dad and Stella in while I'm seeing to the chickens. If I've time I'll have a piece of toast." She hurried outside to let the chickens out and feed them.

As she crossed the yard her father and Stella emerged from the tractor shed deep in conversation.

Larry smiled when he saw her. "I think this young lady's going to be a godsend," he said. "Do you know, she's just fixed that old tractor? Got her running sweet as a nut, she has."

You've changed your tune, Celia thought. But she didn't say it aloud. Instead she smiled and said, "Breakfast's nearly ready."

As she scattered corn for the hens she felt a lot happier about things. She really liked Joyce and hoped they'd be friends. As for Stella, if she kept Dad happy that was all she could ask for. Who knew, if the girls proved themselves as farmers, Dad might eventually come round to the idea that her working with him would be a good thing, especially as Edgar had no interest in the farm. It would have to wait till after the war though. She glanced at her watch, collected the eggs from the henhouse and hurried indoors.

Dad and the girls were sitting at the kitchen table and didn't look up as she drained her tea and grabbed a slice of toast. Outside she bumped into the postman. "Only one today. It's for you," he said, grinning. She didn't recognize the handwriting and, glancing at the postmark, her heart began to thump as she realized it could only be from Matthew Dangerfield.

She put it into her bag and began cycling down the lane towards town. Thoughts of the land girls and her father melted away as she savoured the anticipation of reading what her brother's friend had to say.

The office was busy with several of the village correspondents phoning their stories in so she didn't get a chance to read her letter until halfway through the morning when she'd finished her typing. She gave it to Mr Allen and went through to the kitchen. While she waited for the kettle to boil, she opened the envelope and took out the single sheet of paper. She'd only got as far as, *Dear Celia, I am keeping my promise and hope that you meant it when you said you would like me to write to you* ... when the door opened and Russell burst in.

His face was flushed and his hair stood on end as if he had run his fingers through it. "Did you know about this?" he shouted, waving a piece of paper at her.

"About what?" Celia asked, annoyed that he'd interrupted her reading.

"This," he said, shoving a letter in her face. "Marion's left me."

"Russell, calm down. You must have misunderstood."

"Read this then."

Celia took the note from him, her eyes widening as she took in the contents. "But I thought —"

"So you did know she was going. Why didn't you warn me?"

"I knew she was going to London. She said she had an interview for a modelling job. I had no idea she wasn't coming back." Celia was shocked. Although Marion had confided her discontent to her friend, she had given no indication that she intended to leave her husband. Despite Russell's flirtatious ways, Celia knew that he genuinely loved his wife. But, like many men, his love did not extend to allowing her to have a life that did not include him. The novelty of being a housewife and running her own home had worn off and Marion had begun to miss her old glamorous life. By being so adamant that she must give it all up, Russell had virtually driven her away.

Seeing him so devastated, Celia couldn't tell him what she'd been thinking. He wouldn't understand anyway. He dropped into a chair opposite her and put his hands over his face. "What am I going to do, Cee?"

She patted him awkwardly on the shoulder. "I'm sure she'll be back, Russell. I know she loves you. She just wants a bit of excitement that's all."

"Is that it, do you think? There isn't another man?" He looked up at her through red-rimmed eyes.

"Of course not, silly. She's having a sulk because you tried to stop her taking the job, that's all." Celia hoped it was true, but she couldn't really be sure. Marion had always been impulsive.

"Do you think that's really it?"

She couldn't help feeling sorry for him and tried to reassure him. "She'll do this modelling job and then she'll be back — you'll see," she said. "Is there an address on the letter?" She thought she might write and ask Marion what she was up to.

"It's on hotel paper — there's a telephone number. Perhaps I'll ring them, see if she's still there." He rushed out and Celia could hear him trying to get through. Like everything else these days, telephoning was difficult and the lines were often engaged. She shrugged and went back to Matt's letter.

Thoughts of her friend and her marital problems faded as she read. Although he merely told her that he and Edgar were settling in and getting to know their new crew, there was a warmth in his words which brought a glow to her cheeks.

"Ed's really thrilled to be flying at last and the other chaps seem a good lot," he wrote and went on to speak enthusiastically about the new "kite" which would be in use in a few months. *Can't say too much — careless talk etc.* He finished by saying that he hoped she'd write back and looked forward to Ed inviting him to High Trees the next time they had leave, "which won't be for a while the way things are going at present".

Celia folded the letter and put it back in her bag. She'd write back this evening — in the privacy of her bedroom. Matt was just a friend she told herself, but she didn't want any teasing remarks about boyfriends from her father or the new lodgers.

She went back to her typewriter and tried to concentrate on the invoices. From time to time she took Matt's letter from her bag and glanced at it until she knew every word by heart. She was just reading it again when Mr Allen called her from the back room and she jumped guiltily. She shoved the letter back in her bag and picked up the proofs to take over to the printing shed.

On the cycle ride home, she stopped at the top of the hill, looking back towards the town and the river snaking between the houses which clustered round the church. An idyllic scene, she thought, one which never failed to raise her spirits at any season of the year. Beyond the town, though the river widened and the land became a flood plain, and far in the distance she could see the control tower of the aerodrome and the glint of the lowering sun on the planes lined up on the runways.

Whenever she stopped here to regain her breath, she would send a mental prayer winging its way south to where her brother and his friends had been doing their bit in the fight against their enemies. She still murmured a prayer for Ed's safety — and Matt's now — a sob catching in her throat as she remembered it had much further to go these days. When Ed had been stationed at Tangmere she'd been able to see him fairly often, getting the bus into Chichester on her day off and meeting him at the Unicorn pub, the favourite haunt of the airmen stationed nearby. The estrangement from their father meant that Ed rarely came out to the farm. And now that he was posted so far away, it could be months or even years before she saw him again.

Thinking about her brother naturally led to thoughts of his friend, but as she continued the short distance to the farm, she shut off thoughts of Matt. She wondered how her father had coped with the land girls. He was not a man to hide his prejudices and Celia had a feeling that life might be a bit awkward from now on.

Supper was an almost silent meal. Celia was used to that. Her father was never very chatty and after a hard day's work, he preferred to eat his meal in peace before settling in his chair by the range and getting out his pipe and baccy. But she had expected the girls to talk about their day.

"How are you settling in?" she asked tentatively.

"All right," Stella said and went back to her shepherd's pie.

"You all right at Mrs Robson's?" Celia asked, turning to Joyce.

"Jean's made me very welcome," Joyce replied, grimacing in Larry's direction.

"Well, it's a load off my mind, I can tell you, having you here to help Dad. We were beginning to find it quite a struggle when the farmhands joined up."

"We'd have managed," Larry growled.

"No Dad, we wouldn't. Even when Mickey leaves school, he'll hardly replace two grown men." She turned to the girls and smiled. "We're lucky to have you."

Stella didn't reply. She stood up and put her plate in the sink. Joyce followed suit, turning to Larry with a cheeky grin. "We'll show you, Mr Raines," she said.

"We'll see," he replied, leaving the table to settle in his chair with the paper.

Celia began to clear the table and wash up and the girls took tea towels and offered to help. "No, thanks," she said. "Joyce, you'd better be getting back to the cottage. You've both got an early start in the morning."

Joyce reluctantly said goodnight and took a torch from the dresser. The bulb was covered with tissue paper, leaving only a faint glow. Even out here in the country, the blackout was enforced. She opened the back door and looked out, shivering a little. "Shall I walk with you?" Celia asked.

"Nah, told you I'm not scared of the dark." She set off down the lane and Celia closed the door behind her.

"I'm off to bed," she announced. "Anyone want cocoa before I go up?"

Her father rustled his paper and grunted assent. Stella merely nodded so Celia put some milk on and got out the mugs. When the drinks were made she picked hers up and said goodnight. She couldn't wait to get to her room and start writing to Matt.

To her surprise, Stella followed her. Glancing back down the stairs, she said, "What's up with your Dad? I thought we were going to get on OK. He seemed pleased this morning when I fixed the tractor, but he's hardly said a word all day — just told us what to do and left us to get on with it."

"That's his way," Celia said. "He's not one for idle chitchat. If he wasn't satisfied with your work he'd say so, believe me."

"Well, a little word of encouragement would help."

Celia gave a short laugh. "That you won't get. Look, Stella, it's hard for him. He's dead against women farmers and he's had to accept your being here. If you have any complaints you can talk to the area adviser when she comes round. Mrs Clifton seems a reasonable sort and if you're not happy here, there're plenty of farms would be glad to have you."

"You won't get rid of us that easy," Stella retorted.

"Good, because I for one, am glad that Dad's got some help. As I told you, I wanted to do farm work myself, but he was against it. And now I'm committed to my job in town."

"I thought you'd resent us," Stella admitted.

Celia reassured her and said goodnight, thankful that she seemed to have reached a more amicable relationship with the other girl.

She switched on her bedside lamp and, after undressing and getting into bed, she re-read Matt's letter. Reaching across to the drawer in her bedside cabinet, she got out a pad and pencil. Leaning on a book, she began to write, first thanking Matt for his letter and then apologizing for writing in pencil. *I'm writing this sitting up in bed and I don't think I could manage not to get ink on the sheets*, she wrote. A flush stole over her cheeks as she thought of him reading her words, perhaps imagining her in her nightgown. Don't be silly, she told herself, biting the end of the pencil as she struggled to think what else to say. Be natural, she thought, imagine you're writing to Ed.

In the end that's just what she did, telling him about the land girls and her father's reaction to them, her surprise that Stella had fixed the tractor and Joyce's revelations that she'd gone hop-picking down in Kent and developed a taste for country life. She told him how busy the printing works was now with the extra work from the ministry, although of course she refrained from saying what that work was.

She ended by saying that she hoped he was settling in at Metworth and getting used to the new crew. *Give my love to Ed and tell him to write, lazy devil. And write yourself, too. I'll look forward to hearing from you.*

It was a long letter, warm and friendly, and she hoped he would answer soon. She sealed it and wrote

48

the address and was about to switch the lamp off when she thought of Marion in her London hotel. She picked up her pad and pencil again and wrote a note to her friend, saying how upset Russell was and hoping that she wasn't serious about leaving her husband. "Don't do anything you'll regret," she told her.

Stifling a yawn she settled down to sleep, reflecting that her usually uneventful life had contained too many surprises in the past few days. But her last thought as she drifted off was of her brother's friend and his warm smile, the easy camaraderie that had sprung up between them in such a short time and the hope that it would lead to something more than friendship.

CHAPTER
FIVE

It was late February and there was no sign of spring yet, although some of the ewes had already started lambing. Celia shivered as her bare feet touched the cold lino. She hurriedly thrust them into her slippers, glancing at the luminous figures on her alarm clock. Only 5.30 and still dark. She yawned and went over to the window, lifting the curtain and looking out into the gloom. No snow, thank goodness. Last year they'd been snowed in for weeks and the bad weather had lingered well into March. She hadn't been able to get in to work and had spent the time digging through the drifts to rescue sheep or splitting logs to feed the range. Dad was glad of my help then, she thought, dropping the curtain and getting dressed. At one time she would have felt bitter at the reflection but she was feeling much more optimistic about her future these days. Since Joyce and Stella had come to High Trees, her father had mellowed in his attitude.

It was Stella who'd brought him round. She might look delicate, with her slim wrists and ankles, her baby-blue eyes and sleek blonde hair, but to see her wrestling with a boisterous ram or swinging the starting handle on the old tractor, gave the lie to her frail appearance. Larry had reluctantly begun to respect her and to trust her to work alone.

He wasn't so sure about Joyce. She worked just as hard as Stella but she treated everything as a joke. And her constant chatter got on his nerves. Just as well the younger girl was staying at the Robsons' cottage, Celia thought.

Still, things were working out much better than she'd feared. Dad still wouldn't let her do very much around the farm saying that she had enough to do working full time and keeping house. But she did feel happier these days. The work at the Press was interesting and she really felt she was contributing something to the war effort too. Best of all were the letters from Matt which arrived every other day. Could you fall in love after just a couple of meetings and a handful of letters, she wondered?

As she cleaned her teeth she smiled at herself in the mirror. "Yes," she murmured. "Dearest Matt, I love you . . ." She shook her head, laughing at her foolishness. No way could she write that in a letter. Friends it would have to be — unless he made the first move.

The smile faded and the constant dread that lurked at the back of her mind came to the fore. As she listened to the news on the wireless each evening and heard about the nightly bombing raids that the RAF were carrying out she knew that both Ed and Matt were doing a very dangerous job indeed. She tried not to think about it but it was hard when every night they could hear the planes going over. Most often it was the enemy on their way to strike terror into the hearts of the people of Portsmouth or Southampton. Her brother and his friends had no choice but to strike back. They started it, she thought like a child in a playground squabble.

Downstairs her sombre thoughts fled as her father came in from the yard. She could see he was upset about something. He stamped the mud off his boots and pulled out a chair. "Lost another lamb last night," he said.

"Oh, Dad. Why didn't you wake me?"

"Nothing you could do, gel," he said.

Stella came in shortly afterwards and Celia wondered if she'd been crying. It was hard when they lost an animal after fighting to save it.

"Bloody cold out there," Stella said, going to the range and pouring herself a cup of tea. "That wind makes your eyes water."

Celia didn't believe her but she admired the girl's tough attitude. "Sit down and let me get your breakfast," she said, busying herself at the range, stirring the porridge and frying eggs, making toast.

Joyce came in as she was dishing up. Jean Robson usually sent her and Len off with a cup of tea and slice of toast and they went straight to the milking shed. When they'd finished and the churns were ready for collection at the end of the lane, Len went back to his cottage for a proper breakfast, but Joyce took her meals at the farmhouse.

Celia ate a hurried breakfast and went to let the chickens out and collect the eggs. Back indoors, her father and the girls had already left and she cleared and washed up, prepared a hotpot for the evening meal and made sandwiches for the farm workers' midday break. Jean Robson often prepared the main meal when she was up at the farmhouse doing the cleaning. But today was washday and Celia knew she would not have time. Thank goodness she didn't have to wrestle with the copper herself, she thought.

By the time she had tidied her hair and put on a bit of lipstick, she felt as though she'd already done a day's work. She got her bike out and bumped down the rutted lane. No letter from Matt today. She swiftly buried the flicker of concern. It wasn't his day for writing anyway. There was sure to be one tomorrow.

As usual on arrival at the works, she went into the shed to pick up the time sheets and proofs. Ray looked up from his linotype machine and gave her a cheerful wave. He started work an hour earlier and had already amassed a stack of type which Danny the remaining apprentice was assembling on the stone.

"Part-timer," he joked as she passed his machine.

She laughed and slapped him on the shoulder. Putting up with the men's teasing had become easier with time and she knew there was no malice in it.

"Where's Russell?" she asked.

"He's not in yet," Ray said. "It's all right for some, being the boss's son and all."

"I'm sure he'll be here soon," Celia said, wondering why she was defending him. Ever since Marion had left him he'd mooned around, hardly doing any work and she was sure he was drinking more than was good for him.

She took the proofs in to Mr Allen, contemplating asking him where Russell was, but she thought better of it when he didn't even look up from the papers he was studying. In her own office she sorted the post, took the cover off her typewriter and settled down to work.

She was enjoying the peace and quiet, for once able to get on without interruption. The telephone didn't ring and no one came in to ask about placing advertisements. Glancing at her watch she saw that it was almost lunchtime and she stretched and stood up. Only then did she wonder what had happened to Russell.

Although he was supposed to be employed in the works across the yard, he spent a lot of time in her office, chatting to her and distracting her from work. And he usually told her if he was going to be away. Not that she missed him. She was getting a bit fed up with him going on about Marion. One minute his wife was a bitch who didn't know when she was well off and how dare she leave him. The next he would be almost in tears, saying he didn't know how he could live without her.

Celia had tried to be sympathetic but her patience was wearing thin after all this time. It was obvious she'd gone for good. It was about time he accepted that and got on with his life. Marion had never answered her letter and she hadn't written again. She was sure her friend would have found a more permanent address by

54

now. She knows where I am if she wants to get in touch, she told herself.

Marion was not at the hotel. She was sharing a flat with Elaine Marsh, a former model with whom she'd worked before her marriage. It had all happened so quickly that she still woke up wondering if she was dreaming.

When she'd gone to London all those months ago it had been a gesture of defiance. Despite promising to "love, honour and obey" she had not thought of her marriage vows in quite such literal terms and she'd been shocked that Russell had put his foot down so firmly against her resuming her modelling career.

She had gone over their argument in her head many times since. Her protestations that everyone had to work these days and that if she already had a job she would not be called up had met with derision.

"You can't compare prancing around in front of a camera with war work," Russell said. His laughter had been like a slap in the face and she had flounced into the bathroom, slamming and locking the door.

"Well, you're not going and that's that. I won't allow it," he shouted through the closed door.

"Won't allow?" she had shrieked. "We'll see about that." Afterwards she regretted losing her temper. But she wouldn't admit that she had been exaggerating when she implied she had been offered a job. It was actually only an audition, but she was hopeful of being chosen. The agency had been asked for publicity shots showing the glamorous side of the various jobs women were being called on to do nowadays. It was felt that pictures showing the reality of work on the land and in the factories would hardly help recruitment.

If she got the job she could truthfully say that she was doing war work. It certainly beat helping out in the WVS canteen. She had felt excited and flattered to be considered. Why didn't Russell share her enthusiasm? After all, when they were courting, he'd been proud to be seen with a well-known model on his arm.

The day after their argument, Marion had packed a small case and gone into the Downland Press office to explain to Russell that it wasn't a permanent job and that she'd be back in a couple of days. She didn't want to leave with bad feeling between them. But he had started laying down the law again and she had lost her temper once more.

On the London train she had held on to her resentment and vowed she would stay in London until he began to see sense.

The interview hadn't gone smoothly and she was told she was "not quite right" for the photographic shots they had in mind. Fighting back tears, she'd rushed out of the building, wondering what to do next. No use trying for another modelling assignment — obviously in the couple of years since her marriage, she had lost her looks, grown fat and ugly. It was all Russell's fault, she told herself, irrationally. But she couldn't go back to Sullingford. She'd stay in London for a day or two — let him sweat, she thought. He didn't have to know that the job hadn't worked out.

As she let the door swing shut behind her, a muffled swear word made her turn round. "Sorry," she said. "I didn't hear you coming down the stairs. Are you all right?"

"Yes, I'm OK," the other woman said. She was about to walk on when she paused and looked closely at Marion. "It's Marion Summers isn't it? We worked together — oh, about five years ago it must be."

"Elaine. Fancy bumping into you."

"Well, we are both models and this is a model agency," Elaine said with a laugh. "Did you come about the poster shoot?"

Marion nodded. "No go, though."

"Me too. Still, I'm not bothered — I've got something else lined up. What will you do?"

"Go back to my husband I expect and be a dreary old housewife."

"I heard you'd got married. No kids yet then?"

Marion shook her head. That was another cause of tension between her and Russell and she didn't want to talk about it.

Elaine took her arm. "Come on, let's go and have a cup of tea and catch up. It's been ages."

Reluctantly Marion agreed although she wasn't sure if they'd have anything in common any more. Elaine hadn't changed a bit; she still had the looks and figure of a model while she herself felt like a country bumpkin, especially after being turned down just now.

They found a little café round the corner from the agency and ordered a pot of tea. As Marion had feared, Elaine was full of the exotic places she'd been and the exciting people she'd met. It made Marion feel life was very humdrum. And yet she'd been happy with Russell, enjoying being the wife of one of the small town's prominent businessmen, with a nice house and plenty of leisure time. It was only when the call from the agency came that she'd realized how boring her life had become.

"So what's this other job then?" she asked before Elaine could start probing.

"Public information films. You know, those short films they show at the cinema between the newsreels and the main feature. I've got a screen test tomorrow."

"Sounds like fun," Marion said enviously.

"Why don't you come too?" Elaine asked. "You don't really want to go back to boring housewifery just yet, do you?"

"Not really," Marion admitted.

"Your husband won't mind will he?"

"He will, but I don't care." Marion made up her mind. It wouldn't hurt to let Russell stew a bit longer. If nothing came of it she'd go home and make it up with him. And if she was lucky enough to be taken on, she could truthfully tell him that she was engaged in war work.

That had been several months ago. It was hard work with long hours of boredom in between intense bouts of filming, having to do the same shots over and over until it was done to the director's satisfaction, but she loved it. She'd felt a little bit guilty for not getting in touch with Russell, especially at Christmas. But truth to tell, she'd been having such a good time she had scarcely given him a thought. Didn't she deserve a little fun after all those years in dreary old Sullingford she asked herself.

After staying at the hotel for a few days she had realized she'd have to find somewhere more permanent and moving in with Elaine had proved the ideal solution.

"Someone to share the rent and the chores — not to mention a friend I get on with so well," Elaine had said, laughing. She explained that her previous flatmate had been a bit of a slut when it came to housework, not to mention in her love life too, bringing boyfriends back to the flat and embarrassing Elaine with their antics. "No fear of that with you," she said, "being a respectable married women."

Marion wasn't so sure about that. She had not contacted Russell at all and with each day that passed it was harder to do so. At first she'd deliberately refrained from getting in touch, still seething at his attitude. Then, when he didn't contact her, she was bitterly hurt. It was her own fault, she knew, remembering the hasty letter she'd written when she was staying at the hotel. But he'd known where she was. If he really wanted her back, he would have come rushing after her. When she'd gone to stay with Elaine, she'd left a note at the hotel reception giving her new address so he could easily have found her — if he wanted to.

Now she told herself she didn't care. She was having fun, doing a job she enjoyed and meeting lots of interesting new people. She wouldn't think about Russell. She and Elaine had been invited to a party and, as she carefully applied her makeup and brushed her shiny golden curls, she was determined to enjoy herself.

Russell got off the train at Victoria and hailed a taxi. He had come to London on impulse. After yet another sleepless night spent torturing himself with images of Marion with another man, he had made up his mind to do something about it.

He missed her more than he'd dreamed possible and he would do anything to get her back. He didn't believe she'd meant it when she wrote that she was leaving him for good. That was just her way — act first think later. She was probably regretting it, he told himself, too proud to admit she was wrong.

In the taxi he consulted the piece of paper with the address of the agency. If they couldn't help him he didn't know what he'd do. Marion had lots of friends from her modelling days, but she had taken her address book with her and he had no idea how to contact them.

The taxi drew up outside a black-painted door sandwiched between a dry cleaners and a delicatessen. A discreet brass plaque informed him he'd come to the right place. He pushed the door open and, taking a deep breath, mounted the steep stairs to the offices above.

A plump middle-aged woman sat at the reception desk reading a magazine. Hardly the image for a top model agency, Russell thought. But when she looked up and smiled he could see vestiges of the beauty she had once been.

He cleared his throat, not sure how to begin and she smiled again. "We only have ladies on our books I'm afraid," she said, no trace of sarcasm in her voice.

He laughed. "Well, I'm not exactly model material am I?"

Her appraising look told him she thought otherwise, but he was in no mood for flirting today. "I'm looking for my wife," he blurted out.

"And what makes you think you'll find her here?"

"Her name's Marion Allen, she's a model. Sorry, I mean Marion Summers."

The receptionist pursed her lips. "I do know the name of course but, I'm sorry, Mr Allen, I can't divulge information about our clients. I wish I could help you."

Russell's shoulders slumped. Had he really expected they would give out her address just like that? "I know she's in London, but she hasn't been in touch for a while and I'm worried about her — the bombing and everything."

"I do understand. It's hard to keep in touch with people these days, everyone's moving around. Are you on leave?"

She must have assumed he was in the forces, although he wasn't in uniform, and he seized the opportunity to gain her sympathy. "I haven't got long. I must find her," he said, a catch in his voice.

It worked. "I can't give you an address I'm afraid, but yes, she did come for an interview. She didn't get the job, but I heard recently that she stayed in town and was doing some film work for the Ministry of

Information," she said. "I'm sorry I can't tell you any more, I hope you find her before you have to go back."

Russell thanked her and left, pausing on the pavement outside and wondering what to do next. He couldn't go home without making one more effort. He decided to try the Ministry, although he doubted they would be prepared to tell him anything.

As he looked round for a taxi, he became aware almost for the first time of the bomb damage. He'd been so wrapped up in himself and his misery on the ride from Victoria that he'd barely noticed the shattered buildings, the sandbags shoring up windows and doorways. The people hurrying past were going about their business as usual, seemingly unaware of the devastation around them.

Of course, he read the papers and listened to the wireless. He'd heard the bombers going over on their way to the cities, but sitting at home in his quiet country town, it was hard to imagine the reality of the blitz. For the first time he stopped thinking about himself and the effect Marion's desertion had had on him and began to worry about her. Suppose she'd been caught up in a raid, injured, possibly killed. He couldn't bear the thought. He must find her.

He turned to go back inside the agency office. That woman on the desk had seemed sympathetic and she must have an address or a telephone number for Marion. How else would the agency contact her if they had work for her? He'd charm the information out of her and if that didn't work, he'd try bullying.

Before he reached the door, however, a taxi drew up nearby and three people got out. One of them was Marion and she was hanging on the arm of a tall American officer. She and the other girl were laughing at something he'd said.

Russell was about to approach the group when Marion stood up on her toes and kissed the American on the cheek. "Don't wait for us, sweetie. We'll see you later at the club," she said.

Russell shrank back into the doorway of the dry cleaners. He was right then. She had met someone else — a bloody Yank at that. He watched as the young man strode away. His wife and her friend linked arms and, giggling, entered the agency.

He was tempted to follow them and demand that Marion come home with him right now. He imagined her delight at seeing him, their tearful reunion. But of course it wouldn't work out like that. He'd learned to his cost that laying down the law only made Marion more stubborn.

He looked up to see the American disappearing in the distance. I'd like to go after him and punch him on the nose, Russell thought. But that wouldn't do any good either.

He began the long walk back to Victoria station, shoulders hunched in despair until the wail of the air raid siren roused him from his self pity. An ARP warden grabbed his arm and pushed him into a brick shelter where he sat trapped between a scruffy old man and a young woman with a crying baby.

It gave him time to think and by the time the "all clear" went he had made up his mind. He'd seen Marion go into the agency so he'd write to her there. They'd have to pass his letter on. And there would be no recriminations, no mention of handsome Americans, just a heartfelt declaration of his love and a promise not to interfere in her career if only she would get in touch and let him know she was safe.

CHAPTER
SIX

With the coming of spring, life on the farm was even busier. Although the Raines's only had a small flock of sheep, lambing had been especially hard that year due to the exceptionally cold weather. They had lost two ewes and the kitchen at High Trees was now home to orphaned twin lambs.

The single lamb was being fostered by a ewe which had lost her own baby. But none of the others could be induced to accept the twins. Celia had taken on the responsibility of feeding them and she was exhausted. Not that she minded. Preparing the bottles and sitting by the range with a small defenceless creature looking at her with trusting eyes was one of the rewards of farming. Being up half the night though, and then cycling into town to do a hard day's work at the office was taking its toll.

She daren't complain though.

"You've got it cushy," Stella said, "sitting on your backside in an office all day. Try weeding kale for hours after getting up at four to do the milking, then you'll be really tired."

Celia didn't argue. To Stella, sitting in an office wasn't real work. She'd been a supervisor in a busy department store before joining the land army and was used to being on her feet all day. But Celia's job, especially with the new assignments from the war ministry, was very demanding. Everything had to be checked and double-checked and the final proofreading of these sensitive documents had been added to her duties.

Since she couldn't talk about her work, she knew she'd never make the other girls understand. She didn't think they really believed her when she protested that she'd far rather be working alongside them.

Until recently her life had been brightened by the regular letters from Matt Dangerfield. They had become steadily longer and warmer in tone as the weeks passed and she had begun to hope that his feelings for her matched her own. Despite their brief acquaintance, she felt she now knew him as well as she knew her brother. He often confided his thoughts and feelings and his hopes and plans for "when it was all over".

She wrote back every day telling him about life on the farm and enclosing little pencil sketches — the first primroses in the hedgerow along the lane, the lambs curled in their basket beside the range, Stella in her dungarees, a hoe in her hand, cigarette dangling from her lips, despite Larry's ban on smoking outside.

Matt told her that the pictures meant a lot to him, somehow bringing her closer as he imagined her going about her relatively normal life in the midst of the chaos of war. He didn't say much about his own life, the missions he'd flown, the friends he'd lost. Celia could read between the lines and she also followed the nightly news bulletins on the wireless far more closely than she used to. She knew that since Sir Arthur Harris had taken over Bomber Command, the bombing of German cities had been stepped up in retaliation for the devastation being wreaked on their own population. Casualties among bomber crews were higher than ever.

Celia knew she was right to worry, but as long as the letters kept coming she knew Matt was safe. For the past two weeks though there had been nothing from either him or Ed. She was becoming really concerned although she told herself he was probably far too busy to write. All that didn't stop her imagination from working overtime as she pedalled into town on that bright spring morning.

It was market day in Sullingford and the town was busier than usual. Stalls lined the main street and where it widened out at the bottom of the hill, there were makeshift pens with calves, chickens, pigs, all cackling and squawking and grunting, adding to the noise of the stall holders shouting their wares and the auctioneer trying to make himself heard over the hubbub.

Celia loved market day and, as she wheeled her bicycle towards the printing works, she recalled happier days when she had gone with Dad to Chichester with its purpose-built cattle ring, thronged with farmers from the surrounding farms and villages. After her mother died Dad had stopped letting her go to market with him.

Sullingford's market was a much smaller affair, but it brought people into the town and generally woke up the sleepy little place. Celia smiled and waved in response to greetings from former school friends who sometimes only came into town on market days.

But there was no time to stop and chat. Now that the works were so busy she hated being late. Besides, work would take her mind off worrying about Matt — she hoped.

After parking her bicycle and picking up the proofs from the works, she entered her office, dismayed to see Russell perched on the corner of her desk. She didn't have time to listen to his problems today. He hardly responded to her "good morning" and, as she hung her coat up and pulled out her chair, she realized he looked dreadful. His eyes were bloodshot and his tie askew. Surely he hadn't been drinking so early in the morning.

He didn't move as she sat down and took the cover off her typewriter and she said, rather impatiently, "Did you want something, Russell?"

He shrugged and shifted his weight. But he didn't stand up. "I want my wife back," he said.

"Well, I'm sorry. I can't help you there." He looked so dejected that she softened a little. "You look as if you haven't slept. We've only got Camp, but I could make you some coffee. You don't want your father to see you like this."

He summoned a smile. "Tea, coffee — your cure-all. How will that help?"

"Where did you get to yesterday?" She hoped he hadn't spent the day trying to drink himself into oblivion. It certainly looked like it.

His answer startled her. "I went to London."

"Did you see Marion?"

He gave a short laugh. "Oh, yes, I saw her." He stood up and began to pace the room. It all came out then — how he'd gone to the agency, seen Marion with another man, laughing, kissing him. "To cap it all it was one of those damned Americans who seem to be popping up everywhere. She was having such a good time with her Yank she didn't even notice me," he said bitterly.

"Did you speak to her?"

"No. What was the point?"

Celia didn't know what to say. She knew her friend was impulsive, flirty, liked a good time. But she couldn't imagine Marion having an affair. If she'd met someone else she would come right out with it, ask Russell for a divorce. There must be an explanation.

Russell was still speaking. "I was going to leave a letter for her at the agency, but I decided not to bother. Doesn't seem like she's missing me."

Although Celia felt sorry for him she couldn't help thinking they were both to blame — both so stubborn and no chance of meeting each other halfway unless they actually met in person. Well, it wasn't her problem and she really must get on with some work before Mr Allen came in and asked what she was playing at.

"Russell," she said gently. "I'm sorry things didn't work out, and I wish I could help. But I can't sit here

69

chatting all day. Your father will be shouting for these proofs in a minute and I haven't even started on them."

"I'm sorry, Cee. Thanks for listening." He leaned over and kissed her cheek. "You're so sweet. I sometimes wish —"

Celia was spared hearing what he wished as the door opened and Barney stuck his head round it. "Oh, there you are, Mr Russell. The flat-bed's jammed again. Can you give me a hand?"

"Be right with you, Barney," Russell said. He turned to Celia. "Can we talk later? After work?"

When he'd gone, Celia still didn't start work. She was confused and a little worried. She could cope with the cheeky flirty Russell, managing to brush him off with a laugh and a joke. But this was different. Was he so ready to forget Marion and turn his attention to someone else? Surely not. He was just depressed and unhappy, wanting a shoulder to cry on.

They'd been friends since childhood — the three of them going to dances and to the pictures in Chichester, Russell escorting the two girls home, an arm round each of them. "A thorn between two roses," he would joke. Celia had been briefly attracted to him when she'd been still at school but since then there had been other short-lived romances. And when it became clear that Marion had won Russell's heart and they got married, she was somewhat relieved, especially when she had started working for his father.

Now she worried that remaining friends with him had given him the wrong idea. Had she encouraged

70

him with her friendly banter, her willingness to stop and chat when he came into the office?

She shrugged and pulled the batch of proofs towards her. There would be no meeting him for a drink after work. He'd have to sort his own marital problems out with no help from her. She had the perfect excuse with lambing in full swing and any spare time she had committed to helping out at High Trees.

Besides, although Matt had not declared himself in so many words and she couldn't really be sure if he returned her feelings, she knew where her heart lay. And she would tell Russell so, if he tried to start anything.

The thought of Matt brought back the nagging worry and she found it even harder to concentrate on her work for the rest of the day. Surely there would be a letter waiting for her when she got home.

Matt shrugged off his flying jacket and flopped down on his bunk. He was totally exhausted. How much longer could they keep this up? He glanced across the room at Edgar who was already asleep. Or was he?

Matt was worried about his friend. He had become increasingly withdrawn over the past few weeks. He hoped none of the other crew members had noticed. Morale was low enough already. They'd lost so many planes and with each mission they flew their odds of surviving lessened. Today the empty places at the tables in the mess were especially noticeable. Seven planes had failed to return this time.

Ed was facing the wall, an arm thrown over his face. But Matt was sure he wasn't really sleeping. He debated going over to ask him out for a drink, try to jolly him along a bit. But to be honest he was too tired himself to make the effort.

He leaned over to his locker and picked up the photograph of Celia in its silver frame. It wasn't the snap that had caught his eye when he and Ed had been stationed at Tangmere. This one had been taken by Joyce, one of the land girls, and showed Celia cradling a new born lamb in her arms. Her hair was uncombed and she was wearing a scruffy old jumper. But the smile as she gazed into the camera lit up her eyes. Every time he looked at it, his heart swelled with love. It was hard to believe that their few meetings had been so brief. Her letters were the one bright spot in his life now and he felt he knew her as well as he knew himself.

He reached into his pocket for her last letter and read it again. It was the one that had enclosed the photo taken by Joyce and gave a detailed account of the joys and heartbreaks of lambing. She said how delighted she was that the twin lambs were flourishing under her care. He smiled. She was born to be a farmer's wife. The smile faded as he thought of his return to civilian life after the war and whether she would be willing to give up her country life to be with him. Daft thought when he didn't even know what he wanted himself. But for now and for the duration of the war, the RAF was his life.

He put the letter in his locker along with the others. How foolish to contemplate a future in the midst of this madness. He knew he ought to write back but how could he write a cheerful letter, talking about his hopes for the future when he had to face the fact that he might not return from their next mission?

Then there was Ed. Celia always asked after her brother, complaining that he never wrote, and Matt had got into the habit of sending news on her brother's behalf. But he feared she would read between the lines and start worrying — another reason for not writing.

He slumped down on his bunk again. He should write though — just a short friendly letter, he thought. And if he mentioned Ed at all he would try to imply that his friend was having too much fun in his off duty hours to waste time writing to his sister. But Matt knew the opposite was true and as he got out paper and pen, the temptation to pour it all out got the better of him.

He described their latest bombing raid, the noise, the churning in his stomach as the flak whizzed around the plane. Worst of all though was that, above the noise, he had been aware of Ed, crouched in his cramped navigator's seat behind the cockpit, muttering prayers over and over. Clive had had to use his most authoritative tone to snap him out of it and get him to respond to the request for a fix on their position.

When they landed nobody had mentioned Ed's moment of panic. Only Matt and Sparks, the wireless operator, had been aware of it. Isolated in their gun turrets, Ginger, Pete and Chalky, had been dealing with their own problems. It wouldn't help morale to discover that one of the crew had gone to pieces at a crucial moment.

Matt poured it all out on paper but reading it through afterwards, he knew he couldn't send it. If only he could get leave. He'd go down to Sussex and see Celia and have a long talk with her. Perhaps she could advise him on how to deal with Ed's depression. He knew it wasn't cowardice. There was something else behind it and Matt wished he knew what it was. He screwed up the sheets of paper and was about to start on another letter when the door opened and his pilot, Clive Mitchell looked in.

"Coming over to the NAAFI for a drink?" he asked.

"Can't be bothered," Matt replied.

"Nonsense. You can't sit here mooning over your girl." He kicked the leg of Edgar's bunk. "You too, Ed. Wakey, wakey."

Edgar sat up and rubbed his eyes. "Not time to go already?" he mumbled.

Clive laughed. "We've only just got back. Time for some fun now. We deserve it after today's little jaunt, don't we?"

"Leave me alone," Ed said.

But Clive would not be deterred and Matt joined him in badgering Edgar to come with them. A drink and a sing-song with the others would take his mind off things, Matt thought. The letter to Celia would have to wait.

The three men, arms round each other's shoulders, ambled between the rows of huts towards the NAAFI, a converted farm building on the edge of the air field. As they neared the building, Clive stopped and said, "Got a surprise for you lads."

Matt grinned. "What?"

"Wait and see." He paused. "No, I'll tell you — girls."

"You're kidding," Matt said.

It had been Clive's constant moan that there were no WAAFs stationed at Metworth and he had to go into town to seek feminine company. "It's true. They're land girls. The powers that be have graciously allowed these daughters of the soil to use our NAAFI. Things are looking up."

"Not interested," Ed said, speaking for the first time.

Clive laughed. "Well, they'll be interested in you, mate — once they hear your pa owns a farm."

They peered across the room through the haze of cigarette smoke, seeing Ginger, their front gunner, at the piano, thumping out a tune. It was hard to tell what it was above the hubbub. He was surrounded by women, singing and laughing. They must have come straight from work, as they were still dressed in their corduroy trousers and green jerseys. Matt was reminded of Celia and the photo of her with the lamb. She may not be in the land army, but he knew from her letters that even with her office job she worked as hard as these girls did. How he wished she were here with them.

A mug of beer was thrust into his hand and he found himself joining in with *Roll out the Barrel*. He noticed that Clive had managed to snag the prettiest of the girls for himself. She wasn't a patch on Celia though, he thought as he looked round the room — none of them were. He peered through the smoky haze, looking for

Ed, pleased to see that he too was talking to a girl. Perhaps a little flirtation would help to take his mind off whatever was bothering him.

"You writing a book?" Stella asked, peering over Celia's shoulder as she sat at the kitchen table. "You're always writing."

Celia put her arm over the page to stop Stella reading what she had written. "It's a letter if you must know," she said. With the paper shortage she had run out of proper notepaper and so was using an old exercise book for her letters to Matt.

"Don't know why you bother. He doesn't write back, does he?" Stella said.

Celia didn't reply. She refused to let the other girl needle her. When Stella had arrived at the farm, she had tried to be friendly but her attempts had been rebuffed. At first she'd thought she had done something to incur Stella's dislike until she realized that Joyce got the same treatment — barbed comments and baleful stares. She was good at her job though, and Celia was pleased that her father seemed to think a lot of her. Stella was gradually helping to change his opinion of woman farm workers and for that Celia was grateful.

She waited until Stella had left the room before continuing with her letter. She was running out of things to say and with a sigh she echoed Stella's words. "Don't know why I bother."

It was three weeks since she'd heard from either Matt or Ed and she was getting worried. She told herself she was being foolish. They would have been informed if anything had happened to Ed and, although any official notification about Matt would go to his family in Devon, Celia was sure that her brother would pass on any news.

She threw the pen down and, almost immediately picked it up again. She was being silly. She'd finish this letter and post it on her way to work tomorrow. But, she vowed, if she didn't get a reply by the end of the week, she'd give up.

CHAPTER
SEVEN

Celia was relieved that as spring turned to summer Russell no longer interrupted her work to ask if she'd heard from Marion. "You must know where she is," he'd said time after time until she was fed up with trying to convince him. If Marion had been in touch she would have told him so, but she wouldn't reveal where her friend was staying if Marion had asked her to keep it secret.

As the weeks passed he appeared to have accepted that his wife had gone for good, although he still seemed very depressed and Celia thought he was drinking heavily. She knew he wasn't pulling his weight in the print room. She'd heard the lads muttering that they couldn't be expected to do the extra work with so few staff and the boss's son ought to muck in and give a hand.

Celia was also a little upset that her friend hadn't written to her. Perhaps Marion thought she'd tell Russell where she was staying. But she ought to know me better than that, Celia thought. I can keep a secret. She wished her friend would get in touch though, especially when she heard about the devastating air raids on the city. She was really worried about her and prayed daily that she was safe.

The works was busier than ever printing public information leaflets and, now that Jim had left to join the navy, they were finding it hard to cope with only a handful of staff. Mr Allen decided to cut the number of pages in the *Advertiser* still further. It meant less typing for Celia but the mountain of proofreading did not seem to lessen.

It was a hot, still day and she had opened the window, but the noise from the market was too distracting and she got up to shut it again. When she sat down and picked up the next sheet of paper, the words swam in front of her eyes. It was just the heat, she told herself.

If only she was out in the fresh air, she was sure she'd feel better. Haymaking had started and she envied Joyce and Stella, picturing them at work in the bottom meadow near the river. It was hard work but it was her favourite time of year — when the weather was right as it was now. She sighed and threw down her red pencil. She should be back at High Trees helping. Who knew when the weather would break and ruin the hay harvest?

She rubbed her eyes and started reading the proofs again, marking the few typographical errors in the margin. When Ray had been doing the typesetting it was hardly necessary, she thought; he was so good at his job. With so few people coming into the office to place advertisements or order stationery and posters these days, Celia felt that if it weren't for the work from the Ministry, they could almost do without her. That was, until Mr Allen had made her responsible for the proofreading. Despite Ray being so meticulous everything still had to be checked thoroughly.

She still wished it was possible to give in her notice and help on the farm. Her father could hardly stick to his assertion that it wasn't woman's work now that he had accepted the land girls and seen how hard they worked. If only she hadn't signed that form, she thought. But she had and now she was committed to working at the *Downland Press* for the duration of the war which looked like dragging on for a long while yet.

When the door opened and Russell came in, she suppressed a sigh, hoping he wasn't in one of his maudlin moods. To her surprise he looked better than he had for weeks. His eyes were clear, his shirt immaculate and he looked as if he'd recently had a haircut. And he was smiling.

Celia smiled back, fully expecting him to say he'd heard from Marion at last.

Instead, he perched on the corner of her desk, as was his habit, and grinned. "You're looking at the new me," he announced. "No more weeping and wailing over my errant wife. Good riddance, I say. From now on, I'm not going to think about her."

"What's brought this on?" she asked with a smile.

Russell looked slightly shamefaced. "The old man tore me off a strip," he muttered, glancing towards his father's office. "Told me to pull my socks up. He said I drove Marion away and must accept that she wants a new life."

"She'll be back," Celia said. "She just wanted to teach you a lesson."

"Well, it's too late. I don't care if she stays away for good."

Celia didn't reply and he stood up abruptly. "Anyway, I just popped in to ask if you'd help me celebrate my determination to pull my socks up as the old man it puts it. Come and have a drink with me after work."

"I don't think a drink's a good idea, Russell."

He gave a short laugh. "Perhaps you're right. No more drinking. What about the pictures then?"

Celia was tempted. She hadn't been to the pictures for ages. After being at work all day and then helping with chores on the farm, she was far too tired. Besides, it was her day for working late.

"I'm sure you haven't got time for the pictures. Have you forgotten it's press day? I don't think Mr Allen would be pleased if the two of us sloped off early."

"I had forgotten actually. Oh well, another day perhaps."

When he'd gone, Celia pondered his change of manner. She was sure he was just putting on a front. She didn't think he'd been serious about their going out together either and she hoped he wouldn't mention it again. Not that there was any harm in it. But he was still a married man after all.

Although it was late by the time the papers were bundled up and loaded on the van it was still quite light and Celia was looking forward to cycling home in the warm summer dusk. The heat of the day had lessened and it was good to get outside.

As she wheeled her bicycle across the yard, Russell called out, "Let me give you a lift." He often drove her home on the days they worked late. If it was dark or wet she would accept his offer, but when it was fine she preferred to cycle. Besides, since he'd asked her out, she felt a bit awkward with him. She was used to his hitherto harmless flirting but since splitting up with Marion he'd been spending more time chatting to her and she wasn't sure how to deal with him.

She mounted her bike and called out, "I need the fresh air. See you tomorrow." And before he could insist, she'd pedalled out of the yard and down the hill towards the river. At the bridge she turned back, but the van was nowhere in sight.

Was she being silly, she asked herself as she changed gear and began the slow climb up the hill towards the Downs and High Trees. She had known Russell since they were at school and they'd always got on well. Of course, she'd had that brief crush on him when she was fifteen, but he hadn't known about that, thank goodness. When he started courting Marion seriously she'd been pleased for them both. They were obviously in love, but they were so different that she had often wondered if they were really right for each other. Still, until recently they'd seemed happy enough.

As she neared the farm she turned onto a track leading towards the meadow beside the river. It often flooded in winter, but the waters soon receded, leaving lush growth. In one field the High Trees herd grazed in summer. The other was left for hay and, as Celia drew near, she saw that her father and the land girls were still at work.

Despite her tiredness she threw her bike down beside the hedge and joined them, rolling up her sleeves and grabbing a pitchfork. She knew they'd appreciate an extra pair of hands.

Stella was driving the tractor while Dad stood on top of the trailer, levelling off the load. When he saw Celia he waved. "Too late, lass," he called. "We've nearly finished."

She didn't answer, just forked the last few remaining piles of hay up to the trailer. There was one more field to do and then haymaking would be over for another year. Two ricks stood in the corner of the field; this load would go into the barn. Tomorrow they would start on the other field, if the weather held.

Joyce grinned. "Glutton for punishment, you."

"Can't have people thinking I don't do my bit," Celia said lightly with a glance at Stella. The other girl was scowling and hadn't even acknowledged her.

They finished working in silence. It was nearly dark when Joyce climbed up beside Larry and Stella started up the tractor.

Celia retrieved her bicycle from the hedge and rode back to the farmhouse. She went inside and started preparing a meal for her father and the girls. She had already eaten at the works while they waited for the papers to roll off the press.

She was pouring the water into the big earthenware teapot when Larry came in. "Joyce is shutting the hens up and Stella's feeding the calves. I was wondering where you'd got to — thought we'd have to feed ourselves tonight," he said.

"You know I work late on Thursdays, Dad. I would have brought some fish and chips home, but I guessed you'd still be hard at it and they would have got cold."

She went to the larder and got out the sausages she'd bought the day before. There was a bowl of ready shelled peas on the shelf and when she took the food over to the range she saw that someone had peeled some potatoes and left them in a saucepan covered with cold water.

That must have been Joyce, she thought. Although Stella worked hard out on the farm, she rarely helped in the house and always left the cooking to Celia.

The meal was almost ready when the others came in and Celia thanked Joyce for preparing the vegetables.

"Oh, that wasn't me," she said. "Stella did it."

Celia apologized and thanked the other girl but all she got in return was a scowl. And when Larry complimented her on the meal, saying, "You make gravy almost as good as your mum's," Stella pushed her chair back and left the table, noisily depositing her plate and cutlery in the sink.

After Joyce had gone back to the Robsons' cottage, Celia sat down to write to Edgar. She had given up on Matt, sad that the relationship which had seemed so promising seemed to have fizzled out. Well, if he didn't answer her letters why should she bother? It hurt all the same though.

As she wrote, she stole occasional glances at Stella who was sitting opposite her father in front of the range, doing her knitting. He was reading the paper as usual and Celia thought what a cosy domestic scene it would seem to an outsider. If only Stella wasn't so moody, she thought, wondering what had brought on that earlier display of petulance.

Joyce had confided to her that Stella had had a hard life before joining the land army, her main motivation being to get away from an unhappy home. She'd also hinted that Stella had been involved with her boss at the department store but things hadn't worked out. Still, however unhappy she'd been before, she seemed to enjoy farm life. Although she had to work hard, she had a comfortable bed, good food and a couple of new friends if only she would respond to their efforts at friendship.

Celia sighed and picked up her pen again only to pause when her father spoke. She looked up but Larry wasn't addressing her. He was pointing out something in the paper to Stella. And she was nodding and smiling in agreement.

Astonished, Celia realized that the smile lit up her face and she looked lovely with the lamp shining on her blonde hair. What was going on? Surely Stella wasn't becoming fond of her father? The idea seemed preposterous and Celia dismissed it and went back to her letter. At least Stella seemed in a better mood now and Celia just hoped it would last. Joyce had mentioned only the other day how hard it was to spend a whole day in the company of such an "old grump" even if she did feel sorry for her.

The hot dry weather continued and soon the last of the hay was safely in. The kale was cut and stacked for winter feed and there was a slight lull in the frantic activity on the farm. There were still sheep to be inspected for foot rot and maggot infestation, cows to be milked, and all the other myriad regular jobs to be done, but after the successful hay harvest Larry thought it was about time the girls had a day off.

It was market day in Chichester and he was taking a couple of heifers to sell. "You can come too if you like," he said at breakfast. "That's if one of you doesn't mind squeezing in the back of the pickup with the animals."

Joyce and Stella stared at each other until Joyce said with a mischievous smile, "Toss you for it." She produced a penny from the pocket of her dungarees and flipped it into the air.

"Heads," Stella muttered.

Laughing, Joyce put the penny back in her pocket. "Sorry, love it was tails. You're in the back."

Stella stood up. "Actually, I don't think I'll come. I've got lots to do — washing, mending and that. I'm happy to stay here. I can cook something for when you get back." She smiled at Larry. "You don't need me, do you?"

"No, lass. I just thought it would be a treat for you going into town. Spend some of that hard-earned money you've been saving up."

"Not that there's much to spend it on with the rationing and all," Joyce said. "Come on, Stella. We can go to the pictures while Mr Raines does his market business." She paused. "I'll even let you sit in the front. I don't mind snuggling up to a heifer. There's no one else to snuggle up to around here."

"Oh, all right then," Stella said.

"Wish you could come too, Cee," said Joyce.

"Some of us have to work," Celia replied, laughing. "And if I don't go now, I'll be in trouble. Have a good time."

As she cycled down the lane she saw Bill the postman coming towards her and her heart lifted. Surely there'd be a letter from Matt today. But as he drew near he shook his head and she pedalled on, trying to control the tears that threatened. Was it that he didn't see any point in continuing their correspondence or was there another, more sinister reason?

Freewheeling down the hill towards the bridge into town usually gave her a feeling of euphoria which sometimes made her laugh aloud, but today such feelings eluded her. The noise of several planes taking off from the nearby airfield did nothing to lighten her mood.

Immersing herself in work usually took Celia's mind off things though today worry nagged at the back of her mind. She didn't really want to believe that Matt was no longer interested, but she wouldn't give in to the fear that something dreadful had happened. Surely she would have heard? And even if he'd decided not to write, Ed would have been in touch. She hadn't heard from him either. Knowing they were in the same bomber crew only added to her sense of dread.

When Russell came into the office with a big grin on his face she could not respond and bent her head to the proofs she was checking.

"Cheer up, it might never happen," he said.

"What are you so cheerful about?" she asked, refusing to smile. Perhaps he had heard from Marion. But his next words were a complete surprise.

"Dad says, as there's not much on at the moment, you can have the afternoon off."

"But I've got all these proofs to do."

"If you finish them by dinner time, you can go. Dad says he's expecting a lot of new work from the Ministry soon and then we'll be flat out, working all hours, so make the most of it," Russell said.

Celia threw down her pen, not sure if he was teasing. It was unlike Mr Allen to give her extra time off. Usually if things were slack he would find something for her to do — weeding out old files or tidying the store cupboards over in the works shed.

"I'm serious, Cee. You really can have the afternoon off."

"I wish I'd known that this morning. I could have arranged to meet Joyce to go to the pictures."

"I thought those land girls worked all the hours God sends," Russell replied.

"They do, but Dad's gone into Chichester to the market and taken them with him. Old Len and Mickey are holding the fort today."

"You can still go into town. I'll take you in the van if you like."

Celia looked at him, wondering if this was just a ploy to get her to go out with him. He hadn't mentioned it since the last time she'd refused.

"Oh, come on, Cee. Just a run into Chichester — no strings, honestly. We'll find your friends in the market and we can all go to the flicks together."

Celia was tempted, but she wasn't going to give in so easily. "Depends which film's showing," she said.

"Don't you read the *Advertiser* then?" Russell teased, waving that week's paper under her nose.

"Don't have time," she said. It was true. Although she checked the proofs, she was looking for printing errors and the actual content of the paper seldom sank in.

"Well, there's Errol Flynn in *Robin Hood* at the Gaumont or *Citizen Kane* at the Picturedrome. Your choice."

"Let's wait till we meet up with the others. I don't fancy Orson Welles and *Robin Hood's* been out for ages. They might have already seen it."

Celia went back to her work, but Russell still hovered nearby. She looked up impatiently. "I've got to finish this first. If you'd just let me get on . . ."

"All right. But don't be long. I'll bring the van round the front."

A few minutes later Celia took the papers through to the works and gave them to Ray. Mr Allen looked up as she passed his office door. "Have a nice afternoon," he said.

"Russell wasn't joking then? I really can have the rest of the day off?"

"You deserve it, my dear. What with slaving away here and then helping on the farm, I don't suppose you get much leisure time. Make the most of it." He dismissed her with a wave of his hand and she fetched her bag and jacket and went out into the High Street.

Conversation was impossible as the noisy old works van chugged up the hill and took the main road to Chichester. Celia was glad Russell didn't try to make conversation and she leaned back in the seat and closed her eyes. She sat up as they came into Eastgate Square and turned into Market Avenue. A laughing group of airmen spilled out of the Unicorn pub as they passed and Celia's heart contracted. How could they seem so carefree given the dangerous job they were doing? Despite her determination to put Matt out of her heart and mind, the sight of those blue uniforms brought a lump to her throat.

Russell glanced at her, but didn't say anything. She had never mentioned Matt to him and he probably assumed she was thinking of her brother. He stopped the van outside the Bull Inn and they got out.

The market was still in full swing. Crowds thronged the stalls in search of bargains while over near the animal pens, the hoarse voice of the auctioneer could be heard above the lowing of cows and bleating of sheep and all the other noises that went to make up a busy market day.

"We'll never find your friends in this lot," Russell said. "Let's go along to the cinema. We'll miss the beginning of the film otherwise."

Celia didn't want to be alone with him for too long and she hesitated. "They'll be over by the cattle ring," she said, pushing her way towards the covered building where the cows were paraded in front of the gathered farmers.

She didn't wait to see if Russell was following. Inside she saw her father with Stella and she went over to them.

"Where's Joyce?" she asked. "Weren't you both going to the pictures?"

Stella turned to her. "And I thought you were working." She noticed Russell, who had come in behind Celia. "Oh, I see," she smirked. "Skiving off with the boss's son, are we?"

Celia was about to make an angry retort, but Russell put his hand on her arm. "Good afternoon, Mr Raines. How are things going?" he asked, ignoring Stella.

"Not too bad," Larry replied.

"We're off to the pictures and wondered if the girls would like to come too — that's if you don't need them here."

Before Larry could reply, Stella said, "No thanks, I'm staying here. Mr Raines's heifers are up next and I'm keen to see what they make."

Celia was astonished. She hadn't thought Stella's interest in farming had progressed that far. "What about Joyce then?" she asked.

"She went to get a pie at the stall. You'll never find her in this crowd." She glanced at Russell, who was talking to Larry and lowered her voice. "Besides, you don't want her playing gooseberry, do you?"

Before Celia could think of a suitable retort, Russell said, "Let's go and find her." She hoped he hadn't heard Stella's remark, but just then the heifers were led in and began their parade round the ring. Larry and Stella's attention was diverted and they didn't seem to notice as Celia and Russell left.

They spotted Joyce by the pie stall, her mouth full of pastry. She waved to them and Celia couldn't help smiling at the disappointed look on Russell's face. So he had been hoping to get her alone. Well, she'd make sure Joyce sat between them. And if Russell wanted someone to take his mind off Marion, he could flirt with her friend. As for Joyce, she often complained jokingly that, apart from Celia's father, the only men she'd spoken to lately were old Len Robson and young Mickey.

Celia had already seen *Robin Hood* but Joyce said she "adored" Errol Flynn. They crossed the square to the cinema where Russell managed to sit between the two girls. Celia couldn't think of an excuse to change places and, hoping he would behave himself, she settled down to enjoy seeing Errol Flynn swashbuckling against the Sheriff of Nottingham. But before the film started they had to sit through the usual advertisements, public information films and a very unfunny cartoon.

Celia felt her eyes closing and jerked herself upright. She hadn't realized how tired she was but she didn't want to miss the big film. She leaned across to whisper to Joyce just as Russell shifted in his seat and let out a gasp.

At first she thought it was because she'd leaned against him until she saw that his gaze was fixed on the screen. The film was about the importance of salvage for the war effort. A rather pompous gentleman was explaining why it was important to save every scrap of paper, metal and kitchen waste. Hanging on his every word was a pretty young woman in a maid's uniform. The camera zoomed in on her as she turned with a smile and there, beaming down at them larger than life, was Marion Allen. So that's what she'd been up to all these weeks.

CHAPTER
EIGHT

Celia was about to speak when Russell pushed his seat up with a clatter, brushed past her and stumbled towards the exit.

Joyce leaned across. "What's up with him?" she whispered.

Celia pointed to the screen. "That's his wife. I told you she'd left him, didn't I?"

"You didn't say she was a film star though."

"I didn't know."

A man in the seat behind leaned forward and tapped Joyce on the shoulder. "Do you mind? Some of us are trying to watch the film."

Joyce ignored him. "Do you think we should go after him?"

"Best leave him alone." Celia turned to the man behind, apologized and they settled into their seats.

By now the short film had finished and music flooded the cinema as the titles for *Robin Hood* flashed up on the screen. The light-hearted adventures of the daring outlaw and his plans to foil the dastardly sheriff should have been a welcome respite from the grim realities of everyday life in wartime, but Celia couldn't concentrate. Despite his protestations that he no longer cared for Marion, Russell had obviously been upset by seeing her. She just hoped he wasn't trying to drown his sorrows in the nearest pub.

The film finished and the two girls followed the other patrons out of the cinema.

"Russell's gone. We'll have to get the last bus," Celia said.

"No, there he is," Joyce replied.

Russell was leaning against the van, smoking a cigarette. To her surprise he was smiling. "Enjoy the film, girls?" he asked.

"It was wonderful," Joyce replied. "I love that Errol Flynn; he's so handsome."

"Come on then, let's get you home." Russell opened the van door. "You can both squeeze in the front with me."

As he got in beside them Celia said, "What a shock. Are you all right, Russ?"

"I'm fine." Russell flicked his cigarette end out of the window and started the van. "Sorry I rushed out like that. I went for a walk, had a good long think."

"Well, at least you know what she's up to and that she's safe."

"I also know that she's made a new life for herself. It's obvious what I had to offer wasn't good enough. Good luck to her in her new career." There was a slight sneer on the last word and Celia knew he was merely trying to convince himself. Anything she said would be no comfort to him.

He was silent for the rest of the journey until they'd dropped Joyce off. A few hours ago Celia had been worrying about how to manage Russell if he made a pass at her. No danger of that now, she told herself. He was far too upset.

But, as he stopped the van and she opened the door, he leaned across and grabbed her hand. "Well, that's it then. From now on I'm going to consider myself a free man. What do you say, Cee? You and me — we've always got on well." He pulled her to him, aiming a clumsy kiss at her lips. She pulled away, realizing that, although he'd seemed quite sober, he'd had a few drinks after rushing out of the cinema.

"Russell, no. As far as I'm concerned you're still a married man." She scrambled out of the van and his voice followed her.

"Where's the harm? You don't have a boyfriend, do you? We could have a bit of fun."

She slammed the door and walked away without replying.

It was early evening by then and she expected that her father and Stella would be home. But the pickup truck wasn't in the yard. Where had they got to?

Len came out of the milking parlour and rolled a milk churn towards the gate. He seemed surprised to see her.

"I heard the motor — thought it was your Dad back from market," he said. "You're home early."

"Had the afternoon off. Joyce and I went to the pictures. We dropped her off at the cottage. She'll be over later to help bed the animals down."

"What about the other one?" Len rarely used Stella's name.

"Last I saw she was still in the market with Dad. I expect they'll be back soon."

They both paused as the pickup pulled into the yard and Larry and Stella got out. Stella was laughing, but her usual scowl returned when she saw Celia and she walked into the house without speaking.

"Good film, Cee?" her father asked.

Celia nodded. "How was the market, Dad?"

"Not bad. Got a reasonable price for those heifers." He turned to Len. "Time you was off home. I'll have a word in the morning about that field."

"What field, Dad?" Celia asked.

"Nothing for you to worry about," he said.

As usual he wouldn't discuss anything to do with running the farm. She shrugged and went indoors, thinking she'd make a start on their supper. Stella was sitting at the kitchen table and Celia felt a spurt of annoyance that she could just sit there expecting someone else to wait on her.

As she opened the larder door, Stella said, "Don't bother doing anything for me and Larry. We stopped for fish and chips on the way home. That's why we were late."

Since when had she start calling my father Larry? Celia thought. Cheeky cow. She didn't let her annoyance show, however. "You were lucky to get fish to go with your chips. Last time I queued up for the lads at the works I ended up with just two measly bits of cod to share between all of us," she said. "Well, it saves me cooking. I'll just have a sandwich. I expect Dad would like a cup of tea though."

"I thought lover boy would have taken you for a meal. Still, it wouldn't have been much fun with a chaperone."

Refusing to rise to the bait, Celia filled the teapot and then got on with fixing her sandwich, using the last of her meagre cheese ration. Stella wasn't going to leave things alone though.

"I thought you were stuck on that friend of your brother." She gave a little laugh. "But he's stopped writing hasn't he? Found himself a little WAAF I expect."

"There are lots of reasons he might not be able to write. He is a bomber pilot you know," Celia snapped. The reason that most haunted her dreams rose up and hit her and she was hardly able to control the threatening tears.

Stella was unperturbed. "Wartime romances seldom work out," she said. "I suppose it doesn't hurt to have another string to your bow, especially the boss's son."

Celia slammed the teapot down on the table, slopping some of the contents on to the tablecloth. "You bitch," she shouted and rushed out of the room.

Upstairs, she sat on her bed, appalled by having lost her temper like that. Why should she worry what Stella said? She knew that her friendship with Russell was harmless. They'd known each other since schooldays after all.

Determined to ignore Stella's sniping, she washed her face and went downstairs. Her father was sitting in his usual chair, drinking tea and reading a letter.

Stella, sitting opposite him, looked up and said, "Your sandwich is on the table and I've poured your tea."

She made it sound as if she'd prepared it, but Celia didn't comment. If Stella was trying to get into Dad's good books she'd have to try a lot harder, she thought. He was the sort of man who took being waited on by women for granted.

As Celia started to eat, Stella continued to needle her. "What about Joyce? She'll want a meal. You'd better start cooking." Although the other girl lodged with the Robsons, she usually had her meals at the farm.

Celia hid a smile. "Len said she could eat with them tonight. Jean's made a shepherd's pie — plenty for all of them," she said. She finished her sandwich and took her plate over to the sink. As she poured hot water onto the dirty crockery her father gave an angry exclamation. "I don't see how they can force me to do that."

She turned round to ask what he meant but Stella was leaning forward, her hand on Larry's arm. "I know it's upsetting having someone tell you what to do with your own land, but they do have the power."

"It's nonsense expecting me to plough that field. What are my sheep going to eat next year when there's no grazing land left?"

"Perhaps they think it's more important to grow wheat. I must say I agree with them. So many ships being sunk — we need to grow more of our own food."

Celia paused, a saucer and dish mop in her hand, seething with anger. How dare Stella tell her father what was good for his farm? The cheek of it. She'd only been here five minutes and Dad's family had farmed here for generations. It was all she could do not to throw the saucer across the room.

Her father sighed and said, "You're right, lass. This war's messing everyone's lives up. I suppose I'll have to do what the Ministry says."

Celia dried her hands and got her jacket off the back door. She'd go and find Joyce and help her with the animals. If she stayed she might say something she'd regret. As she walked down the lane she realized she was more hurt than angry. How often had she tried to persuade her father to involve her in the running of the farm, only to be told that farming wasn't woman's work?

It was a pleasant evening, cooler after the sultry heat of the day, and as she walked her temper cooled too. By the time she met Joyce she was feeling a little better, although a vestige of resentment still lurked at the back of her mind.

"Got rid of lover boy then?" Joyce asked as she came near.

"Don't call him that — you're as bad as Stella," Celia snapped.

"Just joking." She opened the gate and went through into the pasture. "Did your Dad say whether he wanted the cows brought in tonight?"

"Don't ask me, Stella's the one he discusses things with."

"Ooh, don't bite my head off." Joyce held up her hands. "What's got into you tonight? We had a lovely afternoon and now —"

"Oh, don't listen to me. I'm just in a bad mood. Perhaps I'd better leave you to get on with your work."

"Don't be silly. It'll do you good to get it off your chest." She looked up at the darkening sky. "It was so hot earlier I thought we were in for a storm, but it seems to have cleared now. The cows will be OK. Let's go and see to the chickens."

Celia followed her into the farmyard, regretting she'd been so snappy with her friend. They fed the hens and made sure the henhouse was secure and Celia asked if Joyce wanted to come in for some cocoa before going back to the Robsons' cottage.

"No thanks; Jean will make some when I get in. Let's sit out here for a bit — it's such a nice evening."

She sat down on an upturned bucket and Celia found a box and joined her. They sat for a few moments gazing up at the stars. It was a clear night and from the aerodrome they heard the roar of planes taking off. Soon there would be the drone of enemy bombers on their way to the cities further along the coast.

Celia shivered and Joyce said, "Thinking about your feller?"

She nodded, biting her lip. "Except that he's not my feller as you call him. I don't even know if he's a friend any more."

Joyce laughed and nudged Celia in the ribs. "So, the boss's son — Russell — there's nothing . . . ?"

Celia laughed. "It's nothing serious. He's always been one for chatting up the girls. It doesn't mean anything. And since Marion left, I think he's trying to convince himself he doesn't care."

"Well, don't go feeling sorry for him and doing something silly." Joyce paused and looked up at the stars once more. "Better get back to the cottage. Jean will be wanting to lock up."

"I'll walk a little way with you." Celia stood up and they linked arms and began walking down the stony track.

"So, if it isn't Russell, what about this friend of your brother's — Matt — you're really stuck on him, aren't you?"

Celia laughed. "Daft isn't it, I only met him a couple of times. How can you fall for someone . . .?"

"Sometimes it's like that. Hits you like a punch in the stomach."

Something in her voice told Celia it wasn't just a casual remark.

"Bob's a prisoner of war, didn't manage to get as far as Dunkirk. Haven't heard anything for ages." She sighed. "We've known each other since we were kids. It wasn't until he went away we realized how we felt. His mum still hopes he'll turn up, but I'm sure we'd have heard by now if he was a prisoner."

"You mustn't give up hope," Celia said.

They reached the cottage and Joyce said, "Don't say anything to Stella — you know what she's like. I think she's jealous cos she hasn't got anybody."

"I think she's after my Dad," Celia blurted out.

Joyce started to laugh, but when she saw that Celia was serious she stopped. "I think he's too sensible to be taken in by the likes of her."

Celia told her about the conversation she'd overheard. "He takes more notice of her than he ever did of me — about the farm I mean. I must admit it galls me."

"At least he seems to have accepted that we girls can do the work. Don't worry, Cee, the war's got to end some time and Stella will go back to her old life. It'll be your turn then. You can leave your boring old office and take your place on the farm like you always wanted to. Your Dad can hardly stop you then."

"I suppose so." She sighed. "Oh, why does life have to be so complicated?"

"You think too much," Joyce said. "You should go out and enjoy yourself sometimes."

"That's what Russell said."

"I don't mean go out with him — unless you want to of course, but, war or no war, there's plenty going on — dances in Chichester, the pictures. We had a good time today; we should do it more often."

"I don't know where you get your energy, after working all hours on the farm."

"You've got to make the most of things — while you've got the chance."

"You're right." Celia gave her friend an impulsive hug and said goodnight.

As she walked up the dark lane towards home she thought over what Joyce had said. It was true, she was jealous of Stella, but it did no good to dwell on it. She would only make herself more miserable.

They hadn't really talked much about Matt, but he had been on her mind all the while. She realized she'd been behaving like a spoilt child, refusing to write because he hadn't answered her letter. She should take a leaf out of Joyce's book. She must be worrying about Bob constantly, though no one would guess from her cheerful demeanour and willingness to listen to other people's troubles.

Yes, she would write to Matt tonight, she thought, a nice cheerful friendly letter.

Matt was seriously worried about Edgar. His friend had become more and more withdrawn over the past few weeks. He did his job competently enough and Matt didn't think any of his fellow crew members had noticed anything amiss. He sincerely hoped they never would; anything that might affect morale would be dealt with harshly by their pilot. Clive Mitchell would not tolerate a member of the crew if he felt he wasn't fully committed to flying and part of the team. All their lives depended on it.

So far they'd been lucky, although there had been a few narrow escapes. The previous night had been the most hair-raising so far and it was only Clive's skill as a pilot that had brought them safely back to base, although the plane wouldn't be flying again for a long time — if ever.

They'd just been informed that briefing for tonight's mission was at five o'clock and the rest of the crew had gone down to the nearby village pub to enjoy a couple of hours of freedom.

Ed had made an excuse not to go and, so that the others didn't start thinking of his friend as the odd one out, Matt stayed behind too. He had some letters to write, he'd said.

As usual when they had any free time, Ed was stretched out on his bed, gazing at the ceiling, answering in monosyllables when Matt tried to talk to him.

"Have you written to your sister lately?" he asked now.

"Nothing to write about," Ed muttered.

"She'll be worrying about you."

"You write then — tell her I'm all right."

"It's not my job to reassure her about your welfare," Matt said sharply. He was feeling guilty because he hadn't written either. It was weeks since that last brief note. But then, she hadn't written either. Still, he wanted to keep in touch with her, of course he did. He reached over and picked up the photo frame — not that he needed a picture. He could see her in his mind's eye as clearly as if she was in the room with him. Celia, busy at the kitchen range in that lovely old farmhouse; leaning on the gate and laughing, pushing her hair out of her eyes; waving goodbye as he kick started the motorbike and roared off down the lane, Ed clinging to him and laughing.

So much had happened since that autumn day over a year ago when they'd set off with such eagerness to join their new squadron. He looked across at Ed. They'd both changed, become harder, less carefree. But it was something more than that with Ed. Matt had tried getting him to come out with the rest of the crew, to try to forget the horrors they encountered on each mission. It hadn't worked. To be fair, Ed would start off by making an effort. But then he would withdraw into himself, nursing his beer mug in a corner, not joining in with the singing and banter. He was so different now from the young man Matt had befriended in their days at the training camp.

How could he write to Celia without revealing his concern for his friend? His last note had been brief, almost impersonal. Yet he didn't want her to think he didn't care. He would write to her today, he decided, but first he must do something about Ed. He stood up abruptly. "Come on, Ed. We're going out," he said. He grabbed his friend's arm and pulled him upright.

At first Ed resisted, Matt persevered though, and eventually he gave in. "I'm not going to the pub," he said.

"Who said anything about the pub? We'll go for a spin on the old bike. We've got enough petrol for a few miles."

"Oh, all right." Ed grabbed his flying jacket and followed Matt outside.

It was a beautiful afternoon, much like the day he'd gone to High Trees Farm and fallen in love, Matt thought. How he wished at that moment that he could just get on the bike and keep going until Sussex and the South Downs came into view. He pictured himself roaring up to the farm, Celia running out to meet him,

106

throwing herself into his arms. A wry grin twisted his lips. Some chance. She'd probably whack him round the head with that enamel dish she used to feed the chickens. And he wouldn't blame her one bit.

"Where we off to then?" Ed's voice shattered his daydream.

"Let you know when we get there," he said.

At first he just drove aimlessly along country lanes with no clear idea of their direction. Then he turned a corner and caught a glimpse of sunspeckled water between beds of reeds. The marshland stretched towards the sea and in its midst he could see the great tower of an ancient church standing sentinel.

He stopped the bike in the narrow lane outside the church and they both dismounted and walked up a grassy path towards the main door. Matt pushed it open and walked in, Ed close behind him.

"Wow," Ed gasped. "Just look at that."

The church was huge for such a tiny hamlet, and so light, the sunlight pouring through arched clerestory windows. Matt followed Ed's gaze upwards to the hammer beam roof, adorned with carved and gilded angels.

In awestruck silence, their footsteps echoing on the stone flags, they walked down the centre aisle.

A voice made them jump. "Welcome to Blythburgh." An elderly woman stepped from behind a pillar where she'd been arranging some flowers. She eyed their uniforms and smiled. "You're from Metworth, aren't you?"

Matt nodded.

"I always say a prayer for you boys when I hear you go over," she said. She noticed Ed gazing up at the carved angels. "It's a beautiful church, isn't it? They call it the cathedral of the marshes. Would you like me to show you round?"

"That's kind of you," Matt said, glancing at Ed. "But we've got to get back soon. We just stopped to stretch our legs."

Outside, Ed said, "We're not in a hurry, are we?"

"I wasn't expecting to see anyone. I wanted to find somewhere quiet so that we could have a talk."

"Oh, what's the problem then?"

"It's not my problem — it's yours," Matt said.

"Don't know what you're talking about." Ed thrust his hands into his pockets and walked away, his shoulders hunched.

Matt followed and grabbed his shoulder, spinning him round. "You do know — and you're going to tell me."

He led his friend over to a bench set in the angle between two buttresses and made him sit down. Ed leaned forward, his elbows on his knees, refusing to look at Matt.

Undeterred, Matt said, "Now listen to me. I know there's something on your mind and I know it's not a girl, so spill the beans, old chap. We're not going back to base until you do and if we're late for briefing it will be your fault."

"All right, all right. It's me. I made a mistake and . . ." Ed covered his face with his hands and let out a groan.

108

"What mistake? When?"

"Weeks ago — on that mission over Hamburg. You remember. We were badly hit and Clive decided we ought to turn back before we dropped the bombs. He was going to jettison them over the sea. I did the calculations, but they were all wrong. Clive couldn't have known — visibility was almost nil. I told him when to let go, but just as he gave the order, I realized. We were over land — a town. We must have killed hundreds of innocent civilians." Ed buried his face in his hands. "It's been playing on my mind ever since. I'm useless at this job. I should be drummed out of the force."

"Rubbish, Ed. You're a brilliant navigator. It must have been an instrument malfunction and besides, we were over a fairly sparsely populated area."

"It wasn't. I checked when we got back. I know I made a mistake."

"You don't make mistakes — even under pressure. You passed your navigation training with flying colours, top of your group." Matt stood up and paced back and forth for a moment. He stopped and faced his friend. "You should have talked to someone before this. As it is, you've let it worry you till it's got out of hand."

"I can't stop thinking about it. Every time we go up, I think it's going to happen again. I check and re-check until I can hardly see the charts and the instruments. Suppose I make another mistake?"

"You won't. In fact, you'll be extra careful from now on, won't you?" Matt tried to reason with him. But he wouldn't listen.

Once he'd started to talk it all spilled out and Matt listened patiently, realizing what a strain his friend had been under. It could all have been resolved if he'd spoken up before. Now he had to convince Ed that he'd done nothing wrong; things like this happened in wartime and innocent people were bound to suffer. Look at those poor people in London, huddled in the Underground night after night as their homes were blasted to pieces. What else could they do but fight back? He didn't remind his friend that since Harris had taken over, they no longer stuck to strategic targets.

Ed's shaky voice came to a halt and he sat up and wiped his hand over his face. "I'll have to ask for a transfer — to ground crew maybe."

"Don't talk daft. We need you, Ed. You're part of the crew."

"Suppose I go to pieces. I'd be letting them down."

"You'll be letting them down far more by opting out. Not good for morale, old chap. Besides, you know what it would mean, don't you? A mark on your record — 'LMF' — lack of moral fibre. And I don't really think that's your problem. It's happened to some of the chaps I know — refusing to fly and so on. You don't want that, do you?"

"I'm not a coward," Ed said indignantly.

"I know that, but it's what other people might think. Besides, you told me that you want to continue flying after the war. You won't be able to if you have that on your record."

Ed nodded. "I suppose you're right." He stood up.

"So, you'll pull your socks up, start acting like one of the team?"

"I'll try. Thanks Matt." Ed stuck his hand out and Matt shook it.

He glanced at his watch. "Better get back. Mustn't be late for briefing."

Matt started up the bike and they set off back towards Metworth. He was glad he'd insisted on tackling Ed. He just hoped that spilling it all out had helped him. He could have denied there was anything wrong, letting his fears and doubts fester until he became a danger to his fellow crewmen. Matt knew that if he hadn't been able to sort things out he would have had no choice but to speak to their squadron leader. Loyalty to the crew far outweighed loyalty to a friend in these circumstances.

Back at the aerodrome, the two men made their way to the briefing room where most of the squadron was already assembled. They found empty chairs near the back, behind the rest of their crew. As they waited for the stragglers to enter, pilot Clive Mitchell leaned back and grinned. "What have you two been up to on this sunny afternoon?"

Ginger, their front gunner laughed. "Been in to Ipswich to pick up a couple of floozies, I bet. Should have asked us to come along, mate."

"Only room for two on the old bike, I'm afraid. Took her out for a run. Don't want her seizing up from lack of use." Matt nudged Ed in the ribs with his elbow, leaned back in his seat and grinned. Let them think they'd been chasing girls. Ed gave a small nod and grinned back.

CHAPTER
NINE

If it hadn't been for Joyce, Celia would have moved out and found lodgings in Sullingford. How she wished she'd sent Stella to lodge at the Robsons' cottage and asked Joyce to stay at the farmhouse. They'd taken to each other immediately but Stella had resisted all her efforts at friendship. Yet she was all smiles when Dad was around. It was obvious she was trying to worm her way into his affections and, to Celia's dismay, it looked as if she was succeeding. These days Larry discussed all the farm business with Stella, seeking her help with filling in the many forms required by the War Agricultural Committee and discussing the welfare of the animals.

At one time he would have turned to Celia; although he'd never let her do the physical farm work, he'd always been glad of her help with the milk yield records and tax forms. She told herself she wasn't jealous — well, perhaps a little bit, she acknowledged.

It wasn't that she begrudged her father a little happiness. Her mother had died eight years ago and he deserved to find someone else to share his life. But why did it have to be Stella? She was far too young for

Larry, only a few years older than Celia herself. That wouldn't have mattered if they'd got on.

These days Celia almost dreaded going home and, as she got off her bike, she had to brace herself before opening the door. She heard voices coming from the barn and strolled across to see what was going on. There was a loud shriek followed by a burst of laughter. Then Stella's angry voice. "It's not funny."

She opened the door to see both girls wielding pitchforks and her first thought was that they were fighting. Joyce had often told her that she was tempted to "whack her one" when Stella had been particularly annoying.

Joyce turned as sunlight flooded the barn and Celia saw that she had speared a large rat on the end of her pitchfork. The look of revulsion on Stella's face gave Celia a momentary satisfaction. So there was something about farm life that the haughty Miss Wilson couldn't cope with. Her unworthy thought vanished and she leapt back as a large rat almost ran over her foot; she didn't like rodents either.

"There's hundreds of the buggers," Joyce yelled, wielding her pitchfork again.

"I'll go and get Len and his dog," Celia said. She ran across the yard, pausing as her father drove up the track on the tractor.

"Where you off to in such a hurry?" he called.

She explained and he turned off the engine and climbed down. "Thought we'd got rid of the damned things," he said, pushing his cap back and scratching his head.

"You never really do though, do you?"

"Well, Nipper will sort them out — best ratter this side of the Downs. Len's gone home for supper. You'll catch him if you hurry."

Len was just taking his boots off when she reached the cottage. Nipper, his elderly Jack Russell terrier, was lapping water from a bowl outside the back door. Celia bent and scratched his back. "Poor thing, thought you'd done your work for the day."

The old dog went everywhere with Len and spent his time rooting out mice and rabbits. Len laughed. "That's not work to him — he enjoys it." He pulled his boots back on. "Tell Jean I'll be a while, lass," he said, whistling to Nipper.

Celia went into the cottage where Jean was laying the table for supper. "Len's had to go back for a bit. Rats in the barn," she said.

"Pity your Dad didn't ask him before letting him traipse all the way back here," Jean said, pushing the pot of stew to the back of the range. "He's not getting any younger you know."

"I'm sorry. The girls are trying to kill them, but there're too many. We need Nipper."

"Oh, well. I should be used to it by now. We were hoping to retire this year, but this darn war drags on."

"I'll talk to Dad," Celia said. "Now young Mickey's left school, Len shouldn't have to work such long hours."

"It's his arthritis, see? He don't complain, but he's in agony sometimes."

Celia nodded sympathetically wishing she could do more to help. Dad could do with another pair of hands. She cursed the bad timing that had forced her to stay at the printing works for the duration of the war; it seemed to be going on for ever.

Back at the barn chaos reigned. Nipper raced about, barking, his tail wagging furiously, while Len, Dad and the two girls lunged with their pitchforks and shovels and the pile of dead rats grew. It looked as if they were managing very well without her and she went indoors.

As she hung her jacket up behind the back door, she glanced at the sideboard in the forlorn hope that there would be a letter from Matt, or at least from Edgar giving news of his friend. Her heart leapt when she spotted the white envelope among the buff official ones.

She snatched it up, her heart racing, as she recognized the handwriting. As she ripped open the envelope, her eye fell on the postmark — and the date. It had been posted three weeks ago. Why had it taken so long to get here?

Disappointed, she scanned the single sheet, which just said that there had been little leisure time for writing and that sometimes Matt was so tired he fell asleep with the pen in his hand. He passed on Ed's love and asked her to write soon. "*Your letters are what keep me sane*," he wrote. If only he'd written more. Still, it was better than nothing, she thought, wishing she'd written herself. Kissing his signature and holding the paper against her heart, she resolved to answer straight away.

She was still clutching the letter, a dreamy smile on her face, when the door opened and her father came in.

"Oh, good. You found your letter," he said. "I'm sorry, lass. It's my fault. I found it caught up with the forms in that drawer — I must have picked it up when I put them away."

"It's all right, Dad. Can't be helped. I'll answer it tonight." She picked up her bag to put the letter away and, as she did so, she looked up and caught Stella watching her. Could she have hidden the letter out of spite? She hastily dismissed the thought and started to get the meal ready.

Stella washed her hands at the sink and said, "Let me give you a hand with that, Celia. You must be worn out, getting up early to feed the chickens and then cycling all that way into town."

There was no hint of sarcasm in her voice, but Celia couldn't resist saying, "It *is* a long way — uphill on the way home too. And I'm doing longer hours at the works too. So thanks, I appreciate an extra pair of hands."

Stella's lips twisted and Celia thought she was about to make a scornful remark about office work but at that moment Larry opened his eyes and stretched. "Something smells good. I'm a lucky man — having two lovely girls to wait on me."

Joyce came in then, having finished off in the barn. "Nipper's finished them all off, for now," she announced.

"I hope so. I don't fancy going in there while there's rats about." Stella glanced at Larry. "Well, it's all part of farm life, isn't it?" she said with a brilliant smile.

Joyce pulled a face behind her back and began to lay the table as Celia mashed potatoes and Stella dished up the mince and carrots.

As she silently ate her meal Celia mulled over the earlier scene and Stella's change of manner when she'd offered to help with the meal. She could only conclude that the older girl was trying to impress her father. She was beginning to think there might be something in Joyce's assertion that Stella was "sweet on" him.

She began to clear away and Joyce got up to help, but Stella stayed at the table talking to Dad about the milk yields. Celia got on with the washing up in silence.

When they'd finished she put her boots and jacket on and went out to shut the chickens up. As she shooed them into the henhouse, making sure none of the flock had gone astray, she reflected that looking after the poultry was traditionally the farmer's wife's job. Since her mother had died, she had taken on the responsibility herself. Well, she thought, as she fastened the gate, if Stella was after her father, she could jolly well take on the chickens too. Even with Jean Robson's help on washday, she had enough to do cooking and cleaning, as well as her job in town.

Joyce joined her in the farmyard and suggested they walk up the lane together. She jerked her head back at the farmhouse. "Those two in there will be talking milk yields till the cows come home." She laughed at her own joke and Celia couldn't help joining in, ashamed of her earlier petty thoughts.

"I really ought to do some ironing," she said. "I've lots of mending too."

"It'll keep," Joyce said, taking her arm. "We haven't had a good old chinwag since we went to the pictures."

Celia fell into step with her friend. Truth to tell she didn't fancy spending the evening watching Stella fawning over her father.

"So what's the gossip then?" Joyce asked. "What did your bomber pilot have to say for himself?"

"Oh, nothing much. I suppose he can't talk about his work and there's not much else to say, is there?" Celia tried to sound nonchalant.

"No hearts and flowers, protestations of undying love?" Joyce put her hand over her heart and pretended to swoon.

Celia punched her arm, laughing. "Don't be silly — it's nothing like that. Besides, I hardly know him really."

"But you do like him though?"

"I do — very much." She had laughed at Joyce's teasing but she couldn't help wishing that he would reveal more of his feelings in his letters. They were halfway to the Robsons' cottage and Celia stopped and said, "I'd better get back if you don't mind. I want to write to Matt straight away."

She said goodnight to her friend and walked slowly back up the lane. She knew Joyce still wasn't sure what had happened to Bob and she felt bad for going on about Matt. Joyce didn't say much, but she must be so badly upset, not knowing if he was still alive. Yet she still managed to laugh and joke.

She was still writing when she heard her father and Stella come upstairs. She listened intently, her pen poised, but their "goodnights" seemed innocuous. Perhaps she was worrying unduly. Surely Dad wouldn't be taken in by Stella's interest in the farm?

She consoled herself with the thought that the war had to end some time. The land girls would go back to their former lives and things would return to normal. She wouldn't have to put up with Stella's sniping for ever.

With a sigh, she returned to her letter. She had already covered three pages, first apologizing for not replying before and explaining the lost letter. She knew she shouldn't really have waited for Matt to write before writing herself, but she'd been upset at not hearing from him. Besides, she didn't want to sound too eager. So she told him about going to the pictures and the surprise of seeing her old school friend on the screen and finished by saying she hoped to hear from him soon. She sealed the letter with a sigh and, before turning out the light, wrote a quick duty note to Ed, although she had little hope that he would reply.

The next morning, her father was already out in the fields and the two girls were milking the cows when the postman came. Celia's heart leapt when she saw the familiar handwriting and she hurriedly put her father's letters on the sideboard. She wanted to tear it open then and there but it was late and she should be leaving for work. She hurried outside to get her bicycle just as Stella crossed the yard.

"Was that the postman?" she called, eyeing the letter in Celia's hand.

"Yes." Celia thrust the envelope into her bag before Stella could comment and wheeled her bicycle out of the gate without waiting for a reply.

A sudden gust of wind and a flurry of rain made the bicycle wobble and Celia had to concentrate on keeping to the road. Clouds were racing across the top of the Downs and she hoped there would be more than just a shower. Now that the hay was safely in, they needed the rain.

It was press day today so she probably wouldn't get a chance to read Matt's letter until the dinner break. But it was lovely to have something to look forward to and she felt a surge of joy that he had written again, seemingly not put off by her failure to answer his last letter.

Just as she reached the printing works, the rain started in earnest. She ran into the machine shed, laughing and shaking her wet hair out of her face.

Russell was on his way out and she bumped into him. He grabbed her by both arms and smiled down at her. "What are you looking so happy about?" he asked.

She couldn't tell him — her growing feelings for Matt were a secret she'd shared only with Joyce. "It's raining," she said. "Good for the crops."

"Well, I'm glad it makes someone happy," he said. "I've got to go out in it."

"Poor you," she teased.

"You could come with me. I've got to go and see Councillor Watson," Russell said. "We could say you're

120

my secretary — you can take notes. He'll give us slap-up lunch at the Royal Hotel."

Celia shook her head. Much as the idea of a good meal tempted her, given they'd been existing on such boring food since rationing had tightened up, she didn't want to give Russell ideas.

"I'm much too busy. Besides, I don't think your father would approve."

Russell laughed. "Can't blame me for trying," he said, grabbing his hat and dashing out into the rain.

Celia collected the time sheets and proofs, enduring the usual teasing and joking from the printers and ran across to the office, holding a sheet of cardboard over her head to protect her from the downpour. If she hadn't been so distracted by the letter from Matt, she'd have realized that the weather was about to change and worn her hooded raincoat.

She was shivering by the time she got inside and she put the kettle on straight away. Mr Allen was probably ready for his cup of tea anyway — he'd probably been in the office since the crack of dawn. While she waited for the water to boil she tried to tidy her damp hair which had escaped its pins and now framed her face in a frizzy halo.

The kettle whistled and she gave up the attempt, hoping that Mr Allen wouldn't comment on her dishevelled state when she took his cup into him. In fact he scarcely looked up, still concentrating on the headlines he was composing for the front page.

The morning passed quickly and by noon the first pages of the *Advertiser* were flying off the flatbed press.

Mrs Jones came in to help with bundling up the papers ready to go on the van and Celia was kept busy helping her.

When there was a lull in the frantic activity Mr Allen sent Danny out for fish and chips for all of them. Fish was a rare treat these days and the shop had started selling pies and sausages when cod or huss wasn't available. Today Danny came back grinning. "Managed to get cod today," he announced, handing round the newspaper-wrapped packages.

Celia sat on a box next to Mrs Jones and, as they devoured their food, she thought how much more fun this was than sitting in a swanky hotel with Russell and a boring old councillor. At times like these, although she'd always wanted to be a farmer, she really loved her job and the people she worked with. They were a good crowd who worked well together and the sound of laughter and singing often rose above the thump and clatter of the machines.

"This is better than I'd have eaten at home," Mrs Jones said.

"Yes, a real treat," replied Celia.

Mrs Jones laughed. "You do all right living on a farm — no shortages there."

"I'm sorry to say that you're wrong. Town folk think we have it easy in the country but it's not true. Oh, I know we have the chickens and eggs and grow vegetables. But I tell you, Mrs Jones, my vegetable plot is no bigger than your little back garden. And we're only allowed to keep a few eggs for ourselves."

"Is that right? Well, I never." Mrs Jones looked disbelieving.

"It's true," Celia said. "The Ministry tells us what to grow and what to do with our animals. We can't just slaughter a lamb or pig when we fancy some meat. The regulations are very strict — it's a nightmare." Celia paused for breath. It was rare that she got so heated, but it made her cross the way people made assumptions.

Mr Allen chipped in. "She's right you know, Mrs Jones. This war is hard on everyone."

"I hadn't thought of it like that," the older woman admitted. "It's just that I'm so fed up with this rationing."

"Aren't we all?" said Ray. "My missus is always grumbling — but she still manages to put a meal on the table every day."

"You cook for your Dad and those land girls, don't you? How do you manage then?" Mrs Jones asked.

"Well, I'm lucky. The land girls get extra rations — not much mind, but it does help. They need it, working so hard." Celia laughed. "You should see some of the concoctions I've made. Still, they seem to like it. Well, they eat it all anyway."

Mrs Jones asked what a concoction was and Celia told her about her own version of Woolton pie. "They didn't complain, so I gave it to them again," she said.

"You must write it down for me. I'll try it on my lot," said Mrs Jones.

"When you've tried it, will you let me know what you thought of it, Mrs Jones?" Mr Allen asked.

"What on earth for? I thought you men were only interested once it got on the plate. Not thinking of cooking it yourself are you?"

"Actually, it's for the paper. I've been thinking of running a kind of housewife's diary about how people are coping with the rationing. If you like Celia's recipe I'll get her to type it up and put it in the paper." He turned to Celia. "Would you be happy to do that?"

"I don't mind," she said, finishing the last chip and licking her fingers.

Mr Allen gave a satisfied nod. "We'll put it in next week then."

Celia screwed up her chip paper and reached into her handbag for a handkerchief, her heart skipping a beat as her fingers brushed against Matt's letter. How could she have forgotten it? She went back to the office to read it in private. She could just imagine the comments she'd get from Ray and Danny and the others.

The letter was everything she'd been longing for. She read it quickly, her eyes lighting up and her heart starting to beat faster. She smoothed the pages out and read it again, more slowly this time, savouring every sentence.

I can't tell you how desolate I felt when each day passed with no letter from you. Your descriptions of farm life and your work remind me what we're fighting for. It's against regulations for me to tell you about my own life for we're not allowed to give details of our missions. However, living so close to an airfield, I know that you have some idea of it.

124

He went on to tell her of his motorcycle ride with Ed and their visit to the beautiful Suffolk church, saying he wished she could have been with him.

"I know your brother doesn't write much — the lazy so-and-so, but you mustn't worry about him. I've told him to get his pen out and write," Matt went on.

Celia smiled. Ed had never been much of a letter-writer and when he'd been stationed at Tangmere it wasn't so bad as she was able to see him quite often. She bit her lip, frowning. Although Dad had never forgiven his only son for joining the RAF, she knew that deep down he worried about him doing such a dangerous job. She felt Ed had a duty to write occasionally to let them know he was all right. A tremor went through her as she realized that if he wasn't all right, they would soon know about it. The old adage that no news was good news seemed truer than ever these days.

She turned the page and read once more Matt's heartfelt plea to continue writing to him.

Your letters are a lifeline. I look forward to them with such pleasure and anticipation. I feel as if I've known you for ever and when this tour of ops is over I plan to get on the bike and be on the road to High Trees Farm as soon as the old man gives us leave. I hope you will make me as welcome as you did last time.

The "old man" was their commanding officer, he'd told her in a previous letter. As she tucked the letter into her bag and got ready to go back to the machine room, she smiled at that last sentence. Of course she would make him welcome.

CHAPTER
TEN

She almost danced across the yard, careless of the rain which had eased off to a steady drizzle. The day was far from over and, as the papers came off the folding machine, and she and Mrs Jones did up the bundles, for the first time in ages she was impatient for the time to pass.

Although she'd only written to Matt last night and posted the letter on her way to work that morning, she couldn't wait to write again.

For the next few weeks she felt as if she was spending all her time writing. Every evening when the chores were done she went up to her room and wrote to Matt, filling page after page with anecdotes about the works and the farm and trying to turn them into amusing stories. She knew from the nightly wireless news what he must be going through. Her stomach would tense with fear and her mouth fill with bile as the measured tones of the announcer informed them of bombing raids where "one of our aircraft failed to return".

She desperately held on to the hope that Matt and Ed's plane would not be among them, and in an effort to keep Matt's spirits up, she tried to keep her letters light-hearted. Although she wanted to tell him everything about her life, she didn't mention Russell or Stella's increasing influence over her father.

When she wasn't writing to Matt and her brother, she was busily scribbling down recipes and household tips. After their conversation about Woolton pie, she had made one for Mr Allen, using her own ingredients, and he had enjoyed it very much.

So, at his insistence, she had typed out the recipe adding some humorous notes. He had included those in the paper too, calling the piece *Diary of a Wartime Housewife*. The response had been good, with readers writing in and people stopping the editor in the street to say how much they'd enjoyed reading it. The result was that Celia had been asked to write a regular column.

"I don't think I could do that, Mr Allen," she said when he approached her.

"Nonsense, my dear. You have a way with words, of putting things in a light-hearted way yet getting a serious point across."

"But I can't think up a new recipe every week," she protested.

"It doesn't have to be a recipe. You could give tips on make do and mend, ways of coping with the blackout — that sort of thing." He smiled at her. "Just write about the things I've heard you discussing with Mrs Jones."

"But there're leaflets, and those films at the pictures. Do you really think people will want to read it in the paper as well? Don't you think everyone's fed up with the government telling us what to do?" Celia protested.

"But you didn't do that — your piece made people smile. We need a bit of cheering up these days. I'll bet our readers will start to look forward to it every week."

Mr Allen seemed so enthusiastic that she had agreed and, to her surprise she was enjoying it. She had no difficulty thinking up a topic each week, even when she ran out of recipes. She started including some of the little anecdotes that she put in her letters to Matt. He always said that they cheered him up and made him realize what they were fighting for. Why not do the same for the readers of the *Advertiser?*

She was just finishing off the current week's column when Mr Allen entered the office. She pulled the paper out of the typewriter and leaned back with a sigh.

"All done?" her boss asked, holding out his hand for the copy.

She held on to the sheets of paper and cleared her throat. "Mr Allen, I've been thinking — about the column."

"Don't tell me you want to stop doing it," he said. "It's become a very popular feature of the paper already."

Celia blushed and smiled. "I love doing it, but . . ." She paused. "I'd like to make some changes." She held her breath, hoping he wouldn't be annoyed at her cheek.

"Go on," he said.

"Well, for a start I don't like the heading. I'm not a housewife and besides, I think it's too restricting."

"Perhaps we could call it *Diary of a Farmer's Wife*." Mr Allen suggested.

"Or what about *A Countrywoman's War?*" She held her breath for his reply.

"Good idea," he said with a smile. "It would broaden the scope of the column and, with your tips and recipes as well as your tales of farm life, it will still fulfil its purpose." He held out his hand for the typewritten sheets. "I've been thinking too. You ought to be paid for this, the same as we pay our other contributors. And I'll put your name on it; you deserve a by-line."

"Oh, no, please don't, Mr Allen."

"Why ever not? Most journalists would kill for a by-line."

"For a start I'm not a journalist — not a real one anyway. And for another I don't want people to know it's me writing it. I wouldn't be able to write about the farm and the things the land girls get up to. As it is I don't use their real names and what I write could apply to any farm in the area. Besides, I don't think Dad would like it if he knew I was writing about High Trees."

"I see your point," Mr Allen said. "Very well, an anonymous countrywoman you shall be."

She didn't stay anonymous for long. Joyce guessed that Celia was the "countrywoman" after reading one of her farm stories. "I thought I'd disguised it," she said. "Please, Joyce, don't tell Dad will you?"

"Why not? I think you're very clever. Surely he'd be proud of you."

"Maybe. But if he knows, I won't feel so free to write about our farm. As it is, it could be any farm in the area. And don't tell Stella either," she added.

Joyce had reluctantly agreed to keep her secret. However, she took a keen interest in the column and sometimes came up with ideas when Celia got stuck.

Writing the weekly column proved a lifeline for Celia although sometimes it was hard to think up something amusing to write and she was glad of Joyce's help. She tried to relieve the serious tips on coping with food rationing and other shortages with diverting stories of life on the farm. Autumn had come round again and the hedges were heavy with blackberries so this week she was writing about this abundance of free food and including a couple of recipes which used a minimum of sugar. This was accompanied by a description of a fictional Joyce's fall into the bramble thicket and the resulting colourful language.

Celia smiled, remembering their helpless laughter as she'd helped Joyce out of the ditch. They had not actually been blackberrying but her friend really had fallen, emerging dishevelled and scratched, after plunging in to rescue a wayward ewe. Celia had seen the potential for an amusing story for her column. And so had Joyce.

"Don't you dare write about this," she warned, trying to keep a straight face.

"I wouldn't dream of it," Celia said.

"Bet you will," Joyce replied. "Just as long as you make sure nobody recognizes me."

Celia had promised. Besides, she knew Joyce didn't really mind.

Keeping so busy helped keep the worry about Matt and her brother at bay but thoughts of the men in her life were never far away. Ed had written more often lately and she suspected that Matt had prodded him to keep in touch. Although he never said much and never referred to their father, she hoped that when the war was over and he came home they would settle their differences. Larry seemed to have mellowed lately and perhaps he would at last accept that Ed was not cut out for the farming life. She knew that in a way he was proud of his son, though he would never say so.

But it was Matt's letters that Celia looked forward to and the sight of postman Bill pushing his bike through the gate each morning brought a ripple of excitement. Matt wrote nearly every day now, but there were some days when no letters came. Then Celia would spend the day worrying, a hollow feeling in her stomach. She dreaded the day when instead of Bill, it would be the telegraph boy coming up the lane with the dreaded yellow envelope in his hand. And that would give her not one, but two reasons, to grieve. Any news of Matt would go to his family, but she knew that whatever happened to Edgar, would have happened to Matt as well.

The only way to quell this gnawing anxiety was to keep as busy as possible. That wasn't hard with her regular work at the printer's and her writing, added to her housekeeping duties and helping on the farm when needed.

A bout of cold, damp weather had aggravated Len's arthritis and he was unable to work, much to his frustration. Joyce confided to Celia that he had got very grumpy and poor Jean was bearing the brunt of it.

"Thank goodness for young Mickey. Not only is he a good worker, it cheers Jean up, having someone to fuss over," she said. Despite her avowal that she didn't want to "run around after youngsters" as she'd put it, Jean had agreed to Mickey moving in to the cottage and made up a camp bed for him in the tiny front room.

Celia was sorry for Len, who had worked at High Trees for as long as she could remember. Still, it did mean that, even with Mickey now working full time, there was more for her to do these days. The upside was that her father no longer went about muttering that "Farm work wasn't for girls".

Maybe it was Stella's influence, she thought, or perhaps he had just had to accept that, with the war, things had changed.

Like most people these days Celia felt permanently tired, but at least she wasn't kept awake at night by bombing raids as they were in the towns. Nearby Chichester and Bognor had suffered several raids with many killed and injured, but so far Sullingford had escaped.

That all changed one night in late September. Celia had become so used to the sound of bombers going over that it no longer disturbed her exhausted sleep. Sometimes the loud chatter of the anti-aircraft guns up on the Downs would startle her awake. Usually she went straight back to sleep, but on this night the noise was loud enough to make her leap out of bed and go to the window.

Cautiously lifting the edge of the blackout curtain, she looked out onto a scene bathed in silver moonlight.

The curve of the Downs behind the farmhouse was faintly outlined against the sky and further down the valley searchlights pierced the night. Now, above the sound of the guns she could hear the drone of a lone plane and the occasional stutter of a damaged engine.

Praying that it wasn't one of theirs, Celia gripped the curtain and watched in fascination as the plane came into view, flying low over the hills. It swooped over the house and she flinched. "It's going to crash," she muttered.

But it didn't and as the sound of the plane faded away another noise filled the air. The scream and whistle of a bomb falling. The crash shook the house, rattling the ornaments on the mantelpiece.

An uneasy silence fell and Celia realized she'd been holding her breath. She relaxed her grip on the curtain and, on trembling legs, opened the door to her room. Other doors on the landing opened and there was a babble of questions as Stella and her father emerged.

"You girls all right?" Larry asked. Then, without waiting for a reply, he hurried downstairs.

Celia and Stella followed and, by the time they reached the kitchen, he had already donned coat and boots. As they made to follow, he waved them back. "Stay here, I'll go and see what's what."

When Celia tried to follow, he barked, "I said stay here." He took his shotgun off the rack and went outside.

Stella sank into a chair by the table. "Why's he taken his gun?" she asked, her voice shaky.

"Perhaps the pilot's baled out," Celia said, going to the range and poking the fire into life. She pulled the kettle on to the hotplate and then, feeling a bit wobbly herself, sat down opposite Stella.

The other girl gave a short laugh. "So, if Larry doesn't shoot him, you'll make him a cup of tea," she said.

"Cocoa, actually." Celia got up again and went to the dresser for crockery, then got the milk jug from the larder. She wasn't in the mood for Stella's sarcasm.

The door opened and Larry came in his face furious. "My best milker," he spluttered, putting his shotgun away.

"What, Dad? What's happened?" Celia took his arm and guided him to his favourite chair beside the range.

Larry wiped a hand over his face, unable to speak for a few moments.

"What about the pilot, did he bale out? Did you find him?" Stella's voice was high, almost panic-stricken. "We could all be murdered in our beds."

Celia gave a disgusted snort. "First off — we're not in bed and secondly, there is no pilot." She wasn't sure about that, but if the pilot had baled out there would have been a second crash and she had heard nothing. She turned to her father. "It was a bomb, wasn't it?"

"Yes, it landed right in the bottom meadow, killed poor old Daisybell. And the others were in such a panic we probably won't get any milk for weeks."

134

"Why drop a bomb out here in the country?" Stella asked, somewhat calmer now.

"The plane was hit by our guns, I thought it was going to crash, but when he released the bomb, it probably gave him a bit of height and he was able to stay airborne," Larry said.

Celia busied herself making the cocoa. "It could have been worse. It could have hit the house."

They sipped the comforting drink in silence, contemplating how much worse it could have been. With a sigh, Larry stood and stretched. "Better get on back to bed, try to get some sleep. We'll be up again soon enough."

Celia gathered up the cups before following the others upstairs. Tired as she was, she could not get to sleep though. A slight frisson of guilt assailed her as she realized that her brain was busily engaged with the idea of turning the night's events into a story for her newspaper article. Was it right to make something amusing out of what was, for her father, a tragedy? Perhaps she would write about something else this week. But, before turning out the light, she reached for the notebook she kept on the bedside table and jotted down a few ideas.

As she drifted off to sleep she recalled something Matt had said in a recent letter. "Morale is very important in wartime and by telling your funny stories you are making people smile and, in your own way, keeping people's spirits up. Keep sending me your cuttings. I pass them round the mess and we all have a chuckle. Keep up the good work."

Daisybell might have been High Trees Farm's best milker but she did not make very good eating. The War Agricultural Committee's regulations said that the death of any farm animal had to be reported and after the usual inspection, permission was given for the poor cow to be butchered for meat. The Raines's were allowed to keep a certain amount for home consumption but Celia couldn't bring herself to eat any of it.

Brought up on a farm, she was not usually sensitive about eating their own animals, but the circumstances of this cow's death made it seem different somehow. Stella had no such qualms and ridiculed her squeamishness.

"Call yourself a farmer's daughter," she sneered as Celia pushed her plate away.

Celia bit back a retort. She was hurt when the other girl made such remarks in front of her father. She knew Stella did it to try and drive a wedge between them and she had schooled herself not to rise to the bait. So far she was succeeding, but she knew she wouldn't be able to keep her temper much longer.

CHAPTER
ELEVEN

Rationing had become even more stringent and consequently farmers were under greater pressure to grow more crops. Larry hated being told what to do on his own farm which had been in his family for three generations and his grumbles were louder than ever when he was forced to plough up yet more grazing land to grow wheat.

But it had been a good growing year and now that it was ready to be harvested, Larry's grumbles took on a different tone. "How do they expect me to get this lot in and threshed before the weather changes?" he asked. Even with the two land girls and young Mickey there were not enough hands to do the job.

Len hobbled up to the farmhouse, leaning on a stick, and said, "I can still drive the tractor, boss."

Stella made to protest — the tractor was her baby now. When Larry agreed to let Len take over her lips set in a pout which quickly turned to a smile when he looked her way.

Celia couldn't help a small smile of her own. It was her day off so she was busy catching up with kitchen chores. When her father and the land girls left to start work, she promised to join them as soon as she could.

She had just finished mopping the kitchen floor when she heard a vehicle in the lane outside. She went outside, shading her eyes against the sun, as a lorry with half a dozen men in the back pulled up. A sergeant jumped down, rifle at the ready, and barked a harsh command. The men clambered down and stood waiting for orders.

It was only then that Celia realized who they were. Their shabby uniforms were distinguished by a large white circle sewn on to the backs of their jackets. Although she was aware that there was an Italian prisoner of war camp a few miles away, she had never seen any of them.

The sergeant turned to Celia and said, "Prisoners of war ready to assist with harvest, ma'am."

She looked at the six men standing with bent heads and hunched shoulders. One of them straightened, looked her in the eye and winked at her. She turned to the sergeant. "I don't think so, sergeant," she said through tight lips. "We've had no notification. Besides, I don't think my father . . ."

Before she could say anything else, Stella came striding up the lane. Ignoring Celia, she called out, "So you're here then. We're in the top field. Follow me."

An officer climbed out of the cab, a clipboard in his hand. "What's the delay, sergeant? Get these men moving," he said. He turned to Celia. "Six eyeties. Sign here, miss. We pick them up at six this evening."

Celia, while pleased that they would have help with the harvest, wondered how much use these bewildered-looking young men would be. Her mind turned to practicalities. "But what are we going to feed them on?" she asked.

The officer pointed out the crate in the back of the lorry. "Food and drink provided for their dinner break."

The sergeant directed two of the prisoners to haul the crate out and between them they carried it up the track towards the field, Stella leading the way. The others followed, the sergeant bringing up the rear, rifle at the ready.

Celia signed the form and the officer thanked her. He got back in the lorry, but before they moved off, he leaned out the window and said, "We'll pick them up at six this evening. You'll find they're good workers, used to outdoor work. Don't let them take advantage though."

Celia nodded. Inside she was seething. It was yet another example of her father shutting her out. After all he'd said in the past about not involving her in the farm and what he called men's work, it seemed Stella had won him over. His new found tolerance for female workers however, did not extend to allowing his own daughter a say in how the farm was run. Not that Dad had any say in this latest development, but he could have told her what was happening.

While she continued with her chores, her resentment festered and when she'd finished she made herself a cup of tea and sat down at the kitchen table. Well, now that they had extra men in the field they didn't need her, she thought. She'd have a well-deserved rest and while she had a few spare minutes she'd write to Matt.

She hadn't heard from him at all that week and, although there was always a niggling worry when a few days passed without a letter, she told herself firmly that it wasn't always possible for him to write. She fiddled with her fountain pen and bit her lip, trying to think of the right words. She had already written pages the day before and included a copy of her latest *Advertiser* column, hoping to cheer him up.

There was nothing new to tell him except for the arrival of the Italian prisoners which could be covered in one sentence. Besides, if she wrote while in this bad mood she would spill out her real feelings — her dislike of Stella and the effect she was having on her father, her general frustration with the war and her life in general.

Even writing her weekly column, which Mr Allen had assured her was helping the war effort, seemed pointless in comparison with what others were doing. She thought about Matt and Edgar, the farmhands and printing workers who had joined up, the land girls and former school friends who had joined the ATS and the WAAFs.

Most of all, as she forced herself to write a bright and breezy note, she thought of what she really wanted to say to Matt — that she dreamed of him constantly, worried about him all the time and desperately needed to know if he felt the same way about her. But she couldn't bring herself to reveal her true feelings. Friendship was all he seemed to want at the moment, so friendship it would have to be.

By the time she'd finished her letter and sealed it she felt a bit better. She glanced at the clock and saw that it was nearly midday. The farmhands would be stopping for dinner soon. Perhaps she would join them after all.

She made herself a corned beef sandwich and wrapped it in greaseproof paper, deciding to take it out to the wheat field and join the others.

It was very hot now and Celia realized that, although the Italians had a water container and the girls had taken flasks of tea, they would need more to drink. She got out the big "harvest teapot" which held twelve cupfuls and measured tea leaves into it. When it had brewed she added milk and poured it into one of the small churns. Balancing it on the basket at the front of her bicycle, she wheeled it up the rutted lane to where the workers sat in the shade of the hedge.

One of the Italians spotted her and leapt up, hurrying towards her.

The sergeant jumped up too. "Oi, where do you think you're going?" he yelled, levelling his rifle.

The young man gestured towards Celia. "I go help the lady," he said.

The sergeant shrugged. "OK," he said, sitting down again and mopping his red face with a handkerchief.

The prisoner lifted the churn off the bike and set it down on the path.

Joyce stood up, brushing dried grass off her dungarees. "Tea?" she said, hopefully.

Celia nodded and she turned to the others. "Tea, come on, lads."

They lined up with their tin mugs at the ready and Celia poured for them. Stella stayed where she was, lounging in the shade and nibbling daintily on her sandwich. Larry sat beside her chewing a piece of grass.

"Tea, Dad?" Celia asked.

He held out his mug. "Thanks, lass. That was a kind thought."

Celia poured herself a drink, sat next to Joyce and unwrapped her food. It was a beautiful day, hot but with a cooling breeze. She leaned back on her elbows, looking up at the blue sky where high above larks sang and wispy clouds drifted over the top of the Downs. Her earlier bad mood faded away. How could anyone be miserable on a day like this?

Stella and her father were talking quietly, the prisoners were flirting with Joyce, who was giving as good as she got, and the sergeant was munching his way through a pile of sandwiches. Celia closed her eyes, only half listening. Even when the drone of planes from the nearby airfield drowned out the birdsong she held on to the feeling of contentment. The war had to end soon, Stella would go back to London, she'd meet Matt again, and Edgar would come home to take his place on the farm.

Her daydream was shattered when the anti-aircraft guns across the valley started chattering, the noise mingling with the scream of diving planes. She sat up, watching in horror as two aircraft dived towards each other. Another joined them and the sound of their guns mingled with those on the hilltop.

142

The farm workers rose to their feet, shading their eyes against the sun as the aerial ballet continued. From this distance they could not make out which were friend or foe. Mickey was jumping up and down excitedly. "Go on, get him," he yelled.

One of the planes broke away trailing smoke and Celia gasped, clutching Joyce's arm as the plane disappeared over the brow of the hill. They heard the crash from where they were standing and Mickey was all for rushing off to see if the pilot had survived but Larry restrained him. "Leave it to the proper authorities," he said. "He must have landed near the ack-ack post. Besides, we've got work to do." He chivvied the Italians to finish their drinks and get back to the harvest.

Celia noticed that the prisoner who'd helped her lift the churn was grinning and making excited gestures to his neighbour. They began chattering in their own language until the sergeant waved his rifle threateningly and shouted at them to get on with their work.

As she began to help Joyce gathering up the sheaves of wheat Celia glanced warily at the men, who seemed to be working steadily. Her thoughts were bitter and she began to regret bringing the Italians tea. They were the enemy after all and they seemed to delight in seeing the plane shot down.

The lorry returned for the prisoners at six o'clock but the others worked on till dusk fell, only stopping for a short break. Celia hoped they would soon finish the top field and that there would be no need for the extra hands the following day. She couldn't help thinking

143

that these were the people her brother and Matt were fighting. They had aligned themselves with Germany and in her book that made them as bad as the Nazis.

Larry called a halt when it got too dark to see what they were doing, glancing up at the sky and saying, "Looks like the weather will hold, so get some rest and we'll make an early start tomorrow."

As they trudged back to the farmhouse, Joyce linked arms with Celia. "That eyetie's got his eye on you," she said, giggling.

"Don't be silly," Celia said.

"He's good-looking though. I wouldn't mind."

"Joyce — they're prisoners of war. You wouldn't . . ."

Joyce shrugged. "They're just young lads, far from home. What if it was one of our boys? You'd hope people were being nice to them." Her voice caught and Celia knew she was thinking of Bob. There had still been no word and, although Joyce still clung to the hope that he was a prisoner, her hopes were fading.

Celia squeezed her friend's arm. Although Joyce was an incorrigible flirt and was always talking about having a bit of fun, she knew that it was just a cover for her feelings. But she still thought her friend shouldn't get too friendly with the prisoners.

The harvest was safely in before the rains came but there was no celebratory harvest supper as there had been in previous years. When Russell came into the office one morning shaking raindrops from his hair, he said, "Your Dad must be pleased the weather held."

Celia nodded. Although she was glad that everything on the farm was going well, she still couldn't bring herself to accept the prisoners of war. Her father had overcome his reservations, acknowledging that they could not have managed the harvest without them. But when he announced that they would be back to help with the ploughing and sowing of winter wheat, Celia wasn't happy about it — and she still wasn't. Although Italy had now surrendered, she couldn't get used to the idea that they were no longer the enemy. But there was nothing she could do about it and she had to admit they had proved to be willing workers, eager to be friendly.

Too friendly, she thought. Mario, the young soldier who had winked at her on that first day, had turned his attention to Joyce when Celia ignored him. To her dismay her friend encouraged him and she often saw them talking and laughing together.

Russell was looking at her intently and she realized she had been lost in thought. "What's up, Cee? You seem a bit low."

"Nothing really," she replied. "I'm just a bit worried about Joyce. She's getting too friendly with this Italian."

"What's wrong with that? It's only a bit of fun. No harm in a bit of flirtation," Russell said.

"You would say that," Celia retorted. "You're a bit of a flirt yourself, in spite of being a married man."

Russell sighed. "I don't feel like a married man these days."

"No word from Marion then?"

He shook his head. "Never mind — that's my problem. But, back to your friend — I'm sure there's no harm in it. You could do with letting your hair down a bit yourself, Cee."

"But what about poor Bob? She never talks about him nowadays."

"Perhaps it's taking her mind off him; after all, she doesn't know if he's even still alive."

Celia didn't want to talk about it anymore. Russell flirting with her and any other female he came in contact with was his way of dealing with Marion's defection and perhaps he was right about Joyce. But she just knew that if anything happened to Matt she would not be looking for someone to take his place so soon.

She rolled a sheet of paper into her typewriter and began hitting the keys. Russell watched her in silence for a moment, then shrugged and walked away. A lump came to her throat and she fought back a sob. There was still no letter from either Matt or Ed and she was finding it hard to hide her concern.

There was nothing she could do but try to take her mind off things by getting on with her work. She had barely started on this week's column and Mr Allen would be chivvying her for the copy. How could she write anything light-hearted when she carried this weight of worry like a stone inside her? But her readers were relying on her to make them smile, to help them forget their own troubles in the midst of this war. She got out her notebook and paged through until she found the bit she wanted.

146

Before long she was typing away as fast as she could, trying to keep up with the flow of her thoughts. Finally, with a sigh of satisfaction, she pulled the paper from the machine, quickly read it through and took the finished article through to her boss's office. It was the best one she had ever done and for just a short while she had been so immersed in her words that thoughts of the farm and Joyce, even Matt, had been pushed into the background.

She stood up and stretched, feeling better than she had for quite a while, and told herself firmly that there was sure to be a letter waiting when she got home.

But there was no letter from Matt, just a brief postcard from Ed.

"*Things pretty hairy here. No time to write. Hope to get leave soon. Will come home if I can be sure of a welcome,*" he wrote.

Disappointment vied with elation. Why hadn't Matt written? Well, at least they were both all right. She was pleased Ed would be coming home. Of course he'd be welcome. And, despite their disagreement, Dad surely wanted to see his son. Hopefully, Matt would bring him on his motorbike. Celia did a little dance of joy just as the door opened and Joyce came into the kitchen.

"Someone's happy," she said.

Celia showed her the postcard and Joyce grinned. "I don't think I'd be that excited about seeing my brother," she said. Her eyes widened. "Oh, I see. You're hoping his friend will come too."

"I know it's silly, Joyce. But I can't help it. We've only met once, but his letters . . ." She sighed. "I feel as if

I've known him forever. I'm dying to meet him again but I'm scared too, though."

"I understand," Joyce said. "Let's hope they get leave soon and put you out of your misery." She washed her hands at the sink and began to lay the table. "Enough day dreaming, girl. Your Dad and Stella will be in soon wanting food."

As they worked together preparing the meal, Joyce was uncharacteristically silent. After a few moments she said, "I know you don't approve of me fraternizing with the Italians —"

Celia started to protest, but Joyce went on, "As I said before, they're just young lads, far from home. I've been teaching Mario English and he's told me a bit about his home. His family has a vineyard and they all work on the land — brothers, sisters, uncles, aunts. Besides, they're on our side now."

"I know but I still think you shouldn't get too friendly with him. We don't know how they really feel about us," Celia said. "Look how they cheered when that plane went down."

"He told me about that," Joyce said. "They thought it was the German plane got clobbered. Mario doesn't like the Krauts any more than we do."

Celia still wasn't convinced, but she let it go. She liked Joyce too much to fall out with her over a difference of opinion.

Days passed and there was no sign of Edgar and no post either. Her joyful anticipation gradually gave way to apprehension as it became clear that his leave had

148

either been cancelled or something much worse had happened.

She refused to believe it was the latter. Surely they would have been informed. She doggedly continued to hope that her brother and his friend would turn up one day but it was hard to hold on to that hope after she'd been to the pictures with Joyce one evening. She scarcely took in the main film, her mind filled with the newsreel images of the continuing raids on Cologne and other German cities. So many planes were being lost. Celia bit her knuckles. Were Matt and her brother even now on yet another mission? If only one of them would write.

CHAPTER
TWELVE

The fifth Christmas of the war was almost upon them, but hostilities showed no sign of ending. Celia had received a very brief note from Matt reassuring her that they were both all right and apologizing for not being in touch. *As you can imagine we've had a lot on our minds and little time for letter-writing*, he wrote.

She wrote back immediately saying she understood. They must be exhausted, she thought, as she chewed the end of her pen wondering how she could cheer him up.

It was one of the shortest letters she'd ever written and she hoped Matt wouldn't think she was losing interest. When she'd finished she got out her notebook and jotted down some ideas for next week's column. She was finding it harder to write lately. It seemed wrong to be telling light-hearted tales of farm life when so many people were living through the worst times of their life. She was fast running out of ideas, especially for new ways to use the ever decreasing and rather boring rations. Perhaps it was time to give it up.

The next day she typed up her notes from the previous evening, but reading it through she wasn't really happy with it. Still, she couldn't let Mr Allen down. She ripped the paper from her typewriter and went though to his office.

"Ah, Celia, you've finished?" He looked over his glasses at her. "You have a real talent for this, you know. How about doing a little more reporting for me?"

Celia blushed and shook her head. "I'm happy just doing the office work. Besides, I wouldn't have time. In fact, I've been thinking about this." She indicated the typewritten sheets. "I don't think I can keep it up. I'm running out of ideas."

"Nonsense." He skimmed the page. "This is quite up to your usual standard. Besides, the readers like it. I had another letter this morning complimenting my correspondent. There's a lot of speculation as to who the author is."

Celia found herself blushing even more furiously. "You mustn't tell anyone. My father would be livid if he found out what I was doing. As it is, he only reads the agricultural and war news."

Dennis Allen laughed. "Don't worry. Your secret is safe with me. I don't think even Russell realizes — he thinks you just type up what someone has sent in."

"Let's keep it that way — please."

The editor nodded agreement. "You'd better take these over to Ray." He handed the article and a layout sheet to her and she hurried across the yard to the print shop.

Without stopping to chat to the typesetter she returned to the office, knowing there was a lot to do before the next day's print run. As she entered the room she sighed with impatience. Didn't Russell have any work to do? She just didn't have time to listen to him going on about Marion.

He was standing with his back to her looking out onto the High Street and the low sun streaming through the plate glass silhouetted his figure. It wasn't until he turned round that she saw the blue uniform and her heart started to thump.

"Matt?" she whispered, sinking into her chair as her legs started to shake.

He took a step towards her, his forehead creased with concern. "Celia, are you all right? I didn't mean to upset you."

She stared at him and her hand went to her throat. Her first thought was that he was bringing bad news. She could hardly speak. "Ed?" she whispered.

"He's fine — he stopped off at the pub."

She made an effort at recovery. "When I saw you were alone, I thought . . ."

He took both her hands. "Oh, my sweet, I'm so sorry. I didn't think. I was just so impatient to see you."

As she looked up into his eyes her heart started to thump for a different reason. For more than two years she had tried to pretend that they were just pen-friends although deep in her heart she had known it was far more than that. How often had she imagined their next meeting? Not like this. But it didn't matter — he was here — really here.

"How long . . .?" She hoped this wasn't a flying visit like his first.

"We've got two days. Ed is booking us in at the White Swan."

152

Two whole days, she thought. Would Mr Allen let her have some time off? The brief wave of happiness dissipated somewhat as she took in what Matt had said. Why couldn't they stay at the farm?

"So Ed doesn't want to come home then?" she asked.

Matt looked uncomfortable. "It's not that," he said. "You told me one of your land girls has taken over his room and I don't want to intrude either. Staying at the pub's the best thing for us I think."

Celia sighed. "Oh, I wish he and Dad would make up — it's so silly. They're both so stubborn."

"I think Ed wants to but he's unsure of his reception." He looked at his watch. "Do you think your boss will let you off early? Tell him your brother's home."

"I'll ask." She stood up, suddenly conscious that Matt still had hold of her hands. She pulled away and patted her hair self-consciously.

She went through to Dennis Allen's office and told him that Edgar had arrived home on an unexpected leave, but she didn't mention Matt.

He smiled. "That's wonderful. Yes, of course you must spend some time with him." He waved a hand. "Take the rest of the day."

Celia felt like kissing him, but she managed to restrain herself and said a heartfelt "thank you."

Outside, Matt tucked her hand under his arm. It was as if no time at all had passed since that first meeting at the farm. Thanks to his letters she felt as if she had known him forever. They crossed the road and went towards the old timbered pub. As they approached, Ed came out and waved to them.

"I've booked a couple of rooms and George said he'd do us some sandwiches," he called.

Celia rushed towards him and gave him a hug. "It's so good to see you, big brother," she said.

He ran a hand through his hair and grinned. "I bet you were more pleased to see my mate here," he said.

Celia felt herself blushing again, but she couldn't deny it. Still, the memory of that first shock when she'd thought Matt was bringing bad news, made her realize how much she'd missed her brother too — and worried about him just as much as she had about Matt. "I'm equally pleased to see you both," she said firmly. "Now what about those sandwiches? I'm starving." With an effort at nonchalance she took hold of his arm and led him towards the pub.

She didn't usually go in pubs and to her relief she saw no one she knew. They sat at a table in a corner by the fireplace, where a log fire was burning. There was an awkward silence for a few moments until George appeared with a huge plate of ham sandwiches and glasses of cider. "Not much to choose from these days," the landlord apologized.

"This is fine, George. Thanks," said Ed.

"Good to see you home." He turned to Celia. "How's things up at High Trees then? Your Dad getting on all right with those girls?"

Celia pulled a face. "He's adapting, shall we say."

George grinned and walked away.

Ed turned to Celia. "Is he really managing?"

"Actually, yes. They're both good workers. I think it took him by surprise at first — you know how he's always been."

Ed laughed. "No job for a woman," he quoted. He took a sip of the cider, pulling a face. "Perhaps he'll change his tune after the war then — let you take it on like you've always wanted to."

"But what will you do, Ed?"

"Stay in the RAF of course."

Matt had been silent, eating his sandwiches and taking occasional sips from his glass. Now he looked up at Celia. "Is that what you really want?"

"It's what I've always dreamed of, more so when I realized Ed wasn't keen. I want High Trees to stay in the family."

"I could tell from your letters how much you love it. And those pieces you write for the paper."

Celia glanced at him keenly. His voice had sounded a bit flat and she suddenly realized that he might have been thinking of a different kind of future for them. But they scarcely knew each other really, despite their growing closeness through their letters. He'd never hinted at his true feelings and she had not dared to acknowledge her growing love for him. Besides, who could think about the future while the war raged around them?

Ed seemed to sense the atmosphere and he looked at his watch. "Shouldn't you be getting back to work, Cee?"

"Mr Allen's given me the afternoon off. Shall we go up to the farm so you can see Dad?"

"Not looking forward to it, but yes. I must try to talk to him." He stood up and drained his glass. "Do you mind if I go alone? I'll walk — give me time to think."

"Go ahead. We'll amuse ourselves won't we?" He grinned, turning to Celia. "Fancy a spin on the old bike?"

"I'd love it," she said, her heart leaping at the thought of spending a whole afternoon with him.

Ed paid for the food and drinks and headed off across the bridge, turning to wave. Celia thought he hadn't been his usual self through lunch, hardly touching the sandwiches, but having a second drink. He must be really apprehensive about the coming confrontation with their father.

As she and Matt crossed the road towards where he'd parked the motorbike, he took her hand and smiled down at her. "I can't believe we're really together after all this time. I've imagined it so often."

"And have I lived up to your expectations?" she said, smiling back, and forcing thoughts of her brother from her mind.

"More," he said, pulling her into the narrow passageway that led to the printing works. He put his arms around her and drew her towards him. As his lips met hers he murmured, "I've dreamed of this too."

She leaned into him and her hand caressed his cheek as she returned the kiss.

A cough and a stifled laugh made them spring apart and a hot tide rushed up her face as she turned to see young Danny grinning and jumping up and down.

"Just wait till I tell . . ."

156

She grabbed his collar. "You dare, you little wretch."

"Try and stop me," he said.

"I suppose you want me to tell everyone about you sneaking in by the back door of the Picturedrome and letting your mates in," she said.

His face blanched. "Your secret is safe with me. Cross me heart and hope to die." He scampered up the alley to the printing works, leaving Matt and Celia laughing.

"You are one tough cookie as the yanks say," Matt said. "Poor lad." He stopped laughing and looked at her, his blue eyes serious now. "I'm sorry I embarrassed you, Celia. I couldn't help myself."

"I didn't mind," she said. "In fact I . . ." But, suddenly feeling shy, she couldn't go on and say that she wished they hadn't been interrupted. "It's just — it's a bit soon. Besides, you don't know what it's like being the only girl working with all these men. They're always teasing me and making remarks."

"Do you want me to sort them out?" he said, half joking.

"Don't worry, I can cope."

"I'm sure you can," he said, laughing.

As Edgar walked up the lane towards the farm, he was dreading seeing his father. But he had to have one more try at healing the breach between them. If only Dad would accept that he was doing what he'd always dreamed of — although even he was having his doubts about that now. He hoped Matt wouldn't say anything to Celia. He couldn't avoid a confrontation with him for much longer though and he knew that during this brief leave, Matt was bound to tackle him about his attitude.

But the recent bomber missions were far from his mind as he crossed the bridge and started up the lane, scarcely noticing the steep climb to the top of the Downs. He was trying to work out what he was going to say to Dad. He understood his father's disappointment when he'd decided to join the RAF. It was natural to want his son to follow in his footsteps. It was how it had always been.

But Ed had been fascinated with planes and flying since he'd been a small boy when he'd spent summer evenings after school lying up here on the short Downland turf watching the biplanes landing and taking off at the Goodwood Flying Club down below. He had imagined himself up there in the blue sky, like a bird. The freedom, the excitement — and yes, sometimes the danger — had appealed to him far more than the thought of spending the rest of his life milking cows and worrying about the weather for the harvest. He wasn't afraid of hard work and willingly helped his father on the farm during school holidays. But it wasn't the life he imagined for himself.

At university he'd had the opportunity to learn to fly and it seemed only logical that the next step was to join the RAF. By 1938 everyone was talking about the likelihood of war but it didn't bother Ed. He would be doing his bit and he didn't give a thought to his father's feelings when he implored him to think again.

"Farmers will be just as important if war does come," Larry had said. "Just like in the last war."

"But Dad, you don't understand, I want to fly," Ed had protested.

"You and your planes. You're like a kid with a new toy," said Larry. "What's going to happen to this place if something happens to you?"

"For a start, Dad, we don't know that there will *be* a war. Chamberlain's been over there to talk to old Adolf. Besides, I've signed on for five years. Let me do this and then I'll think about the future."

"That's if any of us have a future," Larry said gloomily. He had no faith in Chamberlain. "I'm just worried about you, son." It was the first time he'd hinted at his true feelings. He wasn't just thinking about the future of the farm.

Ed thought it was just a ploy to make him change his mind and he'd given a careless laugh. "I'll be all right, Dad. Besides, if anything does happen, you've still got Cee. She loves the farm far more than I do. She'll make a good farmer."

Larry had stormed out, but not before he'd made his feelings clear. "No woman will ever take over *this* farm," he said. "It's not right. And as for you, young man, if you hate this place so much, perhaps it would be better to keep away."

Now, remembering that bitter exchange, Ed wondered what sort of reception he'd get this time. He'd tried to make amends for his thoughtlessness several times over the past few years, the last when he and Matt had come to say goodbye to Celia. Stubborn as ever, Larry had refused to discuss it and Ed had gone away holding onto his anger and resentment at his father's refusal even to try to understand. Since then he had avoided going home on the rare occasions he got leave.

But he had to make one last attempt. The way things were going he might not get another chance and he couldn't go back to Metworth with this bitterness between them. As he reached the farm gate and looked down at the old farmhouse nestling in its hollow, a wave of nostalgia swept over him. He remembered himself and Celia as children helping with the hay-making, his mother coming out with the flasks of tea and a basket of freshly-baked scones. He still couldn't get used to the fact that Mum would not be there to greet him, although it was years since she'd died.

His face twisted with remembered grief. How could he explain that this was why he'd left the farm? Dad had always pictured his son marrying, having sons to carry on at High Trees. But the hard life Mum had endured during the bad times, had convinced Edgar that it had contributed to her early death and made him determined that the woman he might eventually marry would not have to go through that.

Hesitantly, he crossed the yard. Perhaps he'd be able to find the words this time — and perhaps Dad would understand. After all, wasn't that one of the reasons he was so against Celia taking over?

160

A few hens clucked around in the late September sunshine and he heard a soft lowing from the nearby cow shed. Milking time already. It had taken him longer to walk up the hill than he'd thought.

He pushed open the door, inhaling the remembered smells of straw, dung and milk. Dad wasn't there, but the two land girls looked up from their work. He had almost forgotten about them, although Celia often mentioned them in her letters.

The smaller one stood up, brushing her hair from her forehead. Her eyes had lit up at the sight of his uniform and she grinned. "Lost your way?" she asked.

The other girl turned to her and said, "Don't be silly, Joyce. This is Mr Raines's son." She smiled at him. "You're Edgar, aren't you? I recognize you from your photograph."

"So you're the mysterious brother," Joyce said with a cheeky grin.

Ed wasn't in the mood for banter and he said abruptly, "Where's my father?"

"He's busy, but if you really can't wait for him to get back, you'll find him down in the bottom field," the other girl said with a scowl.

"I'll show you if you like," said Joyce. "Stella, you don't mind finishing off here do you? I won't be long and I'll do the clearing up when I get back." Without waiting for a reply she took Ed's arm and led him outside.

As they crossed the yard and started down the track, Joyce said, "Don't take any notice of Stella. She's a bit of a misery — except when your father's around."

"I thought he didn't like women farmers."

"He doesn't, but she's always sucking up to him and he seems to like it."

Ed didn't like the sound of that and he didn't reply.

"Sorry," Joyce said. "Perhaps I spoke out of turn. It's none of my business anyway."

"No, it's not," Ed replied.

"Oh, forget it. Speak first, think later, that's me." She pointed down the track. "There he is — a bullock crashed into the fence and they're trying to repair it."

"Who are those men? I thought everyone had been called up."

"Italian prisoners. Well, technically they're not any more since they surrendered a couple of months back. We call them co-operators now. They still have to go back to their camp every night." She stopped at the gate. "I'd better get back otherwise Stella will be sulking all evening. Have you seen Celia yet?"

"We met in town. My mate and I are staying at the White Swan."

Joyce's eyes lit up. "You mean Matt's here too? I bet Celia's on cloud nine."

Ed grinned. "You could say that."

"Well, I'll let you talk to your father. See you later, maybe." She hurried away and he stood watching his father work, totally absorbed in the task. Little chance of them having a heart to heart with those Eyeties about. It would have to wait for another time. With a feeling of relief that he could put it off for a bit longer, he crossed the field, giving a hesitant wave as Dad spotted him.

His father didn't return the gesture but turned back to the Italian he'd been talking to. A lump rose in Ed's throat. He knew coming home had been a mistake.

CHAPTER
THIRTEEN

Matt perched on the edge of the horse trough at the bottom of the hill beside his motorcycle. "Where would you like to go?" he asked.

Still burning from that kiss, she smiled shyly. "I don't mind — as long as I'm with you."

"OK — let's be off then." He put his flying jacket around her shoulders. "Put this on — it'll be cold on the bike."

"I don't need it, I've got a warm coat. You'll freeze without your jacket." She pulled her scarf and gloves out of her pocket and put them on. "Don't forget, I bike to work so I always wrap up warm."

Matt tried to insist but Celia just laughed and handed the flying jacket back to him. He gave in and shrugged it on, turning up the fur collar. Swinging his leg over the bike, he kick-started it and, above the roar of the engine, gestured to her to climb on behind. "Hang on, we're off," he shouted.

Celia clutched at his waist, her heart in her mouth. But, as he roared over the bridge and out of town, she found she was enjoying the speed, the cold wind on her face and above all, being so close to him. As her confidence increased her frantic hold on his waist eased and her arms crept round him. She leaned her cheek against his shoulder and closed her eyes, wishing they could go on forever like this. She hardly noticed when he slowed down and the motorbike coasted to a stop.

As the engine died, she opened her eyes and, in the sudden silence, heard the sound of waves on the shore. She hadn't been to the coast for years and the sounds and smells of the seaside brought a pang of memory of Sunday School outings, sand castles, ice cream, Punch and Judy. She climbed off the pillion and stood looking around as Matt pulled the bike up onto its stand. It was all so different now. Barbed wire lined the beach, concrete tank traps in between; the ice cream kiosk was boarded up, its paint peeling, one shutter banging in the wind. She shivered. Not that they'd want ice cream at this time of year.

Matt was looking out to sea, his face sombre. He turned to her and forced a smile. "Perhaps this wasn't a good idea," he said. "Why did I pick this place?"

"I used to love it here — not that we got away very often. It was always so busy on the farm, so we never came in the summer. But I loved it when all the visitors had gone home and we had the beach to ourselves." Celia said.

"I loved seaside holidays too. I suppose I was remembering how it was." He shrugged. "Let's walk."

He took her hand and they strolled along in silence for a few minutes. Celia was just happy to be with him but she had hoped that once they were alone he would say the words she'd been longing to hear.

When he suddenly stopped and turned to her, she smiled in anticipation. He gripped her hand fiercely. "Celia, there's something I must say . . ."

"Yes?" She barely breathed the word.

"It's about Ed."

Her heart plummeted. What did he mean? Thoughts of romance fled in concern for her brother. "What about him?" she asked.

Matt ran his fingers through his hair. "This is so hard, maybe I shouldn't have said anything."

"You can't stop now."

"Let's sit down," he said, leading her to one of the remaining shelters.

They were out of the wind, but Celia still shivered as Matt revealed Ed's confession that some months ago, he'd made a mistake in navigation. "I gave him a good talking to and I thought he was all right, but just lately . . ." Matt paused. "He missed our last mission — reported sick — but I don't think he was really ill."

"Ed wouldn't do that, he's not a shirker," Celia protested.

"Normally, I'd agree with you. But you haven't seen him for such a long time. He's changed, Celia. And he's drinking too much as well."

"Perhaps it's this business with Dad playing on his mind. He'll sort it out today and then he'll be all right."

"I hope so — but I don't think it's that." Matt paused. "I was hoping you'd talk to him, warn him."

"Warn him? About what?"

"If he carries on like this — well, he's jeopardising his flying his career." Matt's voice was hesitant. "I don't want to report him but . . ."

"Report him? He hasn't done anything wrong has he?"

"Not yet. But the way he's carrying on is bad for morale. He's putting the rest of the crew at risk too."

"Are you implying my brother is a coward?" Celia's eyes flashed. "He's supposed to be your friend."

Matt grabbed her wrists and tried to pull her towards him. "He is — you must believe me. I want to help him."

"Fat lot of help it'll be reporting him to your CO," Celia snapped, pushing him away. She stood up. "Perhaps you'll take me home now."

Matt sighed. "I'm sorry. This isn't how I'd planned our meeting."

Me neither, Celia thought, as she walked back to where they'd parked the motorcycle. Her dreams of a romantic interlude had fled. How could she have misjudged Matt so? If he were a true friend, surely he'd support her brother — not go running to their commanding officer with tales of his incompetence? And drinking? That couldn't be right — Ed had never been a drinker.

She climbed on to the pillion reluctantly, holding on to Matt's belt instead of clasping her arms round his waist. Tears stung her cheeks as they weaved their way through the country lanes back to the town. It was the wind making her cry, she told herself. Matt Dangerfield wasn't worth crying over — she hardly knew him after all.

It was dark by the time they pulled up outside the pub, Celia jumped down and said, "I'll go and get my bike from the works."

"No need, Celia. I'll take you home. But I want to see if Ed's back yet. You will talk to him, won't you?"

"Of course I will." She paused. "Oh, Matt — I'm sure you're wrong and even if you're right what do you expect me to say to him?"

"Just try to make him see it's serious. He's got to pull his socks up or else . . ."

Celia's temper flared once more. "He's not a coward. I expect even the great Matt Dangerfield gets scared sometimes."

Matt threw up his hands and strode towards the pub without another word. Celia followed slowly. She didn't like going into the public bar. The landlord saw her and beckoned. "Your brother's in the saloon. He's had a drop too much I think."

"Oh dear. Thank you, George. I'll go and talk to him." The meeting with her father couldn't have gone well then, she thought.

Matt held the door for her and she followed him into the quiet saloon bar. Ed was sitting beside the log fire deep in conversation with Russell. She wondered what they were talking about — they'd never been friends and had little in common.

She went over and joined them, leaving Matt to order his drink. Pasting a smile on her face she said brightly, "What are you two up to?"

"Your brother's telling me what life in a bomber squadron is really like," Russell said.

Ed looked up at her, waving his tankard of beer in front of her face. "It's not like you see on the newsreels, Cee," he slurred. "We're not all bloody heroes."

Matt came over and laid a hand on his shoulder. "Come on, old chap. Let's not get maudlin," he said, his voice mild.

Ed shook him off. "People have a right to know what's going on," he said.

Celia sat down next to him. "Ed, you shouldn't be talking like this." She took his hand. "Why don't you tell me how you got on with Dad? Did you talk to him?"

He looked up at her with bleary eyes. "Yes — I talked to him. Fat lot of good it did." He grinned. "Never mind — I got to meet that little Joyce. Pretty little thing." His voice slurred and his head dropped forward onto the table.

Matt pulled at his arm. "I think we'd better get you to bed," he said.

Russell stood up. "I'll give you a hand."

Together they hauled him to his feet and led him upstairs. Celia hesitated, wondering if Matt would come down again. Now that she'd seen the state of her brother she realized she might have been a bit hasty. It seemed Matt really had cause for concern. Perhaps she ought to apologize.

George came through to collect the glasses, raising his eyebrows when he saw the men had gone. Celia gestured upwards. "They're putting Ed to bed," she said.

"I've never seen him in such a state," George said. "This war's got a lot to answer for."

Celia nodded. "Good job he booked to stay here. I wouldn't want Dad to see him like that." She picked up her handbag. "Will you tell them I've gone home? I'll get my bike from the works." She opened the door just as Russell came downstairs. He seemed surprised to see her.

"I didn't realize you were still here," he said.

"Can you tell them I've gone home?" she said.

"You're not biking in the dark. Let me get the van."

"No — I'll be all right. You know I'm used to riding at night."

Russell shrugged. "Suit yourself. I've got something to do anyway." He held the door open for her and they walked across to the printing works. He waited while she got her bike. "Sure you'll be OK?" he asked.

She nodded and set off, glancing across to the White Swan, hoping for a glimpse of Matt. She wished now she hadn't lost her temper earlier but she'd had to defend her brother, hadn't she. But now she had to admit that there was something on his mind and it wasn't the confrontation with their father. Perhaps he'd confided in Russell, but she had the impression they'd been arguing about something.

Perhaps she'd ask Russell in the morning, she thought, glancing behind her to see that a light had

170

come on in the *Advertiser* office. It was quickly extinguished as he drew the blackout curtain. As she crossed the bridge and cycled up the hill towards High Trees she wondered what had been so urgent that Russell had to go back to the office at this hour.

CHAPTER
FOURTEEN

It was late when Celia arrived home and Joyce had already gone back to the Robsons' cottage. Her father was in bed but Stella was still in the kitchen making cocoa.

She turned as Celia came in, a sour expression on her face. "I don't know why your brother bothers coming home when all he does is upset your father," she said.

Celia had to admit that the same thought had crossed her mind, but she was moved to defend him. After all, Dad's stubbornness was just as much to blame for the tension between them. "Ed wanted to try and make things right. After all, he's doing a dangerous job — he might not get another chance." It was the first time she'd voiced aloud the dread that clutched at her heart whenever she heard a bomber go over, whether it was one of theirs or the enemy's.

"Don't you think Larry knows that?" Stella snapped. "Why do you think he wanted him to stay out of the war? After all, he had the chance with farming being a reserved occupation."

Celia bristled with indignation as she did every time Stella used her father's Christian name. "You know nothing about it," she snapped and before Stella could reply she rushed out of the kitchen and shut herself in her room.

As she threw her clothes off and jumped into bed without bothering to brush her hair or clean her teeth, her body shook with heart-broken sobs. How could what had promised to be such a wonderful day have turned so quickly to anger and despair? Hunched under the covers she went through everything, from her conversation — no it was a quarrel, she amended — with Matt, to her petty sniping at Stella. But uppermost in her mind was her worry about Ed. For, now that she'd had time to think about the concerns Matt had voiced, she realized he was really worried about his friend. She shouldn't have doubted him and she vowed to apologize the moment she had the chance. Because, knowing her brother as she did, she was forced to acknowledge that there could be something in what Matt had hinted.

She turned over in bed and punched her pillow in frustration. What could she do about it? Ed was hardly likely to take notice of her and besides, she didn't want him to know that Matt had been talking behind his back. Perhaps she shouldn't have rushed off like that. Well, she'd be seeing Matt in the morning. She'd have a chance to apologize for her hasty reaction. I'll decide what to do then, she thought.

Despite having little sleep the night before, Celia was up early and had finished her chores before her father and the land girls came in for breakfast. She was getting her bicycle out of the shed as they came up the track and she gave them a wave. "I've left it all ready for you," she called. "See you later."

She was off down the track before anyone could ask her why she was leaving for work so early. Joyce was probably grinning, thinking she was in a hurry to see Matt, and Stella would have that sarcastic look on her face. As for Dad, she had no idea what he was thinking. She'd had no opportunity to ask him how he'd got on with Ed and her brother has been in no state to tell her either. From what Stella had said last night, it hadn't gone well. She couldn't face Dad at the moment and besides, she wanted to talk to Ed first. She'd try to smooth things over with their father when she got home from work.

As she rode over the bridge into the High Street she glanced across to the horse trough where Matt had parked his motorcycle the evening before. Her heart lurched when she saw the empty space. Despite the way they had parted, she couldn't believe he would leave without saying goodbye.

She crossed the road to the White Swan and called out to George who was stacking some crates. He turned, a look of surprise on his face. "You've just missed them," he said. "They checked out this morning. Said they were off to Exeter. I thought they'd gone up to the farm first to say goodbye," he said.

Celia blinked back a rush of tears. She could understand Matt wanting to go home and see his parents. But he could have waited and said goodbye.

174

Now she'd never get the chance to make up with him. It hurt, more than she'd dreamed it would.

She realized that George was looking at her sympathetically and managed a careless smile. "I should have got up earlier," she said. "They've gone to see Matt's family and it's a long ride down to Devon." With that, she hurried away.

Without acknowledging the greetings of the men in the works, she put her bike away and went into the office. She sat at her desk and put her head in her hands, determined not to cry. But she did.

She was just drying her eyes when Mr Allen came into the office holding a sheaf of copy paper. "Have you seen this?" he asked.

She shook her head. "I've only just got here," she said, taking the sheets of paper from him. It was an editorial — a comment piece — written by Russell. Usually Mr Allen wrote them but occasionally Russell would stir himself to sit at the typewriter and hammer out a column. So that's what he'd been up to last night, Celia thought, as her eyes skimmed down the page.

It was headed "our brave boys in blue" and spoke of the dangers faced by the bomber squadrons on their nightly raids over enemy territory. It wasn't until she turned to the second page that she realized what Russell was really saying. She gasped. Now she knew what Ed had been getting so het up about in the pub. He'd spilled it all out, in particular his doubts about the ethics of mass bombing involving innocent civilians rather than strategic targets. He felt such tactics wouldn't shorten the war, but rather lead to more retaliation on the part of the enemy.

And Russell had written it all down quoting "an anonymous airman" and asking their readers if they agreed. It was bound to stir up controversy, which is what she knew he intended. And, in such a small town, where everyone knew Edgar Raines and had probably seen him talking to the editor's son, he would not remain anonymous for long.

Now Celia knew why Matt had been so concerned. Then it had just been a matter for the air crew and Ed's CO. But if it became known that he had been speaking out of turn he could be in serious trouble.

"You can't print this," she said, shoving the copy back at her boss with a shaking hand.

"Of course we can't. We'd be in real trouble if we did." Mr Allen said. "I don't know what Russ was thinking of. What's he got against your brother?"

"They were talking in the pub last night. He doesn't really want to get Ed into trouble. But I do know he feels strongly about this."

Mr Allen tore the sheets of paper in half and dropped them in the waste bin. "With all this work we're doing for the Ministry, we can't afford to draw attention to ourselves. Besides, it's spreading alarm and despondency as they say."

Celia fished the paper out of the bin and said, "I think we ought to burn this. Don't want anyone else reading it."

"I'll put it on the fire upstairs. When Russell comes in, tell him I want a word." He pushed his glasses up on his forehead and sighed. "I didn't know he felt like that."

Celia bit her lip and nodded. "I think it's because of Marion being in London and the terrible raids there. But we should be trying to raise morale, not make people have doubts about what we're doing."

Celia returned to her desk, finding it hard to concentrate. Yesterday she'd been happy, full of hope for the future, despite the nagging worry about Ed and Matt's safety. How had it so quickly turned to a nightmare? Now, she bitterly regretted her hasty reaction to Matt's concerns. After hearing Ed's drunken ramblings last night, she realized she should have listened to him. If only they hadn't left so hastily.

And now here was Russell stirring up trouble. She'd give him a piece of her mind when he came in. Thank goodness Mr Allen had refused to publish it.

A few minutes later Russell burst in, a big grin on his face. "Got a good quote from Councillor Watson," he said.

"Quite the dedicated journalist, aren't you?" Celia said, her lips tight.

His face fell. "Oh, Dad showed it to you."

"Russell, how could you? Didn't you think about what it would do to me?"

He had the grace to look a little ashamed, but he still tried to justify himself. "I said 'an anonymous airman' — no one will connect it with Ed."

"Of course they will. The public bar was full last night. Everyone heard you and him arguing, even if they didn't hear the actual words. Besides, it doesn't take much detective work to work out who you were getting at."

"I wasn't getting at Ed particularly," Russell said. "It's just a controversial issue that I felt needed to be addressed."

"Well it won't be addressed in the *Advertiser*. Your father won't print it."

"We'll see about that." He stormed out of the office, slamming the door.

Celia tried not to listen to the raised voices from next door but she smiled grimly at the thought that this time Russell wouldn't get his own way.

When he came back into her office he looked a little chastened. "Dad's right," he said. "I was so angry with Ed, I didn't stop to think." He perched on her desk and reached for her hand. "I was angry with you too. When I saw you going off with Ed's friend, I was jealous."

She snatched her hand away. "You've no right to be jealous. What about Marion?"

He blew out a loud breath. "Marion! She doesn't care about me, swanning off to London with her showbiz friends."

"She's not exactly having fun working for the Ministry of Information."

"Working you call it — making films." He paced the room. "She hasn't even let me know if she's all right."

"Have you tried contacting her?"

"Not since I saw her kissing that Yank."

It was no use telling him he'd probably misunderstood. Knowing Marion, it probably hadn't meant anything. She sighed, not sure what to say.

178

Russell came and sat down again. "Anyway, that's not the point," he said. "Seriously, Celia, I've accepted she's not coming back. She's made a new life for herself. I might have known she'd never settle for small town life. She was made for the bright lights."

Celia could tell what he was leading up to. But she didn't really believe he'd accepted his marriage was over and until it was she would never agree to even a casual date with him. But his next words chilled her heart. "I know Dad won't print that editorial, but I'm not sure if I shouldn't report that conversation with your brother. You wouldn't want him to get into trouble would you?"

"That's blackmail, Russell," she said, her voice cold.

"Call it what you like. But you know how I feel about you — how I've always felt."

"That's nonsense, Russell and you know it. It was always Marion you loved," she pointed out.

"She wasn't right for me — everyone said so. It just took me a long time to find out." He shrugged carelessly, but Celia wasn't taken in.

He stood up to leave. "Anyway, she's made a new life and it's time I did too. Taking you out to dinner will be a start."

"And if I agree, you'll keep quiet about Ed?"

"I give you my word."

Celia took a deep breath. "All right. But don't go reading anything into it, mind."

The grin that lit up his face was almost triumphant. He'd got his own way after months of pestering her and she wondered if she'd done the right thing. If he thought he could wear her down with a few dinners he was wrong. She might have given up on Matt, but she wasn't ready to fall in love again — if ever. Besides, she didn't like being manipulated like this, although it was worth putting up with it for a while to protect her brother from the threat of scandal.

She had just finished typing the reports Mr Allen had left for her when he came in and asked if she'd done her column for that week's paper.

"I've jotted down some notes and I'll write it up this evening," she said.

"On my desk — first thing," he said, speaking more sharply than usual. He'd never been so abrupt with her before. Was he blaming her for her brother's indiscretions?

After he'd gone she remembered her date with Russell that evening. She had to keep her side of the bargain so she'd have to work on her column in her dinner hour. She had no idea what she was going to write. Recipes and make do and mend tips seemed trivial now, considering the more important issues she had on her mind. For, reading Russell's article, she couldn't help thinking about the women and children living with the terror of daily bombing — both in Germany and at home.

As with her father and Ed's disagreement over the farm, she could see both sides of the question. In some ways she agreed with Matt. They had a job to do and must get on with it, whatever their personal feelings. To do otherwise would be letting their crew down and be bad for morale. But she understood Ed's feelings. He'd always been soft-hearted, as a child crying over lost lambs and hiding away when the calves were being loaded for market. She remembered teasing him, getting impatient with him. But when it came down it, she loved her brother and her first loyalty was to him. She decided to write to him tonight and reassure him that whatever happened she would support him. And Matt Dangerfield could jump in the lake, she thought, a little sob catching in her throat.

CHAPTER
FIFTEEN

When Celia read through what she'd written, she felt that it wasn't up to her usual standard. It was hard to be bright and amusing when she had so much else on her mind. But it wasn't her job to write about the weightier issues of the war. Her argument with Matt as well as her brother's rant in the pub, had made her think though. The trouble was, she could see both sides of the question.

She sighed and shrugged. What could she do about it after all? She should just get on and do her job, trying to convince herself she was doing her bit. Her brother would have to make his own mind up about what was right.

She read through her column again and decided it would have to do. Mr Allen wanted her to make people smile, to brighten up their austere lives and take their mind off their worries. She could manage that all right. There was always something happening on the farm which she could turn into an amusing anecdote. It was the recipes and tips — the more serious side of her weekly column — that were more difficult. She felt that she was beginning to repeat herself.

At least she'd managed to finish it. Now, she turned her thoughts to the evening and her date with Russell. He was taking her into Chichester and there wouldn't be time to go home and change. She looked down at her serviceable jumper and skirt. They would have to do. No one dressed up for dinner these days, she told herself.

She picked up the telephone, hoping she'd be able to get through to the farm and that there would be someone there to answer it. She was about to give up when an impatient voice said, "Yes?"

It was Stella. "Is my father there?" Celia asked.

"He's busy. What do you want?"

Celia certainly wasn't going to tell her why she wouldn't be home for the evening meal. Let her think she was working late. "I just wanted to let you all know you'll have to get your own tea tonight. I'll be late — no idea what time."

"Haven't you left something ready?"

"I didn't know I'd be late. You'll just have to manage." Celia put the phone down. She knew she shouldn't have been so abrupt. After all, she usually made sure there was a meal waiting when Dad and the girls came in from the fields after a hard day's work. But she worked hard too, even if Stella didn't think working in an office compared with farm work.

Suddenly, the prospect of a nice dinner in a hotel, even if it was with Russell, seemed more appealing. It would be nice to sit down to eat without Stella glaring at her or having to watch her suck up to Dad.

At 5.30 she read through her column once more and took it through to Mr Allen's office. He barely looked up as she put it on his desk and said "goodnight".

He nodded and she returned to her own office, took her compact from her handbag and looked in the mirror, patting her hair into place. That would have to do, she thought. She wasn't about to make an effort for Russell. The fleeting thought that it would be different if she were meeting Matt crossed her mind, but she shut it off, pasting a smile on her face as Russell came in, jingling the van keys.

He was uncharacteristically quiet on the drive to Chichester and Celia wasn't feeling very chatty either. She hoped she hadn't made a mistake in agreeing to go out with him. The evening could very well turn out to be a disaster. She opened the van door quickly as Russell parked in front of the Cathedral and crossed the road to the Dolphin and Anchor Hotel. She had been there once before to a friend's wedding reception and she strode confidently through the lobby to the dining room.

Russell caught up with her and seized her arm. "It's a bit early to eat. I thought we'd have a drink in the bar first."

"You know I'm not a drinker, Russ," she protested.

"One won't hurt. I'm not trying to get you tiddly," he said, frowning. "Besides, it's hard to get a decent drink these days."

It was true that spirits were now in short supply and the beer was so weak it hardly tasted of anything. It would take a lot to get Russell legless, especially if they were eating too. Celia stopped worrying about him driving her home and shrugged. "All right, just a small sherry," she said.

They sat in the lounge in front of a log fire and Celia began to relax. Russell could be an amusing companion, although she only half-listened as he began telling some story about his meeting with a local councillor. She just hoped he wouldn't mention his leader column and their disagreement over her brother's remarks. At least he seemed to have accepted the separation from Marion and had stopped going on about her perceived treachery. The problem now of course was that he thought of himself as a free man — free to pursue Celia.

If it hadn't been for Matt, she might have been vulnerable to his advances, despite her determination not to get involved with a married man. But, despite the row with Matt and her sadness at the way they had parted, she knew she still loved him. She sighed and forced a smile as Russell asked if she wanted another drink.

"No thanks," she said.

"You're a bit quiet tonight," Russell said. "Not regretting our date are you?"

She shook her head, although in fact part of her was regretting it. Still, what was the harm? It was only a dinner and Russell had promised "no strings". She smiled and offered the only excuse she could think of for her inattention. "I'm just a bit tired, that's all — working and helping on the farm, not to mention cooking and cleaning."

"You're not still annoyed with me?" He leaned forward and touched her knee. "I was a bit hasty writing that article but I was angry with Ed. I didn't think about upsetting you."

"Well I was upset," Celia said, wishing he hadn't brought it up. She was just as annoyed with Ed as she was with Russell. If he hadn't been sounding off in the pub . . .

The thought brought her back to Matt once more. From what she had seen of Ed during his brief visit it seemed he was right to be concerned. She'd write an apology to Matt when she got home, however late it was and however tired she felt.

Russell put his glass down. "Maybe this wasn't a good idea," he said. "I can tell you're uncomfortable being with me. But there's no one here to see or care."

"It's not that — I told you, I'm tired." Celia protested.

"Let's go in to dinner then. The sooner I get you home the better. Don't want Dad on my back if you're too bushed to work properly tomorrow," he said with an attempt at a laugh.

The meal was good and Celia felt she owed it to Russell to be a bit more sociable so she roused herself to talk about the works and impact of the war on the business as well as life on the farm. She even succeeded in making him laugh with an anecdote about Joyce's altercation with a bull.

"Sounds like one of those Countrywoman stories," he said and Celia felt herself blushing. Did he know she was the columnist? She had begged his father to keep her secret but, of course, Russell knew everything that went on in the business.

She recovered quickly and said, "That sort of thing happens on farms. But it's amazing how the writer, whoever she is, manages to find humour in the worst situations."

Russell didn't comment, but she was sure he knew that she was actually the writer. She just hoped that he wouldn't broadcast his knowledge. She wouldn't feel so free to write what she wanted if she couldn't remain anonymous.

On the drive home Russell had gone quiet again, saying that he had to concentrate on manoeuvring up the narrow lane. The hooded headlamps shed little light on the road and it was a miracle they didn't end up in the ditch, but Celia thought it had more to do with the amount he had drunk. He'd managed to wheedle a whisky out of the barman and had also drunk two or three pints of beer.

They drew up in the farmyard and she made to get out of the van but as she reached for the door handle he grasped her shoulder and aimed a clumsy kiss at her lips. She shook him off, saying angrily, "You promised to behave, Russ."

"What's wrong with a little kiss between friends?" he said, slurring his words.

She didn't reply, scrambling out of the van and hurrying across the yard. She paused at the door, waiting until he started the vehicle up with a crunch of the gears.

Indoors, she reflected that she had enjoyed the meal and, most of the time, Russell's company. If he wasn't married — and if she had never met Matt — she might have been tempted to have a fling with him. But, she decided, there would be no more dinners or outings to the pictures. She didn't want to give him the wrong idea.

It wasn't until she was sitting up in bed, chewing the end of her pencil as she tried to find the words to apologise to Matt, that she remembered Russell's sly look when he'd mentioned the Countrywoman column in the paper. He must have guessed she was the writer — and the reason she wanted to keep it secret. Would he use that knowledge to talk her into accepting another date?

Celia overslept and came downstairs the next morning rubbing her eyes and yawning. Stella was in the kitchen making a pot of tea. She had hoped the other girl would still be in the milking parlour so that she wouldn't have to endure any remarks about her late homecoming.

"I haven't got time for breakfast," she said. "Any post?"

Stella grinned. "Out on the tiles last night?" she said, ignoring Celia's question.

Celia ignored her in turn and grabbed her handbag from the sideboard. There was a pile of letters beside it, most of them official-looking brown envelopes as usual. She flicked through them forlornly. There wouldn't be one from Matt, she was sure. Should she post the one she had written to him? And would he answer it? She wondered. She was about to replace the letters on the sideboard when she noticed one from Ed. She stuffed it into her bag and took her coat from the back door.

Much as Celia hated cycling home in the dark these days she refused Russell's offer of a lift. "I thought petrol was rationed," she said.

"Don't worry about that," he said with a grin. "I've got plenty."

"Save it," she said tartly. "You've got to deliver the papers tomorrow."

As she got her bike from the works shed she couldn't help wondering if he was dealing on the black market. It was the sort of thing he would do, she thought. Well, it wasn't her problem. She had enough to think about since reading Ed's letter. Pedalling head down against the icy wind she almost regretted refusing Russell's offer of a ride home especially when she had to get off her bike and push it up the hill. But, apart from her suspicions about his seemingly limitless supply of petrol, she didn't want him getting ideas about their relationship.

She pushed open the back door and took a deep breath of the comforting smell of stew emanating from the pan bubbling on the hob.

Her father was sitting in his usual chair, bending to pull off his boots. "Bitter out there, girl," he said, looking up at her. "Be a heavy frost tonight."

"Cold on the bike," Celia agreed, rubbing her hands. "Something smells good."

"I didn't know what time you'd be home so I asked Stella to cook for us."

Celia bit her lip, determined not to let her feelings show. Was Stella trying to take over in the kitchen too? She knew she was being unreasonable. Hadn't she often thought it wouldn't hurt her to do more in the house?

She forced a smile. "Well, I'm ready for it, Dad. I'll lay the table, shall I?" She got out the cutlery and put plates to warm on the range. "Where are the girls?"

"Just finishing in the barn. They'll be here in a minute. By the way, Stella said there was a letter from Ed. What did he have to say for himself?"

"Not a lot. He just apologized for going off without saying goodbye, that's all." Normally she would have given him the letter to read for himself. But she couldn't share what Ed had confided in his long rambling letter which she'd read in her dinner hour. Dad would probably start ranting about Ed's place being on the farm. It was as if he'd read her thoughts for, as usual whenever her brother was mentioned, he started his usual tirade.

"Bloody war," Larry said. "If it hadn't been for that, he'd have got this flying nonsense out of his head by now and be back here where he belongs."

Celia didn't bother to point out that Ed had never had any interest in the farm. Dad would never accept it, just as he couldn't accept the idea of her taking it on one day.

Just as she finished laying the table, Stella came in and, ignoring her, spoke to Larry about the milk yield.

I might as well not be here, Celia thought, as she dished up the stew.

It was a relief when Joyce entered the room and sat at the table, exclaiming over the appetising aroma emanating from the stew pot. "Can't wait to get stuck in. I'm starving," she said. "This one of your special recipes?" she asked.

"Not this time. I've only just got in. Stella cooked this evening," Celia said and, with an attempt at friendliness turned to the other girl. "It smells delicious, Stella. Thank you."

"Well, we need a good meal after a heavy day ploughing and milking. And I thought you might be out with your young man again," Stella said.

The words were spoken mildly, but Celia knew Stella was having a dig at her over her date with Russell. She knew she shouldn't rise to the bait, but she couldn't stop herself. "He's not my young man — he's just a work colleague," she said.

"That's not the impression I got," Stella said.

Celia suppressed an angry retort. Had Stella been looking out of the window last night and seen Russell's clumsy attempt at a kiss? She bit her lip, determined not to reply.

But Stella gave a sly smile and said, "I suppose it can't do any harm to have two strings to your bow."

Celia almost choked on her food. She half-rose from her chair, wanting to smack the smug smile off Stella's face. Fortunately, Joyce laid a restraining hand on her arm, forcing her to stay seated. "Take no notice of the jealous cow," she murmured.

The rest of the meal passed in silence and the two land girls went outside to shut up the chickens and make sure all was secure for the night while Celia washed up and tidied the kitchen. Her father sat in his chair by the range, reading the paper and occasionally making caustic remarks about the war and those running it. He still felt aggrieved about having to plough up yet another hay meadow. "What are my cows supposed to eat next year?" he muttered.

Joyce put her head round the door and said she was going back to the cottage. "See you in the morning," she said.

Stella sat down and picked up Larry's abandoned newspaper. Might as well go upstairs and answer Ed's letter, Celia thought. She didn't want to sit and write at the kitchen table and watch Stella cosying up to Dad.

"I'm going up," she announced. "Night, Dad."

"Aren't you going to let me see Ed's letter?" Larry asked.

"It's upstairs in my bag. Besides, he didn't say much — I told you."

"Don't know why he bothers to write at all," Larry said.

Celia didn't reply. These days, her brother couldn't do anything right in Dad's eyes. Upstairs she sat at her dressing table and took the letter out of her bag. But she couldn't let Dad read this.

He rambled on for several pages, reiterating what she'd overheard in the pub. She wondered if he'd been drinking when he wrote it. Although she sympathized with his distress over the mass bombing of German cities, she couldn't help thinking of the victims here at home. Being out in the country it was sometimes hard to imagine what people in the big cities were going through. The newsreels at the pictures painted a picture of jolly Londoners singing in their underground shelters, their message "we can take it" giving a lift to the spirits. But she knew the reality was far worse. Russell had told her what it had been like when he'd gone to London in search of Marion. And she knew that, despite trying to convey the impression that he didn't care, he was seriously worried about her.

The knowledge didn't help when it came to replying to her brother's letter but after much furrowing of the brow and chewing of the end of her pencil she managed to fill a couple of pages, conveying her sympathy and understanding, but at the same time urging him to sort himself out. She now understood why Matt had been so concerned and she heartily wished she had not been so hasty with him. She was glad now that she'd overcome her annoyance and written to apologize. She only hoped he would accept her apology and write back.

She finished her letter to Ed advising him to talk to someone about his feelings even if it meant being taken off flying duties. Matt had spoken out of concern for his friend as well as worry about the effect on his crew's morale, but if Ed couldn't confide in him there must be someone — a padre or chaplain — who could help.

After assuring him of her love and support whatever happened, Celia signed off and sealed the envelope. She flexed her frozen fingers and shivered. She ought to get into bed, but she had little hope of sleeping with so much on her mind. She turned to a fresh page in her writing pad and started another letter — this time to Matt telling him she'd heard from Ed and explaining that now she understood what he had been trying to tell her. *I know you have Ed's best interests at heart,* she wrote. *Please try to help him. I know he doesn't really want to let you or the crew down.*

Although she was shivering with cold, by the time she'd finished writing she felt a lot better. As she undressed for bed she hoped Matt would understand why she'd taken her brother's side and realize that it did not detract from her feelings for him.

She settled down under the layers of blankets, hoping that the weather would not get any worse. She did not relish the cycle ride to work next day.

Her fears were realized when she woke next morning. She knew by the quality of the light glowing behind the curtains and the stillness in the air that it had snowed in the night. She got out of bed, wincing as her feet touched the cold floor. She threw the old cardigan that she used as a dressing gown around her shoulders, pulling it closely around her. She went to the window and drew back the curtain, rubbing away the frost that patterned the glass. To the east the sun was just rising over the hills, casting a magical sheen over the farmyard and outhouses. The fields leading down to the river were still in shadow, covered by a silvery blanket.

She heard the clank of a bucket and her father's voice calling to one of the girls. Thank goodness they'd brought the cows in last night, Celia thought. But the sheep were still out there on the hills.

She dressed hurriedly. There was no way she could get in to work today and Dad would need help rescuing any sheep that were trapped in drifts out on the Downs. He'd appreciate an extra pair of hands.

I'll phone Mr Allen later, she thought, hurrying downstairs to the kitchen, still warm from the range which had been banked up the night before. She rattled the poker between the bars trying to coax some life into the embers. When a flame briefly flared, she added kindling and small knobs of coal, filled a kettle and put it on the hob. They'd need a hot drink when they came in, breakfast too. She fried bacon and sausages and fried bread, putting the plates to keep hot at the back of the range. She'd fry the eggs when they came in.

By the time she'd laid the table there was still no sign of Dad and the girls so she took her coat from the hook behind the door and thrust her feet into her Wellington boots. The blast of cold air as she opened the back door had her reaching for her scarf and she stepped out into the yard, already churned to a brown sludge.

As she reached the milking parlour she heard Joyce's laugh and the two land girls came out leading the cows.

"Where's Dad?" Celia asked.

"He's gone to check on the sheep," Joyce said. "We'll join him when we've got the cows back in the barn."

"I'll help," Celia said.

"We can manage," Stella snapped. "Anyway, aren't you supposed to be going to work?"

"Don't be daft, Stell," Joyce said. "How do you expect her to get into town in this lot?" She waved her arm to indicate the snowy landscape and turned to Celia with a grin. "Good excuse for a day off, eh?"

"That's what I thought," Celia replied, smiling. She was determined not let Stella's attitude get under her skin. "I'll go and find Dad."

She opened the gate and trudged up the lane, following in the tracks her father had made earlier. The snow was deeper here and she hoped the sheep had had the sense to shelter from the storm, either in the hedge-rows or the pens that they'd erected earlier.

It was warm work tramping uphill, hampered by the deep snow. At the top she paused and scanned the landscape but there was no sign of her father. Up here on the Downs the wind cut through her and she began to shiver. Best keep on the move, she thought. She breasted the hill and was relieved to see her father, a dark shape against the whiteness with Mickey's slight figure beside him. They were struggling to release one of the ewes who'd become almost buried in a drift. She hurried over to help. As they pulled the animal out of the drift, Mickey fell over backwards, almost disappearing as he sank into the snow drift.

The boy protested indignantly as Celia started to laugh but she couldn't help it. Even Larry gave a wry grin. "Better get back to your gran's, boy," he said. "Get out of those wet clothes and then go and help Stella in the barn."

The sheep had pulled away from them and with an angry bleat moved off towards the remainder of the flock who were huddled in the lee of a stand of hawthorn scrub.

"Shall we get them into the pens?" Celia asked.

Larry looked up at the sky. "No — better bring them down. Looks like we might get some more snow. I had hoped we could leave them out for a bit longer. Thank goodness the lambs aren't due for another couple of months."

Wish we still had old Flossie, Celia thought, but she did not say it aloud. The old sheepdog had died some years ago and her father still hadn't got over her loss, although he rarely mentioned it nowadays. When she had broached getting and training a new puppy he had refused to think about it, saying that now they only had a few sheep it was hardly worth the trouble.

As they tried to coax the unwilling animals away from the shelter of the hedge and into the open field she couldn't help feeling a bit annoyed by her father's stubbornness. They had just got the flock through the gate and on the track leading down to the farm when Joyce and Stella came into view.

"You didn't need us after all," Joyce called cheerfully.

Stella scowled and remained silent.

It was becoming more obvious every day that she was jealous of Celia and resented her helping with farm work. The only good thing about her being here was that she seemed to have caused Dad to mellow a bit. But would he have changed enough to let her work full time at High Trees after the war?

As they trudged back through the snow to the farmhouse, Celia suddenly realized that it wasn't so important to her any more. She told herself it had nothing to do with her feelings for Matt — after all, he hadn't written to her since that disastrous leave. But deep down, she knew that if a miracle happened and he asked her, she would leave High Trees behind without a qualm.

Her thoughts were interrupted when they entered the yard and her father said, "Thanks, Cee. Get on in the warm. We'll finish up here."

"Yeah, get that kettle on," Joyce said with a laugh.

"Breakfast is almost ready. I prepared most of it before I came out," Celia answered. Hurrying inside, she put the kettle on one hot plate and the frying pan on the other, then went to the phone in the hall to let Mr Allen know she would not be in the office that day.

Russell answered and immediately offered to come and fetch her in the van. "It's not that bad, is it?" he asked. "It's nearly gone already."

"It may be all right down in town, but you know how it can get up here, Russ. It's impossible," she said. "You'd never get up the hill. Perhaps if the milk lorry makes it, I'll get a lift."

"We'll just have to manage without you then," Russell said with a laugh. "Enjoy your day off."

"Some day off," Celia muttered, looking round at the kitchen. It could do with a good clean. And she'd have a go at some of the make do and mend recipes while she was home. Normally, this close to Christmas, the pantry would be full of cakes and puddings and jars of homemade mincemeat. This year, thanks to the rationing, as well as the demands on her time, Celia had not given it a thought. It might give her an idea for next week's column. And she could work on that too if she was off work for more than one day. She'd already handed her copy for this week to Mr Allen.

As she bustled round the kitchen, frying eggs and reheating the bacon and sausages, she thought that the weather and the rescue of the sheep would make a good topic for her weekly anecdote. But she was running out of ideas for the recipe that her readers had come to expect.

Well, something would come to her if she spent the morning cooking and cleaning. She was determined to keep busy. That way she wouldn't keep looking out of the window waiting for the postman. After all, if she couldn't get into town, she couldn't expect Bill to struggle up the lane with the post.

When the breakfast was ready she went to the back door to call the girls in. It was very quiet and Celia suddenly realized why. They had become so used to the sound of planes taking off and landing at the nearby airfield that the sudden silence was almost unnerving. Celia smiled. If it was as bad as this up in Norfolk the boys wouldn't be flying either. She could stop worrying for a while. Perhaps the respite would give Ed time to pull himself together.

She stood there for a moment, lost in thought. Matt had said he was letting himself down as well as the crew, but she knew it wasn't cowardice on Ed's part. He had always been a sensitive lad. She could remember him crying when the lambs were sent to market and he'd first realized why they had to go. Dad had been disgusted, telling him to grow up, and to be fair he had tried.

Wanting to please Dad, he had worked hard during the school holidays. But when the flying bug bit him he'd known what he wanted to do. Would he have still been so keen to join the airforce though if he'd known what he'd have to do? Celia wondered. She turned back indoors, shivering as a few flakes of snow drifted down.

When Dad and the girls came in, stamping the snow off their boots, she was busy at the stove. She put on a cheerful face as she dished up, joking about having a day off work. She didn't want them asking what was wrong.

Stella seemed to sense her mood though, and couldn't resist having another dig at her. "No post today," she said. "Not that you were expecting anything were you?" she asked.

"I'm not daft enough to expect Bill to come all the way out here in this," Celia retorted.

"It's not the snow. You haven't heard from him since he went back have you?"

Celia concentrated on pouring the tea. But Stella wouldn't let it go.

"I wonder what he'd think if he knew you'd been to the pictures and out for dinner with the boss's son — going to the pictures, out for dinner . . ." she said with a malicious gleam in her eye.

"One dinner doesn't mean they're courting and we both went to the pictures with Russell," Joyce said. "How do you know it's not me he's interested in?"

Stella laughed. "You?" she said.

Joyce didn't rise to the bait, but turned to Celia saying, "Perhaps we could all do it again when the snow's gone. It was fun."

Before Celia could reply, Larry joined them and Stella immediately turned on the charm. "These eggs are good. How do you manage it on that old range?" she asked.

"Practice," Celia replied. She wasn't going to let Stella needle her. But she couldn't help wondering about the other girl's earlier remark. What had she meant by it? How could Matt know she had been out with Russell? And what would he care anyway after the way they'd parted all those weeks ago? She had half a mind not to post the letter she'd written last night. After all, if he cared, he would have written first — wouldn't he?

CHAPTER
SIXTEEN

It had begun to snow and the propellers were in danger of icing up. Matt peered ahead, trying to see where they were as the snow flakes whirled around the plane. "Why don't they ever get the weather forecast right?" he muttered. They should never have taken off in these conditions. But then, it hadn't been snowing when they'd set off on their mission. They'd actually been grateful for the thick cloud which would enable them to reach their destination undetected. Well, they'd done it and now they were on their way home.

Matt took a swig from his flask of coffee and sighed with relief. This was his last op of the current tour of duty. No more trips to Berlin for a while. He and the crew deserved a break, he thought. Night after night they'd taken off with their heavy bomb load, hampered by some of the worst winter weather he could recall. Night after night of rain and fog. And now snow.

They'd been right on target tonight. No mistakes in Ed's navigation this time. They had almost reached the Dutch coast and there was an exultant mood in the cabin as pilot Clive Mitchell relayed congratulations to his crew.

He broke off abruptly. "Wait up, lads — trouble," he said.

A German fighter had appeared almost out of nowhere. What were enemy fighters doing flying in this sort of weather? Bad enough trying to dodge the flak. Clive plunged the Lancaster into a bank of cloud and turned to grin at Matt. "Lost him," he said. But he had spoken too soon. There was a rattle of gunfire from below followed by several loud bangs.

A burst of return fire sounded from behind and the rear-gunner, Chalky White, shouted, "Got the bastard."

It was too late, though. As the plane lurched, Clive let go off the controls and slumped back in his seat. Glancing across at him, Matt groaned. His friend had taken a hit and blood was pouring down his face.

Matt took over the controls, shouting, "Sparks, get up here and have a look at the skipper."

The fighter had destroyed one engine and he daren't take his eyes off the controls to see if Clive was all right. It was all he could do to keep the plane on course.

And then it had started to snow. "Ed, where are we?" he called over the intercom.

"Should be passing over the Dutch coast any minute," Ed replied, giving the co-ordinates. His voice was calm and efficient, Matt noted with relief. Still, he'd known that Ed would pull his weight in a crisis. After their last visit to High Trees, their friendship had wavered and Matt still hadn't quite forgiven him for being the cause of the rift between him and Celia. But they'd had a long talk and eventually Ed had apologized for his behaviour in the pub.

Since then, although he remained quiet and introspective, he seemed committed to the job they had to do. Thank God for that, Matt thought. It wouldn't do to have him going to pieces right now. With no visual aids to show them where they were, their lives depended on Ed's navigation skills.

"Is he badly hurt?" he asked. The wireless operator had scrambled into the cockpit and was examining Clive's head wound.

"I'm fine," Clive muttered, pushing the other man away. "I can take over now."

"Beg you pardon, skipper, but you're not fine. You've got a nasty cut on your head. Just keep still and let me put a dressing on it. Matt will get us home," Sparks said firmly.

Matt wasn't so sure. The blizzard was increasing by the minute and the propellers were behaving erratically as ice formed. Any minute now one or all of them could seize up. He could get them back on the remaining three engines all right, but not if any more of them conked out too. He hung on to the controls, fighting to keep the plane steady.

"Where are we now, Ed?" he asked.

"Should be coming up to the coast pretty soon. There's a small town off to the east — Terneuzen. Can you see anything?"

Shut away in his little compartment, Ed had no way of knowing that visibility was down to nil. Matt hadn't wanted to burden him with the knowledge that so much depended on his navigational skills. Now, he couldn't help swearing. "I can't see a bloody thing," he said. "You sure we're on course?"

"Course I'm sure," Ed replied.

Matt thought he'd sounded a bit hesitant and he cursed under his breath. He hadn't meant to speak so sharply. It didn't take much to dent Ed's fragile self-confidence. But he had other things to worry about now and he didn't reply. He was too busy trying to keep the plane level as, with a stutter and a rattle, another engine failed. How long before the other two followed suit? Would he have to ditch the plane in the sea? He hoped not. They wouldn't stand much chance in this weather.

Perhaps they should bale out now. Being prisoners of war was surely preferable to perishing in the icy North Sea. Was Terneuzen a large town? He didn't want to risk crashing in a densely populated area. He thought about consulting Ed but knowing his friend's concerns about innocent civilians, he decided not to. Besides, if he remembered rightly, there weren't many towns along this stretch of coast.

He glanced across at Clive. What would he do in this situation? His friend was now semi-conscious, but he was in charge. The decision was his. He had to decide quickly. They were losing height and another engine could go at any moment.

"Get ready to bale out," he instructed the crew, then set the course out to sea.

"What about the skipper?" Sparks asked.

"I'll take care of him," Matt promised.

"You sure?"

Before he could reply, Ed interrupted. "I think we're passing over Terneuzen. Can you see anything?"

"Black as pitch," Matt said. "We'll just have to take a chance." He took a deep breath and ordered the men to bale. When he was sure they were clear, he struggled out of his seat. He shook Clive, hoping he was sufficiently conscious to jump. The pilot mumbled and Matt began to panic. "Come on, skipper. We've got to get out."

As he began to pull Clive out of his seat he became aware of someone else trying to help. "Ed, I thought you'd gone," he said.

"Couldn't leave my mate to struggle," Ed replied.

With no breath for further talk, they manoeuvred their friend out of his seat and into the body of the plane. "Go on, Ed, I'll be right behind you," Matt said.

"I'm not jumping." Ed's voice was firm.

"What? Go on, that's an order."

"There's a town down there, innocent people under occupation by the enemy. I don't want the plane crashing on them. I'll take her out to sea and ditch her."

"No, Ed. I can't let you do that."

"You're wasting time." Ed scrambled into the cockpit and took the controls. "Go on, Matt. Good luck and give my love to Cee."

Making sure that their parachutes were firmly strapped on, Matt wrapped his arms around Clive and stepped out of the plane into the icy air. He hit the release on Clive's chute and watched as the canopy unfolded above him.

With a sigh of relief that Clive seemed to be OK, he deployed his own parachute and drifted down, listening for the crash. But there was only the sound of the wind rushing past his ears. What was he going to tell Celia when he got back? That's if he ever got back, he thought, as the ground rushed up to meet him.

Celia was enjoying being alone in the farmhouse for a change. Dad and Mickey had gone up to the woods with the tractor and trailer to fetch logs for the fire, while the two land girls were working in the barn. It was good to have a couple of hours to herself and to be free of Stella's sarcastic remarks. She turned the wireless on and sang along to *Music While You Work* as she scrubbed the big wooden table.

When the kitchen was cleaned to her satisfaction she made an inspection of the pantry. There wasn't much in there — at least it didn't seem a lot when she compared it with her memory of the days before her mother died. Then the deep walk-in cupboard had been filled with rows of preserves, bottled fruit and jams, salted down runner beans and dried onions.

Since she had left school and gone to work full time there just weren't enough hours in the day. Before cycling into town she had to see to the chickens and tidy the kitchen after breakfast. Then on her return, often cold and wet after riding up the steep lane, there was the meal to prepare. Despite Jean Robson's help with the laundry, there was still a lot to do. Not that she was complaining, Celia thought now. Life on the farm was hard but she loved it. She just wished she had more time. Well, she had time now, she thought, as she began taking things from the shelves and setting them on the table.

Right at the back of the pantry were a couple of jars that looked as if they'd been there for months. She opened one and recoiled at the growth of mould on top.

"Better not let Stella see this," she muttered, picturing the other girl's superior look and the comment she would make about wasting food when it was rationed.

After scooping the unidentifiable mess into the pig bin, she washed the jar and then wiped down the shelves. As she started to put everything back she realized to her surprise that there were more usable ingredients than she'd thought, including a box of dried peas, some lentils and a jar of preserved tomatoes that had somehow been overlooked.

That's tomorrow's dinner, she thought, putting the dried vegetables in a pan to soak overnight.

She glanced at the clock. Plenty of time before everyone came in for their midday meal. She made a cup of tea and sat at the table with her notebook and pencil, trying to word the recipe she would cook tomorrow as well as use in her weekly column. After a moment's thought, she threw down the pencil with a sigh. It was no good. Her recipes were becoming boring and repetitive, no different from the cookery tips given in the magazines and on the wireless.

"Damn," she muttered as she picked up the pencil and noticed that the lead had broken. There would be another one in the dresser drawer, she thought, getting up and rummaging among the litter of old envelopes, bits of string and other oddments. No pencil. She opened the other drawer where her father kept the letters and forms to do with the running of the farm. As she pushed her hand to the back of the drawer she remembered the letter from Matt that had accidentally got caught up with Dad's letters. Why hadn't she heard from him?

Dismissing the thought, she pulled the drawer right out, tipped its contents onto the table and began to sort through them. She tidied the papers into a neat pile, not sure whether to feel relieved or sorry that there was no letter addressed to her. As she returned everything to the drawer, her heart skipped a beat and her fingers closed over a slim notebook. The neat handwriting on the front was her mother's.

With a lump in her throat, Celia sat down and opened the book. There were few reminders of her mother left in the farmhouse. After her death a grief-stricken Larry had disposed of her clothing and personal belongings without a thought for his daughter. The only keepsake Celia had was a small brooch in the form of a posy of spring flowers as well as a faded photograph which she kept on her bedside table.

Now, as she leafed through the pages, the memories came thick and fast. How could she have forgotten standing at the kitchen table, watching as Mum pounded rose petals in a bowl, adding glycerine and other ingredients to make the soothing hand cream that softened her work-worn hands?

She turned the pages, her heart beating faster as she realized that this was Mum's recipe book. There were remedies for sunburn, chilblains, coughs and colds and almost every ailment you could think of — all made from plants that grew in the garden and hedgerow.

This would liven up her newspaper column, she thought excitedly.

Lost in thought, she jumped when the back door opened and Joyce came in, closely followed by Stella. She hadn't realized how late it was and the table wasn't even laid. Fortunately she had made some soup earlier on and it was now bubbling merrily on the range.

She shoved the notebook into her apron pocket and closed the drawer. "Grub's nearly ready," she said with a smile.

Stella glanced at the range, her mouth turned down. "I thought as you were at home today we'd have a proper dinner for once," she said. "We need something on a cold day like today."

Usually they had sandwiches out in the field if they were away from the house or, in bad weather, came indoors to eat. Celia always cooked in the evening or left something to be re-heated if she wasn't going to be home in time. They were lucky to be getting hot soup this lunchtime, she thought. But she wasn't going to let Stella get to her so she bit back her angry report and began setting out the soup bowls.

Joyce had already gone over to the range and was stirring the pot. "This'll warm us up," she said, winking at Celia behind Stella's back.

Larry and Mickey came in, rubbing their hands, their faces glowing from the cold. "Something smells good," Larry said.

Stella's mood changed immediately and she smiled. "Celia's made some soup. Makes a change from sandwiches," she said. "Come and eat while it's hot." She pulled out a chair beside Larry and carried on talking as if Celia wasn't there.

She's behaving as if she's the lady of the house and I'm the servant, Celia thought as she dished up the food. Perhaps that's what she's after. It wasn't that Celia objected to her father taking an interest in another woman. After all, it was some years since Mum had died. But why did it have to be Stella?

She deliberately closed her ears to what she and Dad were saying. She couldn't believe how chatty her normally dour father became in the presence of the land girl. She turned to Joyce who was, as usual, teasing young Mickey and joined in the banter.

"Better not go up on the Downs again till the snow's gone," she said.

"Why not?" Mickey asked, his mouth full.

"Well, it's snowing again. If it gets any deeper, you'll disappear completely and we'll have to dig you out like the sheep."

"I ain't that small," Mickey protested. "I'm nearly as tall as Grandad now."

Celia and Joyce both collapsed with laughter. Len Robson was a small wiry man and Mickey was shaping up to be just like him.

"Leave the lad alone," Larry said. "He's a good worker — that's what counts."

Mickey smirked and stuck his tongue out at Joyce who immediately retaliated.

They all laughed, except for Stella, whose sour expression put a damper on the atmosphere. Celia was relieved when the meal came to an end and they all got up from the table.

Wind rattled the windows and when Larry opened the door, snowflakes drifted indoors. Joyce shuddered and wrapped her scarf round her face, turning to Celia before following the others outside.

"Lucky you, staying here in the warm," she said. "Not that I mind as we'll be working in the barn. It's spending the next few hours with old sourpuss I don't fancy."

"Don't take any notice of her — I don't," Celia said.

"Still it must get to you, seeing her sucking up to your Dad," Joyce said. "And she's not putting all her eggs in one basket, you know."

"What do you mean?"

"Well, she's definitely got her eye on poor old Larry. But she'd been writing to Ed as well. I saw the address on the envelope."

Celia tried not to let Joyce see how upset she was. "I can't stop her, I suppose," she said with a shrug. "Now shut that door, before my kitchen's knee deep in snow."

Joyce hurried across the yard to the barn and Celia looked up at the sky. It was already getting dark and she would have to go out and feed the chickens soon. Best get it done now, she thought, putting on her boots and huddling herself into her coat.

When all the chores were done, an almost meatless pie in the oven and the potatoes peeled ready, Celia made herself a cup of tea and sat down to read her mother's notebook.

As she flicked through it, she became more excited as she realized that here was the answer to livening up her column. The recipes she included every week didn't just have to be for food. She could write up these beauty treatments, the recipes for creams and lotions for minor injuries — arnica for bruises, elderflower cream for sunburn.

Not that we need that at the moment, Celia thought with a smile, glancing up at the darkening windows. If only I'd found Mum's book in the summer. Joyce could have done with some of that cream back then. Many of the recipes used the wild herbs and flowers that grew abundantly along the lanes and in the woods around the farm.

There were food recipes too and Celia remembered the little bottles of peppermint oil and orange essence she had found lurking at the back of the pantry that morning.

Her column was taking shape in her head now. Last week, she'd given tips on making Christmas presents and decorations from scraps of wool and material. This week she would include a recipe for carrot fudge made from very simple ingredients and not needing any sugar. Packed in a small box and tied with a piece of colourful ribbon, it would make a nice present, she thought.

"Thanks, Mum," she whispered. After dinner she would go up to her room and write. Rescuing the sheep this morning would make an amusing anecdote and the recipe would fill the rest of her column.

Well satisfied with her so-called "day off", she set about getting the meal ready. If the snow cleared tomorrow, she would try to get in to work and type it all up.

It wasn't until she was dishing up that the implication of what Joyce had said earlier dawned on her. If Stella was writing to Ed, she had probably told him that Celia had gone out to dinner with Russell. That was what she had meant by her remark about Matt not liking it if he knew.

The urge to confront the other girl was almost overwhelming, but that was probably what she wanted. She wouldn't give her the satisfaction of rising to the bait. Instead, she put the plate down on the table in front of her father. "Steak and kidney, Dad — your favourite. Not much meat I'm afraid though."

"Never mind, lass. You do your best I know."

Celia had escaped upstairs to get on with her writing while the ideas were still fresh. It was bitterly cold and she sat at the table with a blanket round her shoulders and her feet on a hot water bottle. It would be warmer downstairs, but she knew that if she tried to write with Stella in the room, the other girl wouldn't rest until she had found out what she was up to. Joyce was the only one who knew that she was writing for the paper and had promised to keep her secret. Her anonymity gave her the freedom to write about incidents on the farm and besides, she dreaded her father finding out. She knew he would not approve, especially if he knew she was using her mother's old book for ideas.

She stood up and stretched, going over to the window. It had stopped snowing and the clouds were gradually dispersing, allowing faint moonlight to illuminate the fields beyond the farm. While she appreciated the beauty of the scene, Celia knew that this sort of weather was hated by farmers, as well as those who had to travel to earn a living. She hoped the snow would have melted enough to allow her to go in to work, although she didn't relish riding her bike. If the milk lorry made it up the hill, she would cadge a lift into town, she thought.

All was quiet, no planes overhead and Celia once more thought that at least the weather meant Matt and Ed would not be flying tonight. Surely they couldn't take off in all this snow? Sadly, she thought back to the autumn when she and Matt had spent those blissful hours together. Once more she savoured his kisses, wondering if she'd ever know such happiness again. Why had they let her brother's problems come between them, she asked herself.

Perhaps she'd write again, she thought, as she started downstairs to prepare her father's bedtime cocoa. But no. She'd wait and see what he said. That's if he answered at all.

CHAPTER
SEVENTEEN

Matt hit the ground and rolled several times before coming to rest at the foot of a sand dune. At least he thought it was a sand dune. It was pitch black and he felt around in the darkness to release his parachute harness.

Had the others got down safely too? He risked calling out and was answered with a faint groan. He felt his way towards the sound and encountered the body of the pilot. "You all right, skipper?" he asked.

"Not sure. Where are we?" Clive mumbled.

Well, at least he was still alive, Matt thought. "Don't try to move," he said. "I need to think what to do."

He felt around in the darkness and bundled the parachutes up, debating whether to try to bury them. Suppose the beach was mined? Well, he'd just have to take a chance. He scooped a hole in the sand and pushed the material in, holding his breath when his fingers encountered a hard object. He felt around carefully but it turned out to be large pebble. Sighing with relief he filled in the hole and stood up.

"Perhaps we should stay put till it's light," he whispered to Clive.

His friend muttered incoherently and Matt knew he needed help. Besides, it was freezing and they'd die of hypothermia if they didn't move soon.

Cautiously, he scrambled to the top of the dune. Only a few flakes of snow now drifted down and far off in the east a faint glimmer of light illuminated the sea which stretched in front of him. They were nearer the coast than he thought. How far away was Terneuzen, he wondered. And how heavily occupied by the enemy?

He gave a thought to Ed, who had so bravely stayed behind to prevent the plane possibly crashing on the town. What could he tell Celia, he wondered? Would it be a comfort to her to know of her brother's courage?

He thrust the thought from him and turned away from the sea, peering inland through the darkness. There was no sign of the rest of his crew but they couldn't be far away. He hoped they would meet up when it got light. He slid down the sand dune to where Clive was still muttering deliriously.

"Quiet, skipper," he said, shaking the pilot by the shoulder. "Can you stand up?" When daylight came they would be too exposed and he had decided that they should risk the mines and get off the beach. They would head inland and hope to come across some friendly Dutch people before they were picked up by the Germans. It wasn't a vain hope — a few months earlier a couple of chaps from their squadron had been helped by the resistance and found their way home after baling out over enemy-occupied territory.

Perhaps they'd be lucky too, he thought. But as he helped the skipper to his feet, a bright light shone out and a voice shouted, "Halt, *Hände hoch*."

Still supporting Clive with one arm around him, he raised his other hand. "Skipper," he whispered. "Put your hands up."

"What?" Clive muttered.

"*Hände hoch*," the German soldier shouted, louder this time.

Matt let go of Clive, hoping his friend could stand alone, and put his hands in the air. "Don't shoot, he's injured," he called out.

The torch was dazzling him and he couldn't see how many of them there were. If there was just one he might be able to tackle him, Matt thought. But as he made a slight movement, two others materialized out of the darkness and grabbed him. Others took Clive by the arms and the two of them were hustled up the beach, their feet sinking into the loose sand and making them stumble.

Prodded by rifle butts, they were made to climb into the back of a waiting truck where, to Matt's dismay, he saw the rest of the crew — Chalky, Sparks, Ginger and Pete. Well, at least they'd landed safely. It was just a pity they'd all been caught.

"So they got you too? Bad luck, mate," Ginger said, peering through the darkness at Matt's companion. "Is that the skipper? Is he all right?"

"Not sure," Matt replied. "He was hit, I think. His head's bleeding."

A German soldier poked his head into the truck and barked, "No talking."

"Where's Ed?" Ginger whispered defiantly.

"He didn't bale. Tell you later," Matt replied.

They sat huddled together against the cold for what seemed like hours until it became light, when there was a burst of conversation in German and the truck began to move off. Matt guessed they'd been searching for the remaining crew member.

Two guards sat at the rear, their rifles at the ready. But the men were too exhausted to make a move. Not that they'd have a hope of getting away without being shot, Matt thought, as each of them succumbed to an uneasy doze.

He couldn't sleep though, his mind churning with thoughts as to whether he'd done the right thing in baling out. At least they were all still alive — except for poor old Ed. Could they have made it back to the English coast though? No. He was sure they'd been about to crash and that baling out over land was their best chance. He should have insisted that Ed bale too though. What was he going to tell Celia? That's if they ever got the chance to meet again.

After a day at home, Celia couldn't wait to get back to work. Although she'd enjoyed the unaccustomed day off and was glowing with satisfaction at all the jobs she'd managed to complete, she didn't feel she could put up with Stella for much longer.

So when she went outside to feed the hens before breakfast, she was pleased that, although the snow still lay thick in the hedgerows and on the tops of the downs, it was beginning to thaw. She didn't think it was safe to ride her bike just yet though.

Having resigned herself to another day of housework, she breathed a sigh of relief when she saw the milk lorry creeping up the hill. High Trees was the last farm on Fred's round. She was sure he'd give her a lift into town on his way to the station.

By the time he and Dad and the girls had loaded the churns, she'd prepared their breakfast and had a quick bite to eat herself. Fred said he didn't mind lingering over a cup of tea while she got herself ready for work. "So long as I get the churns to the station in time," he said.

"How will you get home?" Dad asked as she got her coat off the hook behind the door.

"I expect Russell will give her a lift," Stella said with a smirk.

In the lorry she replied absently to Fred's comments about the weather. Despite the beginning thaw she hadn't expected the post to come, but she was still disappointed that she hadn't heard from Matt. If only she hadn't reacted so hastily to his concerns about her brother. And if only he'd stayed long enough for her to put things right.

She was so lost in thought she almost didn't realize they had reached the turning into town until Fred spoke. "Can I drop you off here, love? The road's fairly clear and it's only a little way into town so you'll be all right."

"Yes, of course. Thanks, Fred." She forced a smile and opened the cab door.

"Mind how you go," he said, "and don't worry about that brother of yours — or his friend. They'll be all right."

Celia felt herself blushing. "What do you mean?" she asked.

"Your Dad said you'd started writing to one of Ed's mates. He's worried you might get hurt . . ." His voice trailed off and Celia knew what he was thinking. It was something she tried not to think about herself, especially when Dad turned the news on and they heard the ominous words, "several of our aircraft failed to return".

"He's only a pen friend," she said, blushing again when Fred grinned.

She said goodbye to him and began the walk into town while he turned onto the main road towards the station. As she trudged through the snow which was rapidly turning to slush, she comforted herself with the thought that for the past couple of nights at least Matt and her brother would not have been flying, given the terrible weather conditions.

"Sorry about yesterday, Mr Allen," she said when she entered the office. "Hope everything's all right."

"We managed," her boss said. "Ray didn't turn up either but he's in today. I'm surprised you got here — not on your bike, I hope?"

"I got a lift on the milk lorry."

"Well, Russ will take you home so don't worry about getting back."

Celia thanked him and went to put the kettle on. Mr Allen was always ready for a cup of tea and she could do with warming up after walking from the junction.

"I wrote my column while I was at home yesterday — just need to type it up," she said when she took Mr Allen's tea into his office.

"Don't bother typing it, Celia. I'm sure Ray can read your writing."

"I'd rather type it — there're lots of crossings out and it's a bit of a scribble. It won't take long," Celia was still anxious to keep her authorship a secret and knew Ray would recognize her writing.

The linotype operator wasn't exactly a gossip, but he might mention it to someone. In this small town where everyone knew everyone else word would soon get round and she didn't want her father to know about it. She just knew he wouldn't approve.

After typing her article she took it through to the works, smiling at the printers but making no attempt at conversation over the noise of the big press which was churning out more leaflets for the War Ministry. She handed the typewritten sheets to Ray and went back to her office to open the post.

She was extra busy, having missed a day's work and the time flew. Dusk had fallen even earlier today and as she got up to switch on the lights, the outside door opened. Her heart gave the usual lurch when the telegraph boy came in, stamping snow from his shoes. But telegrams often came to the works — usually official ones concerned with their work for the ministry — and she managed to smile at the lad.

222

"Miss Raines?" he asked.

She gasped and sat down quickly. "That's me. What is it?"

"This is addressed to Mr L Raines, High Trees Farm," the boy said. "I can't get up there on my bike 'cause of the snow so the postmaster said to give it you."

She took the small yellow envelope and tore it open, her eyes misting as she took in the dreaded words. *Flight Sergeant Edgar Raines — missing.*

"Any reply, miss?"

Celia shook her head and the boy left.

She was still sitting with the telegram in her hand, when Russell came in bringing a blast of cold air with him.

"Nippy out there, Cee," he said, rubbing his hands. "You ready to go? Dad said to get you home before it snows again."

She didn't reply and Russell came over to the desk, putting his hand on her shoulder. "You OK?" he asked, noticing the paper in her hand. "Oh, no. Is it Ed?"

She nodded. "It says missing . . ."

"Well then, I'm sure that's all it is. There'll be more news soon."

His voice sounded too hearty, Celia thought, as if he's trying to convince himself as well as me. She hoped he was right. But meantime, what was she going to say to Dad?

She was quiet in the van going home and she was grateful that for once Russell didn't tease or try to flirt with her.

It had turned colder and the remaining slushy snow had frozen in the rutted lane leading up to the farm. The drive took much longer than usual and it was fully dark by the time they pulled up at the house.

Celia felt she should ask Russell in for a hot drink before letting him drive back to town, although she wanted to get indoors and break the news to her father as soon as possible.

To her relief, he refused, but then spoiled it by grabbing her hand and saying, "It's not a hot drink I want from you, Celia."

"I know what you want, Russell, and I've told you before, it's not on."

"Still dreaming about your pilot, I suppose," he said.

Anger welled up at his insensitivity. "I've just heard that my brother is missing in action and you know Matt is in the same crew. Whatever has happened to Ed has happened to him too . . ." Her voice broke and she choked back tears.

Russell was immediately contrite. "Oh, Cee, forgive me. I didn't think —"

"No, you didn't, did you?" She grabbed her bag and opened the van door.

He leaned over as she got out. "Do you want me to pick you up tomorrow if it's still like this?" he asked.

"I'll come in on the milk lorry as I did this morning." She slammed the van door and watched as he drove away.

Celia's anger evaporated as swiftly as it had come. She knew she shouldn't take Russell seriously; she felt that a lot of his womanizing was a cover for his unhappiness about his wife's defection. She'd always taken his flirting with a pinch of salt, confident that he meant nothing by it and still enjoyed his company. Despite his cheeky ways, she knew how devoted he was to Marion. But since his wife had left him and he had accepted that she wasn't coming back, he'd become more dogged in his pursuit of her. She wished she could avoid him, but it was difficult when they worked together, even more so when his father seemed to have no idea of the situation and almost insisted on her being taken home in the works van.

Before going indoors, she looked up at the sky, praying that they would not get more snow. The sooner she could start riding her bike into town again the better, she thought. And there would be no more dinners or visit to the pictures with Russell, even with Joyce as chaperone.

She hung her coat up and took off her wet shoes, feeling in her bag for the dreaded telegram. She should stop thinking about her own petty problems and concentrate on her father. No matter that he and her brother had not been on good terms lately, she knew that the news would be a severe blow to him.

As she entered the kitchen, she heard laughter and she tensed, hating the idea that she would be the cause of changing the mood inside the farmhouse.

Dad was in his chair by the range and the two land girls were sitting at the table. The laughter was coming from the wireless which was tuned to the *Light Programme* and the comedy sketch show *ITMA*. Even Stella was smiling.

But her face must have told them something was wrong and the smiles faded as they turned towards her.

Larry's hands whitened on the arms of his chair and he half-rose as he spotted the telegram in her hand. "Ed?" he whispered.

Stella pushed her chair back and came over to him, putting her arm around his shoulders. She looked up at Celia. "What is it?" she asked.

Celia held out the telegram. "It says missing — just missing, not . . ." For once she felt no resentment as Stella tried to comfort her father. She wouldn't have known what to say anyway.

Larry snatched the telegram from her and read it, his hands trembling.

Only Joyce stayed calm. She pushed Celia into a chair and poured her a cup of tea. "You've had a shock too," she said, patting her arm.

Celia picked up the cup, but her hands were shaking and she put it down again.

Stella was murmuring to Larry, reassuring him that "missing" meant just that. "He probably baled out. Sometimes it's weeks before you hear anything," she said.

"She's right," Joyce said. "You mustn't give up hope." She turned to Celia and whispered, "It's not just Ed, is it?"

She shook her head. "I couldn't bear it if . . ." She couldn't bring herself to say Matt's name.

None of them felt like eating and very soon, Joyce left to go back to the Robsons' cottage. Between them, Stella and Celia persuaded Larry to go to bed too.

After a brief protest he said, "Suppose I'd better try to sleep. Farm work goes on whatever happens."

Stella nodded agreement and Celia knew they were both right. There was nothing they could do except hope for more news, probably a letter from Ed's commanding officer saying what had happened.

As she got ready for bed, Celia's thoughts were with Matt. She grieved for her brother, too, but her prayers were for the man she had fallen in love with. How she wished they hadn't quarrelled on his last visit. It all seemed so trivial now.

She climbed into bed and closed her eyes, but sleep wouldn't come. She tried to convince herself that Matt had survived, even if it meant he was now a prisoner, and that one day she would get the chance to make it up with him.

The next morning Celia woke to find to her relief that the snow had almost gone. She'd be able to cycle to work after all. As she drew back the curtains and looked out, the memory of the telegram and its dreadful news rushed back to her and she hesitated before going downstairs, reluctant to face her father and the girls.

The kitchen was empty, her father and the land girls were outside dealing with the livestock. She went about her usual morning jobs mechanically, her thoughts with Matt and Ed and the rest of the Lancaster's crew. Had they been taken prisoner? She knew that sometimes planes crashed in the sea and the crews survived in their dinghies. But given the dreadful weather conditions of the past few days she hoped that hadn't happened. Even if they'd managed to scramble into the dinghy, she knew their chances of being picked up before they succumbed to the bitter cold were very slim. Perhaps it was better to hope they'd baled out and been taken prisoner.

She banged the kettle down on the hotplate. How much longer could this war last? The last one had dragged on for four years, but this one had already overtaken it.

Her gloomy thoughts were interrupted by Joyce noisily stamping the mud from her boots. "Looks like we won't get a white Christmas after all," she said.

"I don't want to think about it," Celia said. Until the telegram came she'd been looking forward to Christmas. Last year, despite the shortages and rationing, they'd managed to have quite a jolly time. There wasn't much to celebrate now.

Joyce gave her a hug. "I understand. But you mustn't give up hope."

Celia choked back a sob as she remembered Joyce's fiancé Bob, who'd been missing since 1940. She'd clung to the hope that he was still alive, but recently she'd begun to admit that he couldn't have survived. But no one would guess how she felt; she always stayed cheerful. Celia told herself she must be brave too, like her friend.

"It's Dad I'm more worried about," she said.

"Yeah, it's hit him hard."

"I daresay Stella will be a comfort to him." Celia couldn't keep the bitterness out of her voice.

"Don't be like that, Cee. I don't like Stella any more than you do, but let's face it, your Dad gets on with her." Her voice softened. "We all need someone, especially at times like this."

"Perhaps you're right," Celia said. Her father had been alone so long now. He deserved to have a little happiness. She realized it wasn't the thought of another woman in his life that upset her. It was more that Stella had usurped what she'd always thought of as her rightful position on the farm.

Since meeting Matt it hadn't seemed so important that she take over from her father when the time came. Now, realizing that there was little chance of ever seeing him again, her resentment came flooding back. High Trees Farm was all she had.

When her father came in to breakfast with Stella close behind, Celia thought he looked as if he hadn't slept at all. But he was always quiet in the mornings and it was hard to tell how he really felt. Stella chattered on about the milk yield and Celia felt a twinge of annoyance at what she thought was insensitivity. But when her father answered with a trace of animation in his voice, she realized the other girl was trying to distract him from brooding about Ed.

She had thought about staying at home today to keep him company. but he didn't need her, she thought. Besides, keeping busy was best and the farm work had to go on whatever happened. Work would be good for her too, she thought, and after clearing the table she went upstairs to get ready.

Cycling into town, her face numb from the bitter wind, tears stung her cheeks. There'd been no post again today, not that she expected anything now — only the official letter saying what had happened to Ed and his crew. She thought of Matt's family in Devon, wishing that she'd had the chance to meet them. They would have had a telegram too and her heart went out to them.

CHAPTER
EIGHTEEN

Press day had come round again and still there was no news of Ed. The big presses were thumping away in the works shed as Celia parked her bicycle just inside the door and crossed the yard to the office. Mr Allen looked up from the page proof he was studying and beckoned her into his office. "Any news?" he asked

"I haven't given up hope yet. 'Missing' doesn't mean . . ."

Mr Allen coughed as if not sure what to say next. "Are you sure you wouldn't rather be at home with your Dad? He shouldn't be alone."

"He's busy with farm work and he's got the land girls there. He'll feel better if he keeps working."

Mr Allen nodded. "Well, let me know if there's anything . . ."

"Thank you." Celia escaped into her office and closed the door. She'd have to go through this conversation, or one very like it, every time she saw someone she knew. She could just about cope with people's sympathy over her brother, but no one knew of her feelings for his friend and the heartbreak she was enduring.

She fumbled in her bag for a hanky and not finding one, wiped her eyes with a damp glove. She'd feel better once they had more news. It was the not knowing that was so hard to bear. She pulled her typewriter towards her, taking off the cover, determined to take a leaf out of Dad's book and immerse herself in work.

It was a busy morning. Someone came in asking if it was too late to put an advertisement in this week's *Advertiser*, followed a few minutes later by the local auctioneer with his copy for next week's edition. Both chatted cheerfully about the weather, pleased that the snow had gone now.

To Celia's relief neither mentioned Ed, but it wouldn't be long before the news got round. She concentrated on checking the proofs for a new Ministry advertising campaign, determined to banish from her mind all thoughts of the war and what had happened to the men in her life. There was nothing she could do now but hope and pray.

Due to the paper shortage, this week's *Advertiser* contained fewer pages than usual and consequently the presses stopped their racket a little earlier in the afternoon.

Mrs Jones arrived just after their tea break to begin bundling up the newspapers and Celia covered her typewriter and went to help. Mr Allen gave her the list of headlines for the posters, looking over his glasses at her as she scanned them quickly.

When she saw the bottom headline, she let out a strangled gasp. "Must I?" Celia said. How could he expect her to write in bold black letters the words, "*Local airman missing in action*"? The news had come too late for last week's edition and it had not occurred to her that there would be a mention in this week's paper.

"I'm sorry," he said. "It is news and so many people knew him. I'll get Russell to do them."

"No. I'll do them. It's just — it made it real," she said. She got the paper and the bottle of Indian ink and proceeded to paint the headlines on the posters. How many times had she done this without giving a thought to those behind the news? Every week she typed up stories and did the posters. Up until now she'd always been able to tell herself it was her job; it was news. This was different though.

When the last paper had rolled off the press, Celia decided not to stay and eat the usual fish and chips with her colleagues. She wanted to get home and continue with the preparations for Christmas. There were only a couple of days to go now — not that anyone at High Trees felt like celebrating.

As she put on her coat and gloves, she debated whether to take her usual copy of the *Advertiser*. She had typed many of the stories and taken the advertisements down over the phone so she didn't need to read it herself. But her father enjoyed reading the market reports and she knew Joyce looked forward to the *Countrywoman* column.

Would it upset her father to read about his son? Still, if she didn't give him his usual copy he'd probably guess why and be upset about that. With a sigh, she put the paper in her bag, calling out "goodnight" to the men in the works.

By the time she reached High Trees she was frozen and wondering whether she was being a bit pig-headed refusing a lift home. After all, she was confident she could manage Russell.

The cosy farmhouse kitchen was a welcome respite from the cold wind and she hurried over to the range to warm her hands. Her father was already there but there was no sign of the land girls.

"We got the rest of the sheep in, just in case there's more snow. Thank goodness lambing's not for another few weeks," he said. "The girls are finishing up in the barn."

"I'll get the dinner started then," Celia said.

"Got the paper, Cee?" he asked.

She got it out of her bag and passed it over, then busied herself at the range, tense for any comment on the report about her brother.

But, apart from a sharp intake of breath, he didn't say a word. As usual, he was keeping his feelings to himself. Only the rustle of the pages turning and the bubbling of pans on the hob broke the silence until Joyce and Stella came in, rubbing their hands and exclaiming about the cold.

"Won't be long," Celia said after greeting them. "Perhaps you'll lay the table while I mash the potatoes."

"Oh, goodie, sausages and mash today," Joyce said.

After the meal, Joyce got ready to go back to the Robsons' cottage and asked Larry if he'd finished with the Advertiser. She usually took it to read herself and to pass on to Len and Jean.

"Not quite," Larry said. "Give me a few minutes and I'll let you have it."

He went over to his favourite chair and picked up the paper.

"Stay and have another cuppa," Celia said, topping up the teapot with more hot water and Joyce sat down at the table again.

"I want to see what the *Countrywoman* has to say this week," she said, winking at Celia.

Larry rustled the paper. "You don't read that nonsense do you?" he asked. "It's probably written by some flibbertigibbet office girl who knows nothing about farming or country life."

"Well, I know I'm quite a newcomer to this farming lark, but it seems authentic to me. And Jean — Mrs Robson — says the recipes are very helpful," Joyce said.

For once Stella agreed with her. "Celia's used some of them and I must say that version of old Woolton's horrible pie she does is much better than those sausages we've just eaten."

"She probably gets the recipes out of a book," Larry said.

Celia felt her face growing warm. She hadn't confessed to rummaging in her father's desk and finding Mum's old recipe notebook. How would he feel if he knew she had used one of them in the column? He never talked about her mother and virtually every trace of her had been erased from the house soon after her death. At the time Celia had been too young to protest.

Joyce grinned and asked Larry if he had ever actually read the *Countrywoman*.

"Of course I have — anything to do with farming interests me. But this person, whoever it is, makes fun of farm work. Anyone reading it would think we were playing at it."

Celia wanted to protest, but to do so would risk her father realizing she had written it. Given his reaction, she knew she'd been right to keep it a secret.

But before she could speak, Stella stood up for the writer. "I don't think she's making fun — not in a nasty way," she said tentatively. "She just sees the light-hearted side of some of the things we do on the farm. Everything's so dark and gloomy these days, it's good to have something to smile about."

Joyce agreed. "Last time we went to market I heard someone talking about it. They said they look forward to reading the *Countrywoman* every week — it's a nice change from all the doom and gloom."

"That's what Mr Allen says," Celia put in.

"Well, I think it's all a lot of nonsense," Larry insisted. "Listen to this — keeping Christmas festive in spite of rationing. Who's got time to mess about making stuff like carrot fudge?"

"Let me see," Joyce said, grabbing the paper from him and reading the recipe. "Ooh, sounds yummy — not like the real thing though, but better than nothing. I think I'll make some and give it to Jean for Christmas."

Larry took the paper back and carried on reading. Suddenly he looked up at Celia. "Your mum used to make this — it was during the last war when we were first married. There was rationing then you know. She had all sorts of ideas for making little treats for you and Ed." The mention of his son seemed to throw him for a moment and he cleared his throat and looked down at the paper.

There were a few moments silence and Joyce finished her tea and went to get her coat.

"What's this?" Larry suddenly said, thrusting the paper at Celia and poking his finger at the page. "This bit about the sheep getting stuck in the snow — and the farm lad almost up to his neck in it. How did she know about that?" He glared round the room until his eye fell on Celia again. "It's you, isn't it? You're the one writing this rubbish. Well, I won't have it — making fun of me and my farm. How dare you?"

He stood up and towered over her. She hadn't seen him so angry since she was a child and she and Ed had made a tunnel through one of the haystacks and carved out a little nest right in the middle.

"Dad, I'm sorry. I didn't mean any harm. It's meant to cheer people up, make them laugh."

"Well, I'm not laughing. How long has this been going on?"

"Ages. I didn't tell you about it because I didn't want to upset you, Dad."

"So, you must have known I wouldn't approve, yet you carried on with it."

"I'm sorry, Dad."

"Sorry's not good enough, my girl. I should never have let you go and work on that paper. First they splash my dead son's name all over the front page, then I find my daughter has been telling all and sundry about what goes on on my farm." He sat back down and put his head in his hands.

The injustice of his remark stung, especially since it was he who'd insisted she get a job in an office rather than work with him. And Edgar wasn't dead — he was missing. She was about to point this out to her father but, before she could reply, Stella went over to him and put her arm round his shoulders. "Come on, Larry. I know you're upset, but it's not the end of the world. Celia didn't mean any harm."

He shrugged her off and glared at Celia. "Where did you get that recipe?"

"I found Mum's old notebook when I was tidying up."

"Give it to me — I'll chuck it on the fire."

"No, Dad. It's precious to me. I've got nothing of Mum's except that little brooch she won at the fair. Anyway, I left it in my desk at work." She blushed at the lie but she didn't care. Why was he being so unreasonable? His rage seemed out of all proportion to what she had done. Perhaps he was taking out his anger and grief over Ed on her, a convenient vent for his feelings.

She couldn't take any more, suddenly feeling so weary that she could hardly stand. "I'm going to bed," she said abruptly and went out of the room without saying goodnight to anyone. As she climbed the stairs she heard Stella's voice murmuring to her father. She was surprised that Stella had stood up for her. She'd expected her to take Dad's side and try to drive a bigger wedge between them.

She still couldn't take to Stella, but she was grateful for her softening influence on Dad. Perhaps she could make him see that her writing was a way of contributing to the war effort. Pity no one knew about her work for the Ministry, she thought.

She pummelled her pillow trying to get comfortable, but despite being so tired she found herself going over the argument downstairs and wondering how it had got so out of hand. She would apologise once more to Dad in the morning, but whatever he said, she'd continue writing her column. And she would save the cuttings to send to Matt as she always did. She refused to believe that he wasn't coming back. He and Ed must have been captured and soon there must be good news.

CHAPTER
NINETEEN

Ed turned the plane into the wind, praying that Sparks had managed to get off a Mayday signal before baling out. He braced himself as the Lancaster hit the water. Knowing he had only three or four minutes before the plane sank, he scrambled out through the roof hatch, gashing his leg on a jagged fragment of metal where the flak had torn a hole in the fuselage.

He crawled over the fuselage and dropped down onto the wing, anxious to get to the dinghy before the plane sank. Water was already filling the plane as he leaned through the open hatch and operated the manual release. The dinghy popped through the opening and inflated to lie gently bobbing alongside the stricken aircraft.

He scrambled in, inflated his *Mae West* and pushed off, seizing the paddle to get as far away as possible before the plane sank.

Dawn was brightening the eastern sky as the Lancaster disappeared beneath the waves. Luckily, it had stopped snowing, but a damp mist had crept up, isolating the small dinghy in a world silent except for the slap of waves on the side.

Hopes of being picked up faded as he drifted, alone and lost on the grey sea. No one would find him in these conditions. There had been no time to grab the radio. He'd managed to salvage the emergency pack of food and water, but they would have to last until the weather cleared. Perhaps then he'd stand a chance of being spotted.

The gash in his leg was bleeding badly, but when he rummaged among the meagre supplies, he discovered that the first aid kit was missing. He cursed briefly and tore a strip from his shirt, binding it tightly round his calf.

He had been drifting for hours and he dozed fitfully, waking with a start to find that the light had started to fade. It was going to be a long night and a bitterly cold one too. Thank goodness he had his sheepskin flying jacket. But it was his hands and feet that were suffering. As the sea became increasingly choppy, water had sloshed over the sides, soaking through his boots. He pulled his collar up around his ears and tried to sleep.

The gentle bobbing of the dinghy began to lull him into a half-doze and his mind drifted back to his last visit home. If only he'd been able to stay longer, perhaps he'd have been able to make Dad understand. That land girl, Stella, had written to him, saying she was sure his father would come round in time.

He's not one for showing his feelings, as you know, she'd written. *But he loves you and worries about you. I've seen his face when he's listening to the news.*

He'd thought at the time she had a bit of a cheek writing to him like that. And then there was the news about his sister taking up with Russell Allen. He hadn't meant to tell Matt but he'd asked how she was and said he hadn't heard from her. He knew his friend was smitten with Cee and thought it only fair to warn him not to get too involved. Now, he wished he'd kept quiet. Matt hadn't said much, but he'd obviously been upset.

He stirred restlessly, trying to lift his feet out of the water which had collected in the bottom of the dinghy. He kept a tight hold on the flare, ready to let it off if he heard a plane. But nothing disturbed the night.

What had happened to Matt and the others? Had they landed safely? Ed had little confidence in his navigational skills since that disastrous raid a year ago. He'd tried hard since then not to let it show and thought he'd succeeded in convincing the skipper that he was OK. How he wished he'd been selected as a fighter pilot. That way he'd only have had responsibility for himself. It was letting the crew down that played on his mind so much. Well, he'd done his best for them this time, not to mention avoiding the possibility of killing innocent civilians. His conscience was clear, he thought once more, as he drifted into an uneasy sleep.

The dinghy lurched and he jerked awake. Huge waves slapped against the hull and the water in the bottom of the craft now reached past his ankles. He dropped the flare and frantically began to bale, praying that the wind would die down.

As the second day of his ordeal began, he carried on baling, just managing to keep the water level to a safe depth. But his arms were aching and his hands were

242

numb. He didn't know how much longer he could keep it up.

The cut on his leg was throbbing but he didn't dare undo the makeshift bandage for fear of what he would find. He was sure the wound was infected. Still, if he wasn't picked up soon, a gash on his leg would be the least of his worries. As he scooped up more water and threw it over the side, his numb fingers couldn't keep hold of the baler and it slid from his grasp, landing in the bottom of the dinghy. He leaned forward to pick it up but his vision blurred and he slumped back.

He was dreaming about life on the farm — a small boy again, helping Dad with the lambing. He loved the little creatures, thrilled to bits when Dad let him take one indoors and look after it. He smiled in his sleep, feeling the heat from the kitchen range as he sat in Dad's chair, feeding the lamb from a baby's bottle.

He started up, shaking, whispering, "No, Dad, no. Don't take him away." He couldn't bear the thought of his lamb being sent to the slaughterhouse. But Dad had called him a "sissie" and wrested the lamb from his arms.

The dream faded and, fully awake now, he became aware of his hopeless situation as he took in the heaving ocean, the water slapping in the bottom of the dinghy. Too late, he began to realize how he had let Dad down, refusing to take an interest in the farm, insisting on going his own way. But even if he were rescued he knew he would never settle down at High Trees. It wasn't just that he was "soft" to use Dad's word. He loved flying and, even in his present dire situation, he knew he wouldn't have changed a thing.

Cee should take over the farm, he thought, picturing her helping with the hay-making, her face and arms tanned, her hair awry and festooned with stalks of hay. She shouldn't be working in that printing works. She should be at High Trees, working alongside those land girls — Stella and Joyce. Now, if it had been Joyce who had written to him . . .

A pity he wouldn't get the chance to get to know her better, he thought, as he drifted off into a doze once more.

Christmas was a sombre season at High Trees, the shadow of Ed hung over them all and in an effort to inject some cheer she invited the Robsons and Mickey to join them after milking on Boxing Day for high tea. She had scoured her mother's recipe book for sugarless and fatless treats, some of which had gone down better than others. Jean Robson told Celia she'd been delighted with the box of carrot fudge Joyce had given her and said she would try the recipe that had been in the *Advertiser*.

Following the Ministry of Food's injunctions to dig for victory, she and Len had produced a glut of vegetables from their little cottage garden. "If I see another carrot, I'll scream," she said, laughing. "We seem to have them for every meal. But I don't mind them made into sweets."

"I don't believe carrots help you to see in the dark," Mickey said, screwing up his face in disgust.

244

"Well, you'll never know if you don't eat them, will you?" his grandmother retorted. "Now, why don't you have a piece of this cake, lad?"

He grabbed a slice and stuffed it into his mouth. "Mmm, nice," he said, his mouth full. "What's it made of?"

"Carrots," Celia said and they all laughed.

Larry stood up abruptly. "Better make sure everything's shut up properly," he said and went out of the room.

Stella followed him, leaving an uncomfortable silence. Jean spoke first. "He's probably upset with us, laughing and joking at a time like this."

"Well, it's no good sitting around being miserable — that won't bring Ed back," Joyce said. "But I know how he feels, it's not knowing that's hardest."

"Have you given up on Bob then?" Celia asked.

"I suppose I have. It's been too long." She too pushed her chair back and went outside.

"Bloody war," Len said.

After that, there was no chance of continuing with their attempts at jollity and Celia got up to clear the table. Jean helped and they washed up in silence, while Len and Mickey joined the others to finish seeing to the livestock before going back to their cottage.

"Any news of your young man?" Jean asked as they finished stacking the plates on the dresser.

"I haven't got a young man," Celia said, unwilling to confide in the older woman. Joyce must have told her about Matt, she thought.

"Sorry," Jean said, "I thought . . ."

"He's just a pen friend, a mate of Ed's." Celia tried to make light of it. She would break down if anyone showed too much sympathy.

"Oh, they're in the same crew, aren't they?" Jean clapped a hand over her mouth. "Oh, forgive me. I shouldn't have said anything. You must be so worried."

"I'm sure they're both OK — we're bound to hear something soon." Despite her positive attitude there was a catch in her voice and she willed Jean to drop the subject before she went and made a fool of herself.

Jean put the last of the crockery away and patted Celia awkwardly on the shoulder. "I'll get off home," she said. "Thanks for inviting us. It was a lovely meal."

Celia nodded and said a subdued "goodnight". She managed to get up to her room before she gave way to the threatening tears, but once there a storm of sobs overtook her. She went over every moment of that last meeting with Matt, wishing with all her heart that she had been more understanding. She realized now it was concern for her brother that had made him speak out. "Please God, it's not too late to make it up with him," she prayed.

CHAPTER
TWENTY

New Year 1944 dawned with heavy rain and strong winds and Celia wasn't looking forward to going to work, although it would be good to get away from the depressing atmosphere at home.

There had still been no news of Ed and that meant no news of Matt either. Hope was fading fast and, despite Joyce's optimistic encouragement, Celia felt they must surely have heard something by now. She believed it would be better to know for sure, even if it was only confirmation that her brother, as well as the man she loved, was no longer missing but dead.

She hurriedly finished her chores, hoping to be gone before her father and the land girls came in to breakfast. She had been tempted to ask Dad to drive her into town in the lorry, but she knew he was too busy, and besides, he couldn't really spare the petrol. She would just have to brave the wind on her bicycle or walk the three miles.

She wrapped up well against the cold wind and stepped outside, glancing at the sky and wondering if it would be safe to cycle. The trees which bordered the lane were bent almost double and there was a litter of twigs and larger branches blowing across the lane. No bike today then, she thought, dreading the long trek into town. No post either. Bill would never be able to cycle up the hill in this gale.

As she crossed the yard she heard the sound of an engine and she smiled. The milk lorry. She would get a lift in to work after all. But when the vehicle turned into the yard, her heart sank. Pleased as she was to be spared the long cold walk, she didn't think she could cope with Russell in her present frame of mind.

He got out of the van and said, "I didn't think you'd want to get your bike out today."

Celia knew she should be pleased with his thoughtful gesture so she smiled as she thanked him. The smile faded when he held out an envelope and said, "I thought your father would want this as soon as possible. I met Bill at the bottom of the hill, really struggling with his bike so I offered to bring the post."

Celia snatched the letter from him, her heart pounding. Ignoring Russell, she ran across the yard, waving the envelope and shouting, "Dad — there's a letter."

Larry came out of the barn cleaning his hands on a fistful of straw, Joyce and Stella close behind. His hand shook as he reached for the envelope and he dropped it to his side.

"I can't . . . You read it, Cee," he said.

"Shouldn't you go indoors, out of the cold?" Stella asked, taking his arm.

He shook her off impatiently. "Read it now, Cee. I need to know," he said.

She tore the envelope open and quickly scanned the contents. The letter was from Squadron Leader James, the man Matt always referred to as the old man. She gasped and her eyes filled, but she smiled through the tears. "He's all right — Dad, he's alive," she said.

"Thank God," said Larry. He turned to Stella. "Do you hear that, Stell? My boy's safe."

"I'm so pleased for you — both of you," Stella said.

"Hear, hear," said Joyce. "What happened to him. Is he a prisoner?"

Celia was shivering, whether from the cold or emotion she wasn't sure. But she echoed Stella's earlier suggestion. "Let's go indoors. Then I'll read it properly."

Joyce hurried ahead saying she would put the kettle on, while Stella took Larry's arm and urged him inside.

Celia suddenly remembered Russell who was still standing by the van with the engine running. "I gather it's good news," he said.

"Oh, Russell. It's Ed. He's safe. Come on in and I'll tell you about it."

Inside the warm kitchen, Joyce was already busy at the range while Larry was rummaging in the bottom of the dresser. "We don't want tea at a time like this," he said, bringing out a dusty bottle and holding it aloft. "I was saving this for a special occasion."

"Good brandy that," Russell said, eyeing the label.

"Any brandy's good in my book," Joyce said, turning from the stove. "Shall I get some glasses out?"

"Never mind that," Celia said. "Do you want me to read the letter or not?"

"We've got to celebrate," Joyce said, getting glasses and pouring each of them a glass. "Besides, your Dad's had a shock and brandy's good for that."

"None for me," Celia said, sitting at the table and reading aloud from Squadron Leader James's letter. Ed was safe, but it wasn't entirely good news. He'd been picked up by Air Sea Rescue suffering from hypothermia as well as a badly-infected wound. He was now in the Royal Naval Hospital at Gosport. The letter went on to say that the doctors hoped he would recover, although it was not certain at this stage.

Celia's voice faltered as she read the last paragraph. "We don't know what happened to the rest of the crew," she read. "Your son was able to tell us that they baled out before the crash, but there has been no further news of them. If they have been taken prisoner it might be some time before we are officially informed."

Joyce took Celia's hand and squeezed it. "He'll be all right," she whispered.

"I must see him," Larry said, obviously thinking they were talking about Ed.

"Would you like me to come with you to the hospital?" Stella asked, completely ignoring Celia.

Larry shook his head. "Someone's got to stay and look after things here. I'm relying on you to do that — and Joyce, of course. Celia will come with me, won't you, Cee?"

She nodded and turned to Russell. "Will you explain to your father? I'm sure he'll understand if I don't come to work today."

"Of course." Russell downed his tot of brandy and stood up, reaching for his coat. "I'm really glad old Ed's turned up. What's happened to him makes me feel really bad about that spat we had in the pub last year."

"I'm sure he's forgotten about it," Celia replied, trying to reassure him. It wasn't really Russell's fault that Ed had drunk too much and started sounding off. She said goodbye and was about to go back indoors when he called to her.

"I almost forgot — there's a couple more letters."

She scarcely looked at the envelopes he handed to her as, shivering, she returned to the house. Joyce was dishing up the breakfast Celia had prepared earlier and urging Larry to eat something before the drive to Portsmouth.

He stuffed a piece of toast into his mouth and left the table. "Come on, Cee. Sooner we get started, the sooner we get back." He spoke roughly, impatiently, but Celia was sure it was a cover for his anxiety about Ed.

He drove silently, concentrating on the road, which was littered with fallen branches from the gale. The wind had abated somewhat, but when they had gone through Chichester and reached the exposed stretch of road which ran alongside the creeks and marshes of the harbour, the truck was buffeted by strong gusts.

Celia didn't care about the weather as she clung to the belief that if Ed had been rescued, surely Matt must be safe too. She couldn't wait to get to the hospital and hear about what had happened from her brother's lips.

She clenched her fists, suddenly realizing she was still clutching the letters that Russell had handed to her.

She leafed through them and said, "A couple here from the Ministry of Ag, Dad." She placed them on the dashboard and glanced at the last envelope. Her heart began to beat painfully fast as she recognized Matt's writing.

He must have written it before taking off for that last mission. She ripped it open and devoured the contents.

A lump formed in her throat as, despite her forced optimism, she realized this might be the last letter she would ever receive from Matt. She read it again, smiling through her tears. He apologized for not writing before, explaining that he had been hurt by her reaction to his concern for her brother — it was concern for Ed that had made him speak so harshly, he said, ending by begging her to write back.

As she finished reading, she realized that he had probably not received the letter she'd written before Christmas. She hadn't been able to post it for a few days because of the snow and by then he'd probably already set off on that last mission.

She'd had time to think since their meeting back in the autumn and she had come to understand his reasons. She had just been too stubborn to write and say so, waiting for him to make the first move. Now, as she re-read Matt's loving words, the tears flowed freely. It was everything she'd ever dreamed of hearing from him and she prayed desperately that one day she would get the chance to tell him so.

She became aware that her father had pulled the lorry off the road onto the grass verge. He put a hand on her arm. "Celia, love, what's the matter? I know, you're worried about Ed but I'm sure we'll find he's all right. At least he's alive."

Celia thrust the letter at him. "I'm not thinking about Ed. This is from Matt."

"Matt? Oh, that pal of Ed's you've been writing to." Understanding dawned and he said, "Sorry, Cee. I didn't realize. Ed's CO said they didn't know what had happened to the rest of the crew, didn't he?"

"I couldn't bear it if . . ." She couldn't go on.

"But you said he was just a pen friend."

"No, Dad, you don't understand. He's much more than a pen friend."

Larry was silent for a moment, then he patted her hand and started up the engine once more. "I'm sorry, love." He pulled out onto the main road again. "Nearly there now. Perhaps Ed will be able to tell you more."

Celia didn't reply. She read Matt's letter again, then folded it and put it back in the envelope. She glanced at the postmark. It had been sent just before Christmas. Why had it taken so long to reach her? Still, the post was erratic these days, not like before the war when letters always arrived the next day.

The lorry pulled up at the hospital entrance and Celia jumped down almost before it had stopped. She hurried inside and inquired where she could find her brother. When her father had caught up with her they followed an orderly along a corridor with doors leading off it. At the last one he gestured them inside. "He's down there," the man said, pointing to a bed under the window.

Celia paused, trying to gain control of her emotions. She would not have recognized her brother if he has not been pointed out to her. The gaunt, pale-faced young man was lying motionless, a cage over his legs protecting his wounded limb. He was staring vacantly out of the window but, as they approached the bed, his face lit up in a smile. He reached out and grasped his father's arm. "Dad, I'm so pleased you came."

Larry shook him off and stood looking down at his son. "Well, lad, what have you been up to, eh?"

"It's a long story, Dad." He smiled up at Celia. "Sis, good to see you too."

She was less restrained in her greeting, leaning over the bed and hugging him to her. Tears started up again and she brushed them away.

He grinned at her. "No need for tears. I'm here, aren't I?" The grin faded and he grimaced in pain.

"Are you all right? Shall I fetch someone?"

"No need, I've just had a pill — it takes a while to work," he said, gesturing at the cage covering his lower half. "It's this damn leg. Nips something awful."

Larry had crossed the ward and came back carrying a metal-framed chair. "Sit and talk to your brother, Cee," he said. "I'm going to have a word with the doctor."

Ed's gaze followed him as he walked away. "Don't know why he bothered to come. We never have much to say to each other."

"He came because he's concerned about you, Ed. I know he doesn't show it, but he was really upset when we heard you'd been shot down."

"Maybe," Ed muttered. "But why do I get the feeling that everything I do is wrong? You'd think I ditched the bloody plane on purpose."

Celia couldn't think of a suitable response so she took his hand and squeezed it, glancing around the ward at the other injured men. A couple of them were out of bed playing dominoes at a table in the centre of the ward, but others just lay gazing vacantly at the ceiling.

Bloody war, she thought. What a waste of all these young lives.

Ed interrupted her thoughts, pulling at her hand. "You haven't asked about Matt," he said. "Have you heard anything?"

She shook her head. "I was hoping you'd tell me," she said. "Why would I be informed? Any news would go to his family and I don't think they know about me."

"Sorry, sis. I didn't think. Anyway, I can't tell you much." He paused, a frown wrinkling his forehead. "It's all a bit hazy now. I was in that dinghy for two and a half days, baling for dear life, cold, hungry. I was practically unconscious by the time I was finally picked up."

Celia squeezed his hand. "Don't talk about it if it upsets you, Ed."

"It's all right." But his voice was faint and he closed his eyes.

Celia desperately wanted to hear the full story, especially as a cold feeling had gradually stolen over her. Why had Ed been alone in the dinghy? Why hadn't the rest of the crew been with him? She wanted to shake him.

"What happened, Ed?" she asked, her voice sharp with anxiety.

"They baled out — the skipper, Matt, everyone."

Celia sighed, regretting her impatience, as she recalled what Ed's CO had written. But why hadn't Ed baled with them? She waited as Ed took a sip of water and took a deep breath.

"We were hit, about to crash. We were near the coast and Matt decided to bale while we were still over land. He thought we'd stand a better chance as prisoners than if we ditched in the sea — especially at this time of year."

"Do you really think he's a prisoner then?"

"Probably. That part of the coast is heavily defended. There would have been patrols so they'd have been picked up pretty quickly."

"Was it because you were injured that you stayed with the plane? Why didn't your pilot insist you jumped with the rest of them?"

"Skipper was hurt — Matt was in charge. He ordered me to jump but . . ." His voice trailed away and he closed his eyes.

Celia waited for a few moments, but she soon realized that her brother wasn't going to say anything else. He appeared to be asleep, but his face twitched from time to time and his hands grasped the bedclothes as he was assailed with spasms of pain.

She leaned over and kissed his cheek. "Get well soon, Ed," she whispered, straightening as her father re-entered the ward.

Larry came over to the bed and grasped his son's hand. "Glad you're safe, son. Hope to see you back home soon."

Ed's eyes fluttered open. "Thanks for coming, Dad."

Larry cleared his throat as Ed's eyes closed again. "Come on, Cee. Got to get back for the milking," he said gruffly.

Celia kissed her brother again and followed her father. He strode ahead and she hurried to catch up with him, their footsteps echoing on the tiled floor.

Outside she grabbed his arm. "What did the doctor say, Dad?"

He shook her off and didn't reply, climbing up into the pickup and starting the engine.

"Dad — tell me."

"It's not good, Cee. They might have to take his leg off."

"Oh, no." Worry over Matt was swamped by concern for her brother. Would he ever be able to fly again? He would be devastated if he was relegated to a desk job.

As they drove back along the main road to Chichester, Celia wondered what the future held for her brother. She thought about Douglas Bader, who had persuaded the powers that be to let him fly with no legs at all. Celia had met him once when she had joined Ed and his mates for a drink in the Unicorn pub in Chichester. He'd been the life and soul of the party but she couldn't imagine Ed behaving in quite the same way.

CHAPTER
TWENTY-ONE

Ed was in hospital for months while the surgeons tried desperately to save his leg. He had several operations. But after the last one the doctors could not control the infection and in March they decided, reluctantly, to amputate just above the knee.

Celia tried to visit as often as she could but after that first time her father never did. He said he was too busy on the farm and it was true that with lambing and sowing the spring wheat there weren't really enough hours in the day. But she knew he was just making excuses. As had always been the case, Dad and her brother had nothing to say to each other.

Since his injury, it seemed Ed had nothing to say to her either. He had been moved from Gosport to Roehampton Hospital, which specialized in treating amputees and getting them ready to face life again. Although it was a bit further to travel, Celia didn't mind sitting on a train for hours followed by a tedious bus journey to the hospital if it meant she could cheer her brother up. Nothing she said or did, though could rouse him out of his depression.

She had given up her day off once more to come and see him, only to sit with him in silence on the terrace.

She had received only monosyllabic replies to her enquiries about his progress and when he might be allowed to come home and she was rapidly losing patience with him.

"Ed, you can't go on like this. I've spoken to the doctors and they say they've done all they can for you. It's up to you now," she said, holding her breath for his reply. Sometimes he would just shrug and mumble; at others he would lash out in anger. In the early days she had tried to encourage him by reminding him of Douglas Bader's achievements — and he had lost both legs.

Now he just stared at her. "But they keep telling me I'll never fly again, Cee."

"Oh, Ed, I'm sure they're wrong. You just need to get a little stronger."

"I'm doing OK — so the doctors say. Walking a bit better every day but . . ." he turned away from her and gazed out across the hospital gardens, blinking against the strong sunlight.

Celia put her hand on his arm. "I'm pleased to hear that," she said. "But if you're doing so well, why won't they let you come home?"

"You don't understand, Cee. It's not just my leg, it's . . ." He banged the heel of his hand against his temple. "It's up here. I feel I'm being punished."

"You're right — I don't understand." Celia tried to hide her dismay. What was going through her poor brother's head? She remembered that row with Matt, his concern for Ed and the effect his behaviour might have on the crew. Had he made another mistake, caused the plane to crash? Was that why he was so depressed?

She took his hand, hoping he would confide in her, struggling to find the right words. She spoke hesitantly. "I'm sure you've done nothing wrong. It wasn't your fault the plane crashed. And you did what you thought was right — not baling out when the others did. You probably saved lives, ditching in the sea instead of over land."

"I'm not talking about *that*." Ed sat up straighter in the chair, wincing as he jarred his unhealed stump. Then it all spilled out, how he blamed himself for an error in navigation, how it had played on his mind and affected his ability to do his job.

"I know Matt talked to you." Celia swallowed a lump in her throat at the memory. "You must know we quarrelled. I thought he was being too harsh."

Ed leaned towards her and grasped her hand. "No, Cee. He was right. I was letting the side down. Every time we went up, I dreaded it, terrified of making another mistake. I'm sure the others knew as well. I felt they were judging me, waiting for me to fall to pieces . . ." He covered his face with his hands and began to sob, his shoulders shaking with emotion.

Celia knelt beside him, taking him in her arms and murmuring to him, stroking his hair as she had when they were children and he'd come to her for comfort after a telling-off by their father or when one of the animals had been hurt. He'd always been a sensitive boy, but she thought he'd toughened up since joining the RAF.

As the sobs subsided, Ed sat up and wiped his face with his hand. "Sorry about that." He gave a shaky laugh. "Glad Dad's not here to see me acting like a sissie. I'd never hear the last of it."

Celia smiled. "Don't worry, I won't tell him. Anyway, it's understandable after what you've been through. You needed to get it out of your system."

He nodded.

"Do you feel better now?" she asked.

"A bit, I suppose. I wish I could talk to Matt though." He paused. "Still no news?"

Celia shook her head. It had been months. Surely if he was safe, even if he'd been captured, he'd have been able to write to her. "I think you'd hear sooner than me. Surely someone at Metworth would have let you know if the rest of the crew had been taken prisoner."

Ed shivered as a cold wind sprung up. He heaved himself out of the chair, grabbing for his crutches before Celia could help him. "I'm going to speak to the doc. They've got to let me go back to flying. As you said, if Bader can do it, so can I."

Celia followed her brother indoors, pleased that the outburst appeared to have cleared his mind. He might not be fit enough to fly yet, but at least he seemed to be in a more positive frame of mind.

She didn't want to dampen his enthusiasm but she said hesitantly, "They'll probably give you convalescent leave before you return to duty. It will be good to have you home for a while."

"Let's hope Dad feels the same," Ed replied.

* ★ ★

Matt awoke shivering, stiff and aching with cold. The days were getting warmer but the nights were still bitter. Most of the men slept with their clothes on, those who had coats or jackets using them as extra blankets. He was lucky to still have his leather flying jacket, but it had slipped off during the night and now lay in a heap on the floor of the hut. It was still dark and it was a moment before he realized that Ginger was shaking his shoulder.

"Your turn, old man," his friend said.

Matt groaned. They'd been digging that bloody tunnel for weeks and got nowhere. Yesterday there had been another cave-in. He sat up and ran his fingers through his hair. "All right, I'm coming."

He made his way to the end of the hut where Sparks was waiting. They knew the drill by now and no words were exchanged as they lowered themselves into the hole and crawled along the tunnel.

It was slow work, pecking away at the soil with their improvised shovels. How long before they made a breakthrough? And if they did, would they be able to get clean away? Matt knew that several escape attempts had been made before their arrival at the camp, but none of them had been successful. Despite the many setbacks, the men were always willing to try again and Matt had joined in the escape plans enthusiastically. There was always a chance some of them would make it — and he intended to be one of them.

He was tired, hungry and cold and he stopped digging for a moment, flexing his frozen fingers. Then, as always when he became discouraged, he thought of Celia. He pictured her riding her bike in all weathers, working long hours at the print works and then coming home to do her share on the farm. Yet always finding time to write her cheerful column in the paper, as well as the letters to him which had so brightened his life over the past couple of years.

He began to dig again, more enthusiastically now, knowing that every shovelful of frozen soil could be bringing him closer to her. He wondered if she had got his letters. There had been no word from her and he wasn't even sure if she knew what had happened to him. He thought about Ed and his bravery in taking the kite out to ditch in the sea. He had written and told Celia what had happened, hoping that it would help her and her father to bear his loss if they knew what he'd done.

He sighed and continued digging. If she hadn't received his letters — and who knew if their captors even sent them despite the Geneva Convention — she would think the whole crew had gone down.

Sparks tapped him on the shoulder, jerking him out of his reverie. "Better get back up on top," he whispered, pointing to his wristwatch in the dim glow of the lamp.

Matt nodded and began the scramble back to the surface. The others replaced the flagstone and erased all signs of their digging while he and Sparks hurried to get washed and tidied up before roll call. Just in time. Already the guards were going along the rows of huts, banging on the doors and shouting *"Raus, raus."*

As he queued up for his meagre rations, Matt's thoughts turned to Celia again, as they so often did these days. She couldn't have received his letters, he thought. Although they'd argued last time they met, she would have got his letter of apology. And he knew in his heart she would understand and not hold a grudge. She would surely have written to him if she knew where he was.

He decided he would write again and had retreated to the hut for a little privacy when the shout went up. "Mail's come." His heart leapt. Perhaps this time . . .

He rushed outside, hovering expectantly on the fringe of the crowd. The last letter was handed out and he turned away, shoulders slumped. He wanted to rush back to the tunnel and dig, dig, dig till he reached the other side. He must get out of here somehow, must get back to Celia — and back in the war, doing his job. He felt so useless stuck here.

He was striding across the compound, his fists clenched at his sides, when Clive grasped him firmly by the shoulder, swinging him round to face him. "Steady on, old man," he said. "We're all brassed off at getting no letters. None of our lot have heard a word since we got here. I don't know what they're playing at, but we can't let them see how it affects us." He nodded imperceptibly towards the commandant's hut where the German officer stood in the doorway watching the prisoners.

Matt straightened his shoulders and relaxed. "Sorry, mate. Can't help getting a bit het up. It's just worrying about them back home — they must be thinking we went down with poor old Ed."

"You're thinking about that girl of yours, aren't you — Ed's sister," Clive said.

Matt nodded.

"Well, write again. We don't know for sure if they're holding back our letters and one of them might get through."

"I'll do that," Matt said. "Meantime, what about the tunnel? How far . . .?"

"I think there's a fair way to go yet. But we'll get there in the end, don't worry," Clive reassured him. "Besides, the war can't go on for ever. We'll get home one way or another."

Matt wasn't so sure. From what he'd seen there was no end in sight. Bombing the German cities to pieces didn't seem to be having much effect; even the successful raid on the big dams last year hadn't slowed things down. No, Matt thought, he could be stuck in this hole for years — the tunnel was the only answer.

Celia had stopped looking out for the postman weeks ago, although deep down she still hadn't quite given up hope that somehow Matt had survived. Ed had told her that the rest of the crew had baled out. They must have been captured and were now prisoners of war. So why hadn't she heard from him, she wondered as she cycled down the hill into town on this bright spring morning, enjoying the sunshine filtering through the fresh green leaves.

With the primroses and violets starring the grass verge it was enough to give a lift to the heart and inspire hope. Celia smiled as a new thought occurred to her. Perhaps Matt and the others had not been caught, but were in hiding somewhere, or trying to make their way home. Yes, that must be why there had been no news. She was still smiling at the thought as she rode over the bridge into town.

She put her bicycle away and went through to the front office and the smile faded. Russell was sitting on the corner of her desk holding a sheaf of copy paper.

"What do you want?" she asked rather ungraciously.

"I want to talk to you about this," he said, waving the papers under her nose.

Celia flinched when she saw it was the typescript of her latest Countrywoman column. "What about it?" she said.

He grinned. "You wrote it, didn't you? I had my suspicions, but now I know for sure."

"So what?"

"I spoke to Dad about it and he said you didn't want your father to know you were writing about the farm. You were afraid of upsetting him — that's why you wanted to remain anonymous."

Before she could tell him that her father had found out and now seemed to accept what she'd done, he stood up and said, "How about coming out with me tonight? There's a dance in the officers' mess at Tangmere."

"No thanks, Russell. I'm not in the mood for dancing."

"I know you've been a bit down lately, what with your brother being in hospital. You need cheering up."

"Russell — I've told you before. I don't go out with married men and as far as I'm concerned, you're still married."

"Ah. So, if Marion and I divorced, you'd consider it?" His eyes gleamed.

Celia sighed. Would he never give up? "I really don't know," she said. "But seeing as you are not divorced the question doesn't arise does it?"

Russell waved the sheaf of paper at her. "If you still want to remain anonymous, I suggest you accept my invitation." Before she could reply, he went on, "Come on, Cee. I'm starved for female company. What harm can it do?"

"For a start it's not just my company you want, is it?" She waved away his exclamation of protest. "Anyway, that's not the point — and it's no use trying to blackmail me into going out with you."

"Oh, Cee. I wouldn't exactly call it blackmail."

"Well, I would. And it won't work because my father is well aware of what I've been doing and is quite happy for me to continue writing the Countrywoman column." It wasn't strictly true. Although he still didn't really approve, Dad had seemed to accept her reasons for continuing to write.

Russell tried to laugh it off. "I was only teasing, Celia."

She just stared coldly at him. "Perhaps you'll leave me alone now. I have work to do."

He went out, slamming the door behind him and Celia sighed. She wondered how she could ever have been attracted to him, even as a naïve fifteen-year-old. The crush had soon faded and since coming to work for his father, they had got on well — as friends and colleagues, no more than that.

As she cycled home that evening she felt relief that she had finally put Russell in his place. At least she hoped so. She doubted he would try that again. It hadn't worked when he'd written that article about Ed and it hadn't now.

If only Marion would come home or at least get in touch with her husband. She was positive that Russell still cared for her and that if they ever got together again he would be faithful to her. His pestering of her was just to prove something to himself, Celia thought. But if he needed a woman that badly, why had he set his sights on her when there were plenty of girls around who'd enjoy his attentions?

Celia's thoughts turned to Matt once more and she prayed that he was all right. How she wished that she would hear from him and be able to tell Russell truthfully that there was another man in her life.

She cycled into the farmyard and looked around, wondering where everyone was. It was still fairly light but a bit late for them to be out in the fields still. A soft lowing came from the cowshed, but she had seen the churns stacked up by the gate so she knew the afternoon milking had been done.

Then she remembered that one of the ewes had been a bit late dropping her lamb and Dad had brought her into the barn so that he could keep an eye on her. The rest of the flock had given birth with little trouble this year despite the appalling weather which had continued well into March.

If her father and the girls were busy tending to the ewe they wouldn't welcome an interruption, Celia thought, deciding to make a start on the evening meal. She took the bag of groceries which she had bought in her dinner hour out of the bicycle basket and went indoors. She plonked the bag down on the kitchen table and turned to put her gloves and handbag down on the dresser. With a gasp she noticed the pile of letters — not one, but three identical envelopes, all addressed in Matt's distinctive sloping handwriting.

Without bothering to take off her coat, she snatched them up and sank into a chair at the table, her heart pounding. Thank God. He was safe — or at least he had been at the time of writing. The official stamps and seals told her the letters had been sent from a POW camp and with a shaking hand she tore open the topmost envelope.

My dearest Celia, he began, and tears welled up at the endearment so that she could scarcely make out the next few words. She sniffed and brushed a hand across her eyes, scanning the page quickly as he explained that he and the rest of the crew had baled out and immediately been taken prisoner. *Clive got a crack on the head but the rest of us are all right*, he wrote, and went on to say how sorry he was that Ed had not baled out with them. *He was very brave to stay behind and take the plane out to sea. His action surely saved lives.*

269

Celia looked at the date on the letter, realizing it had been written at about the same time they'd received the news of Ed's rescue. Poor Matt. He must think that Ed had been killed. I must write back straight away and put his mind at rest, she thought.

She pressed the page with his signature to her lips, then quickly tore open the second letter. In this one he said that he hoped the reason she hadn't written was that she'd never received his letter and not because of their earlier quarrel. *Anyway, I will keep writing until I do hear from you, one way or another*, he concluded.

The final letter was almost a repeat of the other two and ended with the hope that at least one of them would reach her. *I will not give up hoping to hear from you*, he wrote. *And I also hope that you have forgiven me for the harsh words between us when we last met. But my most earnest wish is that when I get out of this awful place I will be able to return to High Trees Farm and find a welcome there.*

"Oh, Matt. Of course you'll be welcome," she murmured.

She was about to re-read the last letter when the door opened abruptly bringing a cold draught and Stella's mocking laugh. "So, you found your letters then?" she said. "Lover boy's stirred himself to get in touch at last."

Before Celia could reply, Joyce said, "Give it a rest, Stell. It's obvious he's written from a POW camp. It's a miracle the letters got here at all."

She turned away abruptly and filled the kettle, banging it down on the hob. She knew that Joyce had now accepted that her fiancé had probably not survived, although she still clung to the faint hope that he was a POW. It must be so hard for her.

Joyce's happy-go-lucky attitude to life made it easy to forget what she must be going through. She was very good at hiding her true feelings, flirting with the Italians and going out to dances at the nearby air base, but Celia knew that inwardly she was still grieving for Bob.

Knowing that her friend would shrug off any expression of sympathy, she began to unpack the groceries while Joyce got out the cups and saucers for tea.

The door opened again and Larry came in. His shoulders were hunched and he looked thoroughly fed up. Before Celia could ask what was wrong, Stella said, "I'm so sorry about the ewe, Larry. I know you did your best to save her."

"Nobody's fault — these things happen in farming," he said, sitting down to take his boots off.

"What about the lamb?" Celia asked.

Her father shook his head. "Both gone," he said.

"I'm sorry, Dad." There was nothing else to say and Celia carried on getting the meal ready. Her joy at hearing from Matt at last had completely evaporated after hearing her father's bad news.

Joyce left to go back to the Robsons' cottage leaving the three of them to eat their supper in silence.

As she cleared away Celia said, "I'm going to visit Ed on Sunday. He'll be pleased to hear that Matt and the rest of the crew are safe. I'll tell him about the sheep too."

"He won't care," Larry said and relapsed into silence again.

Celia swallowed the lump in her throat. All Dad thought about was the farm — not a word about how she was feeling or how her day had been. Losing a lamb and its mother was a blow to be sure, but he could have said something about Matt. And despite having made some sort of reconciliation with Ed, it seemed he still didn't have much time for his son.

"Just because Ed doesn't want to be a farmer doesn't mean he's not interested in what goes on at High Trees," she said. "In fact, I think he's beginning to change his mind."

"It's a bit late for that. Fat use he'll be around the farm with only one leg," Larry said.

Celia whirled round. "Dad! What a thing to say. I hope you won't take that tone when Ed comes home."

He didn't reply and Celia threw down the tea towel she'd been using. Snatching up Matt's letters, she rushed out of the room. Upstairs she burst into tears. Why did Dad have to be like that? Those few moments of happiness had been quite eclipsed by her family's problems.

CHAPTER
TWENTY-TWO

Spring was turning to summer by the time Ed was finally allowed home from hospital. He was a long way from being fit for return to duty and had been granted convalescent leave, although he would have to return to Roehampton for regular fittings of his artificial leg and for assessment of his progress. Even when he returned to Metworth he had been told it was unlikely he would be allowed to fly.

Celia was still worried about his mental state for he seemed to be in the grip of deep depression. On a damp and dismal day in late spring she got home from a long day at the printing works, tired and irritable after battling up the hill in the rain. Her bad mood wasn't helped when she found her brother slumped in the armchair in front of the range.

His eyes were closed, but he jerked upright when he heard the door slam. "Cee — home already?" he asked, his voice slurred.

She felt a burst of irritation. "It's nearly seven o'clock, Ed. Where is everybody?"

"Don't ask me. Still out in the fields, I suppose."

"Oh, for goodness' sake. This farm will be yours one day. You could try to take an interest." When he began to protest, she held up a hand. "All right, I know how you feel. But you could at least make yourself useful while you're at home — lay the table, put the kettle on . . ."

"But, Cee, I'm on leave."

"And I've been at work all day," she snapped. "Never mind," she waved him back to his chair as he made an attempt to rise. "I know you're still convalescing. Don't mind me. I'm just tired."

"I'm sorry. I've been sitting here brooding on my situation when I should be thanking my lucky stars I'm home. There's Matt and Skipper and the others stuck in a prison camp. I should be thinking about them." He struggled out of the chair and reached for his crutches. "You're right, Cee. I could do a bit more around the house — and I have been trying."

He went over to the dresser and began getting plates down, while Celia hung her jacket up and put on an apron.

After a few moments silence, Ed said, "I've had time to think while I've been sitting here. I've got to face up to the fact that I'll probably not be allowed to fly again and I don't think I could stand a desk job."

"So what will you do then? They won't discharge you while the war's still on will they?"

"I don't know. But the war can't last much longer anyway. You've seen for yourself that something's in the wind with all the extra traffic around here. It's all supposed to be hush-hush, but it's obvious the powers that be are gearing up for an invasion. I even heard rumours at the hospital."

274

Celia thought he was probably right. Dad had told her about the encampment of soldiers on the other side of the Downs. From the increased activity going on all around it was obvious this wasn't just another exercise. Perhaps the end of the war really was in sight.

"So, Ed, what about when it's all over then?" she asked.

Ed rapped his knuckles on his tin leg. "It depends on how I get on with this," he said. "As you said, there's lots I could do if I put my mind to it — not just in the house. Perhaps it's time I gave some thought to helping on the farm."

"So you've decided you want to be a farmer after all?"

"Well, it's not what I really want, but I don't have much choice, do I?"

Celia didn't know what to say. She hadn't been expecting this. "Dad'll be pleased," she said. But in view of his earlier remarks about Ed's uselessness, she wasn't so sure.

"Don't say anything to him yet, please. I want to be sure I can cope with it first," Ed said.

Celia nodded, glancing at the clock. "I'd better get on. They'll be in soon wanting to be fed."

"No need to cook anything. Stella made us a shepherd's pie for dinner," Ed said, heaving himself out of the chair.

Celia knew she should be grateful but she couldn't suppress the little spurt of irritation at the other girl taking over what she thought of as her kitchen. "Did she save any for me?" she asked.

Ed looked a little embarrassed. "There was some left over, but I finished it. Sorry, I didn't think."

"Thanks a lot. I've only had a couple of sandwiches all day." She filled the kettle and banged it down on the hob, then noisily began rummaging in the pantry.

Ed hobbled over and pushed her to one side. "Sit down — I'll do it."

After a token protest she sat at the table watching in some bemusement as her brother whisked eggs in a bowl and sliced bread for toast.

"Thank goodness for the hens. Will this do?" he asked a few moments later, placing a plate of steaming scrambled eggs in front of her.

"You're a dark horse," she said, picking up her knife and fork. "I didn't know you could cook."

"This is all I can manage — Joyce showed me," he said colouring slightly. "So you see, I *have* been trying to help out a bit since I got home."

Celia was immediately ashamed of her earlier annoyance. What else had been going on while she was away all day in Sullingford? What with Stella sucking up to Dad and now Ed and Joyce apparently becoming friendly, she was beginning to feel as if she wasn't needed around the farm. She gave herself a mental shake, telling herself not to be so silly, and smiled warmly at her brother. "This is delicious," she said, tucking into the food.

"I'll do some for the others when they come in," he said.

She looked at him more closely, realizing she had been jumping to conclusions when she had seen him slumped in the chair. She had become so accustomed to seeing him sunk into depression but now she noticed the renewed sparkle in his eyes, the colour in his cheeks. This was a new Ed — he was looking to the future and trying to make the best of his loss of a limb.

What had brought about the change in him? It must be Joyce, she thought with a smile. Perhaps her friend had finally accepted that Bob wouldn't be coming back and was becoming interested in Ed. Celia hoped it wasn't just a flirtation on Joyce's part. She did not want her brother to be hurt. If it was serious it would be a good thing for Ed, and the farm. Celia would welcome Joyce as a sister-in-law. As for Stella, she hoped the other land girl would return to her former life when the war was over. There certainly wasn't room for three women at High Trees.

Later that evening she went to her room to write her daily letter to Matt, struggling to find something cheerful to say to him. Of course, she couldn't tell him of the feeling in the air that an invasion of France was imminent. In fact she made little mention of the war just as he in turn did not talk about prison life. She usually filled her letters with amusing anecdotes such as those she put in her weekly newspaper article, but tonight she just could not dream up anything amusing.

She really wanted to pour out her feelings on paper, to tell him about her fears for the future. Would it be with Matt? He hadn't said so in so many words although she was sure that he returned her love. But were a few meetings and letters enough to build a life on? She truly hoped so. When he'd been reported missing and she thought she might never see him again she had realized she truly loved him. But did he feel the same?

His letters from the POW camp were warm and friendly, affectionate even, but there had been no actual words of love. Perhaps, being uncertain of what the future held for him, he was reluctant to declare himself. Or perhaps he still felt that his disagreement with Ed and their differing views on the conduct of the war would come between them, she thought, biting the end of her pencil.

She could see both sides of the question when it came to the bombing, but she couldn't let an argument between the people she loved most dearly stand in the way of her happiness. Families had been torn apart for less. She would not let that happen.

She gripped her pencil firmly and began to write, filling page after page and ended by writing, *Dearest Matt, I can't imagine what it must be like for you but I hope that knowing I will be here waiting for you when you come home will help you to get through it.* She paused and gazed out of the window, wrapped in fantasies of that homecoming. After a few moments she brought herself down to earth with a sigh and added the words . . . *that's if you want me.*

It was up to him now.

They were nearing the end of the tunnel — at least they hoped so, provided their calculations were correct. Enthusiasm had been flagging for the past couple of weeks after the guards had become suspicious and begun making more frequent inspections of the huts. Some of the lads were all for abandoning it altogether since the commandant had made it clear that the penalty for trying to escape was death.

Matt was one of those who wanted to press on, buoyed up by the frequent letters he was now getting from Celia. That last one had really cheered him up and he was determined to get out and make his way home to her. Then he could show her in person all the feelings and emotions he had been reluctant to commit to paper.

"Come on, Ginger," he said. "Let's get on with it. Only a few more yards to go and then we'll be free."

Sparks called across the hut. "You'd better wait a bit. I spotted Fat Hermann nosing around a little while ago."

"He's always nosing round," Matt said. "I'm relying on you to keep him occupied while Ginger and I get on with it. Ask him to show you the pictures of his wife and children. He loves that."

"Oh, all right then. But be careful," Sparks said. He helped Matt and Ginger to uncover the hole and waited while they lowered themselves down into the tunnel.

Working as quickly and as quietly as they could, Matt and Ginger managed to complete another few yards before the signal came to stop. They had just managed to cover up all traces of their activity and were sitting on their bunks trying to look unconcerned when the guard they called Fat Hermann stomped in.

He glared suspiciously round at the occupants of the hut — Clive stretched out on his bunk reading a letter;

Ginger and Matt engaged in a game of cards; Sparks stirring something in a pot on the stove.

He said nothing for a few moments and the men continued with their activities as if unaware of his presence. Holding an imaginary rifle up to his shoulder and crooking his trigger finger, the guard gave a harsh laugh and said, "Remember — no escapes." Then, with a final searching look round the hut, he went out.

"I'm sure he knows," Sparks said.

"If he knew, we'd be for it already," Clive said, looking up from his letter.

"He's waiting to catch us in the act."

"We'll just have to be careful," Matt said. "But I don't care. I'm getting out of here one way or another." He went over to the window. "Anyway, he's gone. Come on, let's get cracking."

"No," Clive said. "Give it a rest for a while. Don't give Fat Hermann any reason to keep an eye on us."

Matt started to protest, but he gave in with a resigned shrug of his shoulders. Clive was right. It wouldn't do to get caught at this late stage.

Later, after lights out, Sparks left his bunk and got the wireless out of its the hiding place. The men huddled round as he fiddled with the controls, holding their breath until he managed to get a signal. After the usual coded messages, some of which made no sense to the listening men, came the one they had all been waiting and praying for.

It was all they could do not to let out a whoop and a cheer. But they hugged and shook each other's hands, wide grins splitting their faces. It had happened at last.

Allied troops had landed in France. Matt glanced at the makeshift calendar pinned above his bunk. It was 6 June, 1944.

The longed-for summer weather took its time coming and Celia knew her father was worried about the hay harvest. It had been raining on and off for several days and the blustery wind last night was sure to have added to the damage.

"There're always something to worry about in farming," Celia said as she got ready for work.

"It's not just the harvest," Ed said when, after a gloomy look at the sky, their father had gone out to inspect the grass in the meadow down by the river. "They won't be able to get across the Channel if this keeps up," he said.

"Do you really think they're going to try an invasion?" Celia asked.

"You've seen the trucks coming through and yesterday I went up to the top of the Downs. There's signs everywhere if you know where to look. How they expect it to remain a secret I don't know."

"Let's hope the weather clears soon then," Celia said. She had been feeling a bit down lately as there had been no letter from Matt for a couple of weeks. Now she felt a little lift of her heart. Things were hotting up at last and it seemed that finally the end of the war was in sight. Surely he would soon be home.

Considerably cheered by the thought she said goodbye to Ed and got on her bicycle. Even the misty rain which plastered her hair across her face did not spoil her mood as she freewheeled down the hill with the wind behind her.

There seemed to be less work from the Ministry these days to Celia's relief. She was becoming a bit fed up with all the directives and rules and regulations she'd had to proofread over the past few years. Of course, she realized the necessity for them, but she much preferred to do work connected with the newspaper.

At least the works had been able to keep going thanks to the official government work and the lads who'd gone off to fight would have jobs to come back to, she thought, as she sat down at her desk to sort the post.

During the afternoon she had time to work on her own column, thumbing through the little notebook she always kept with her for ideas. She had run out of beauty tips and recipes and was finding it harder to find something to write about each week.

After a few moments lost in thought, she gave up and went through to the kitchen to make Mr Allen's afternoon tea. Her copy did not need to be on the boss's desk till the next day. She'd have a chat with Joyce tonight. Perhaps she would come up with an idea.

The rest of the day dragged with not even an interruption from Russell to break the monotony and it was with relief that she was able to put the cover on her typewriter and fetch her bicycle from the works shed. The rain had stopped, although it was still quite windy and she did not relish the ride uphill.

As she reached the bridge she was forced to get off her bicycle and stand to the side as a column of Army vehicles swept past her. It seemed never-ending and she stood patiently until they'd gone past, smiling in response to the whistles and calls of the men in the back of the trucks.

Where were they off too, she wondered. She thought she could guess. This time it wasn't just another exercise. She felt a flutter in her stomach at the thought of what lay ahead for these smiling young men. Was this the long-awaited invasion at last?

Over the past few months, she had become used to seeing columns of marching soldiers, jeeps and tanks cluttering up the country lanes. But this seemed different somehow, more purposeful. Her heart lifted at the thought that, if they were successful, Matt and all the other young men who had been held in captivity, might soon be liberated.

She got on her bicycle again and scarcely noticed the wind and the steepness of the hill as she hurried home with a much lighter heart than when she had set out that morning.

After supper, the skies had cleared and she walked down to the Robsons' cottage to have a chat with Joyce. Her friend suggested they went for a walk. "I want to show you something," she said and they trudged up the track past the farm and over the brow of the next hill.

"Look down there," she said, pointing to the hollow in the Downs where until recently there had been an encampment of army tents. Now the field was empty, the tents dismantled, the men gone. There was no sign that it had ever been occupied.

"They've gone," she said.

"So, it's really on then," Celia said.

"Looks like it."

Celia hardly dared think what the end of the war would mean for her and those close to her. Matt would come home but did they have a future together? Ed would have to try and make some sort of life on the farm. Joyce would leave. As for Stella and her father, she didn't want to think about that. Instead of the euphoria she had expected at the prospect of the war's end, she felt slightly depressed, unsettled.

She sighed. "What will you do when it's all over — go back to London?"

"Not on your life. I couldn't wait to get away." She leaned on the gate and looked down at the fields spread out below. The low sun had found its way through the clouds and was casting purple shadows into the hollows. It was a peaceful scene and both girls sighed.

"This is the life for me," Joyce said.

"Me too — I can't imagine living anywhere else."

"What about when Matt comes home?"

"I don't know. We've never discussed the future."

"I know what I want," Joyce said.

Celia wondered if she was still hoping that Bob would come home safely, but she wasn't really surprised when her friend said, "I'd like to stay here working on the farm — even when I'm released from the Land Army. I don't suppose your Dad will allow it though, unless . . ." She shook her head and gave a little laugh.

"I'm not so sure. He seems to have accepted that women can do farm work just as well as men. Pity he didn't realize that earlier," Celia said.

"Shame that. Still, perhaps after the war . . ." Joyce replied. "Anyway, even if I can't stay on at High Trees I'm going to carry on farming." She shrugged and started walking back up the track.

Celia followed without saying anything. It had just occurred to her that Joyce's desire to stay on at High Trees might have something to do with her brother. They had become very friendly over the past few weeks and she was sure that her friend had helped considerably to bring about Ed's change of demeanour.

As they reached the cottage, Joyce said. "I can't make any decisions really, not till I know for sure . . ."

"I understand. It must be so hard for you." Celia knew she was thinking about Bob.

As she walked back to the farmhouse Celia wondered what effect it would have on her brother if Bob turned up alive after all and Joyce decided to honour her engagement to him. It seemed wicked to hope otherwise, but Celia only wanted Ed to be happy. It seemed that everyone had problems these days and she reflected on how fortunate she was. At least she knew that Matt was all right. There was sure to be another letter in the morning.

CHAPTER
TWENTY-THREE

Celia arrived at the works on a July morning to find the main printing shed empty. Where were the lads, she wondered. A burst of chatter from the little room where the men gathered for their tea breaks alerted her that something was going on. She put her head round the door and Ray looked up from where he was crouched in front of the wireless. "There's been an attempt to kill Hitler," he said.

"Pity they didn't get the bastard," Barney muttered, colouring as he saw Celia standing there. "Pardon my French," he said.

"That's all right, Barney. I agree," Celia said. If they'd succeeded it would have brought a swift end to the war. As it was, things seemed to be getting worse. In the past couple of weeks a new threat had appeared in the skies. Flying bombs, christened "doodlebugs", were devastating London, just like in the Blitz a couple of years ago. Would there never be an end to it all?

Celia thought about Marion and prayed that she was safe. Russell, despite professing not to care about his wife, was obviously worried sick and had gone up to London to see for himself. Perhaps he could persuade her to come home this time. However much Russell annoyed her, Celia really wanted him to be happy.

She went in to her office, determined to immerse herself in work and not think about what was going on in the wider world. There had been no word from Matt and she was determined not to think about him either. Obviously she had been wrong to pour her heart out in that last letter. If he felt the same he would have written back straight away. It had been nearly two months and, despite the fact that letters sometimes took weeks to reach them, she would surely have heard by now.

She typed steadily for an hour, managing successfully to put her worries behind her. She was interrupted by Mr Allen who came in with a pile of proofs to be checked.

"Any chance of a cuppa?" he asked.

Celia, glad of a break, stood up and stretched. "I'll put the kettle on," she said.

"Have you heard the news?" he asked.

Celia nodded. "Ray had the wireless on earlier."

"Another botched job," said Mr Allen. "Still, the Americans seem to be making progress in France." He paused. "Any news of that young man of yours?" he asked.

"Not lately," Celia replied.

"Don't worry. It's chaos over there in Europe. You can't expect letters to get through. The krauts have got more on their minds these days than posting prisoners' letters."

Celia smiled, a little comforted by her boss's positive manner. She made the tea and took it in to him, together with the last of the biscuits.

She resumed her typing, becoming so engrossed that she did not hear the outer door open. Someone coughed and she looked up and said, "Can I help you?" before she realized who was standing there.

Ed grinned, leaning on his stick. "I believe you can, miss," he said. "I'm looking for a nice young lady to take to lunch."

Celia laughed. "What about Joyce — she's a nice young lady," she teased.

"She's busy up in the top field with Dad. I offered to help, but Dad gave me that look of his. You know, the one that says, 'what can a helpless cripple do?' So I hitched a lift on the milk lorry and came into town."

"Oh, Ed. Don't let him get to you. He's really pleased you're home safe. It's just — he's never been able to show his feelings, you know that."

Ed shrugged. "Maybe. Anyway, let's go over to the White Swan. George will make us some sandwiches. I need to talk to you."

"I'll just tell Mr Allen I'm popping out." Celia grabbed her handbag and put her head round the boss's door.

He looked up absently from the newspaper he was reading. "Just off? Take your time over lunch. Things are quiet at the moment, but I'll need you to stay late."

In the pub Celia couldn't help remembering the last time she'd been in there. Then she'd been furious with her brother for causing the rift between her and Matt, furious with Matt too. But that was all in the past now. She was just happy to have Ed back. And if Matt was safe too, she would be content. Those two were the most important people in her life now.

Ed joined her at the table, plonking down two glasses of cider. "Best he can do," he said, raising his glass to George behind the bar. "His wife's making us some sandwiches — corned beef." He pulled a face and Celia laughed.

"Lucky to get that," she said. "Now, what did you want to talk to me about?" She hoped he wasn't going to start moaning about their father. She was getting fed up with trying to be the peacemaker.

What he had to say didn't come as a complete surprise however. Ever since she'd visited him in hospital after the amputation of his leg she had sensed a change in him. He no longer spoke about getting back to Metworth and flying. She had also noticed how he was trying to do more around the farm despite their father's dismissive attitude to his attempts.

"You really mean you want to give up the RAF and work on the farm?" she said.

"I had time to do a lot of thinking while I lay in that hospital bed," he said. "Before that too." He took a swig from his glass and was quiet for a moment.

Celia concentrated on her sandwich, unwilling to break into his thoughts. He would confide in her when he was ready.

"You know, Cee. I really love flying and being part of the crew. When we were off duty we had a lot of laughs and then, in the air, working together as a team." He paused. "It was great — until that time . . ." His voice faltered, then he pulled himself together.

Celia put her hand on his arm, but he shook her off. "I've had time to think about that too," he said. "Matt was right. I was doing my job the best I knew how in difficult conditions. It was wrong of me to let my personal feelings get the better of me. I still feel bad about what we were doing, but I accept now that we had no choice."

"I think Matt sympathized. But he was worried about morale and he didn't want you to get in trouble either." Celia sighed. "Anyway, you're out of it now."

"Not quite. That's what I came to tell you. My convalescence is over. I've had orders to report back to Metworth — today."

"You mean — you'll be flying again?"

Ed gave a wry laugh. "No chance. It'll be a desk job for me. Still, it's only till the end of the war. I think I'll be able to stick it out."

"And then you'll come home — work with Dad?"

"If he'll let me."

"Of course he will. It's what he's always wanted. When you've shown him you can manage, he'll be so proud of you."

Ed didn't reply, picking up his glass and draining it. He went up to the bar and asked George for a refill.

Celia sighed. She hoped he wasn't going to start drinking again. But when he came back to the table he grinned and raised his glass. "Here's to young farmer Raines," he said.

"Is that what you really want?"

Ed nodded. "I told you, I've been thinking about it for quite a while. Even before this happened . . ." He tapped his false leg. "I'd be flying over France or Holland and see all those little farms scattered around, people trying to live their lives the way they have for hundreds of years — just like us up at High Trees. It made me realize something. I felt homesick." He gazed earnestly into Celia's eyes. "Oh, I know I said I hated life on the farm but that was partly Dad's doing. He knew how I felt about the animals but he always called me a sissy. I'm still squeamish but I can deal with that now though. I've had to deal with far worse these past few years."

"Are you sure, Ed?"

"Not really." He gave that embarrassed laugh again. "Anyway, since I've been home I've seen how things have changed. We've only got a few cows now, and a smaller flock. Most of the farm's been turned over to arable due to the war . . ."

"But Dad hates it. He'll want to go back to dairy farming as soon as there's a let-up in all these ministry regulations."

"We'll see." There was a determined glint in Ed's eye. He finished his drink and stood up. "Better let you get back to work, I suppose. And I've got a train to catch."

He retrieved his kitbag from behind the bar, shook hands with the landlord and went out into the square. Celia followed him and they crossed the road to the *Advertiser* office. Before she went in she said, "This change of heart wouldn't have anything to do with a certain land girl would it?"

Ed's face reddened. "It might do," he said.

Celia hesitated. Did he know about Bob? Her brother seemed to sense her thoughts.

"Don't worry — Joyce and I have had a long talk. She said that even if her fiancé comes back it's all over between them. But I think she's really accepted that he won't be coming home. She's ready to accept me, but we've agreed to wait."

Celia kissed his cheek. "I'm pleased for you." She put her arms round him and hugged him tight, then pushed him away. "Now go and catch that train," she said.

Back in the office she remained deep in thought. The thought of Stella had her wondering what the other girl's reaction would be. It would certainly make waves and put her schemes in jeopardy — that's if she really was making a play for Dad and the farm. And what about Dad? Would he accept that Ed was finally ready to take his place on the farm — and that he was quite capable of doing so despite having only one leg?

Matt crouched at the edge of the wood looking down at the railway embankment. In the distance he could hear the rumble of the approaching train. "Hurry up," he whispered. "Come on."

He and Ginger ran up the embankment, but they were too late. The train picked up speed and passed them by. He threw himself down in the undergrowth beside Ginger, wondering what had happened to Clive and the others. They had split up after getting out of the camp and he and Ginger had been on the run for weeks.

When the news of the allied landings had reached them in the prison camp, a wave of euphoria swept over the camp. They were sure they'd be freed before long. But as the days passed they began to realize that the Germans would not give in without a determined fight. Escape plans resumed with renewed enthusiasm.

Their original plan had been to make for Switzerland but, with the news of the allied invasion, Clive felt it made more sense to try and get to France. They would stand a better chance of getting home if they could meet up with the advancing allies, he said.

The others agreed and their illicit wireless monitored the progress of the invasion while they completed work on the escape tunnel. At last, after several more weeks of frantic digging, Matt, with Ginger, Clive and six others, broke through. They found themselves in a patch of scrubby woodland some distance from the prison. Breathing a sigh of relief that their calculations had proved correct, they hastily crawled away through the trees.

For the next few days they had moved carefully across country, trusting in their forged papers to get them past the German patrols. Their luck held until they reached the French border, but they weren't safe even then.

Enemy activity was all around them, patrols more vigilant since the allied invasion. Their fears of being caught increased with each mile they travelled and they had decided to split up into twos.

They were sure the Allies must now be forging their way inland. "If we keep going north west, we'll meet up with them soon," Matt said.

They had stumbled on through the woods until, exhausted, they sought refuge in a remote farmhouse. They decided to rest there and had stayed put for three days, surviving on the raw swedes and turnips which were stored in the barn. As they listened to the boom and rattle of heavy artillery in the distance and the rumble of tanks passing on the road two fields away, they had no way of knowing whether it was the enemy or the Allies coming closer.

"We can't stay here," Matt said. "We must find some proper food. Come on, Ginge. Let's get of here," he said.

They had made their way cautiously west, walking by night and hiding during the day, telling themselves that surely they would come upon allied troops eventually. When they neared the railway line they had decided to try to board a passing train.

Now they cowered in the undergrowth as a voice rang out and they crawled reluctantly out of the bushes with their hands up. A grin spread over Matt's face as he realized they were being addressed in French.

It took them some time to convince their rescuers that they were all on the same side; they had then been invited to tag along with the resistance group until they could be handed over to the allies whom they were told were making steady progress towards Paris.

"You'll soon be home," the leader, Raoul, said.

Matt wondered how soon, "soon" would be. He fingered Celia's last letter which he kept in an inside pocket. She had poured her heart out to him, but he hadn't had a chance to write back in the same vein. He just hoped she wouldn't think he didn't care. He vowed that once back in England, after first reassuring his parents of his safety, he would be on his motorbike and down to Sussex before he did anything else.

CHAPTER
TWENTY-FOUR

It was a very hot day and Celia had the back door and windows open to let out some of the steam created by the bubbling pot on the range. She was listening to the wireless while she worked.

After the wet and windy summer, which had ruined most of the wheat, everyone else was out in the fields trying to retrieve what they could. The top of the Downs, where once sheep had grazed, had been sown with wheat, much against Larry Raines's will. Earlier in the day Celia had climbed the steep track intending to offer help but they didn't need her up on the hills and she had decided to go home and make some jam. Despite the bad weather there had been a good crop of plums from the old tree.

Halfway through the morning Joyce came in, sniffing the air appreciatively. "Smells good," she said.

"Don't know if it's going to taste good though. Not enough sugar. I can't get it to set." Celia dipped a ladle into the pan and dropped a little on to a cold plate. "See, it's not right."

"Well, you can't waste it," Joyce said. "Just hope for the best."

Celia couldn't help smiling at Joyce's carefree attitude. "Perhaps you're right. Besides, I can't stand here stirring all day. There're all those tomatoes to bottle yet."

"Rather you than me. It's too hot. I only came in for a drink." She poured herself a glass of water and drained it in one gulp. She filled the water bottle and said, "Better get back to the others."

As she turned away, Celia said, "How's Ed? I never hear from him now he's started writing to you."

"He's fine — says he can't wait to be discharged and get back here. But actually he's loving his new job. He says he didn't realize he had it in him to be a teacher."

"He was dreading they'd put him in an office. But this is different — he's a brilliant navigator and it's good he's passing on his skills to the new recruits."

"Let's hope it won't be for much longer though," Joyce said. "What's the latest news?" She nodded towards the wireless which was now playing some lively music.

Celia glanced at the clock. "There'll be another bulletin in half an hour."

"Can't hang about for that," Joyce said.

Celia returned to her jam-making, her thoughts sombre. The previous day there had been news of a vast explosion in London. It was far worse than the doodlebugs. The official story was that a gas main had exploded, but this was the second one within a couple of days so it seemed unlikely that was true.

Russell had come into the office to tell her about it, worried that the rumours he'd heard about a new more devastating weapon were true. On his visit to London a few weeks earlier he'd persuaded Marion to spend some time with him and they had patched up their differences. He had come home beaming with the news that when she finished filming she would come home. With this new worry about her safety, he had taken the train to London that morning to make sure she was all right.

Celia prayed he was worrying about nothing. She was pleased that her old friends were getting together again. It seemed that everyone was happier these days, more light-hearted now that the end of the war seemed in sight and they could start thinking about the future.

But what about her future, she wondered. Still no word from Matt. Was he all right, or was it that he just didn't want to continue their friendship now that she had revealed her love for him? Had he only wanted someone to write to? She couldn't really believe that — not after that wonderful afternoon by the sea, the tender kiss in the alley beside the works.

But then there had been that awful argument, her angry words and his hasty departure without saying goodbye. Despite resuming their correspondence, Celia still wasn't sure how Matt really felt. It was so hard to tell from a letter. If only they had been able to meet again, to talk about their true feelings before he had gone off on that fateful mission. And now . . .?

Celia gave the jam a last stir and removed the pan from the stove. She turned the wireless up and sang along with *Music While You Work*, trying not to think about Matt. She should be thinking about what she was doing and how she could use it in her next newspaper column, but deep inside she knew she would never forget him and she prayed that he was safe.

True to his promise, Raoul had led Matt and Ginger to a safe house on the outskirts of Rouen. It took several days of hiding in ditches and woodland as they made their way through the German lines. Most of the traffic was going south and Raoul whispered that the enemy must be on the run — in this part of France at least.

Cooped up in the tiny cottage, Matt wished he could go outside for some air. The August heat was becoming unbearable, but they did not dare to open a window for fear of someone hearing the wireless and betraying them.

For days they had been hoping for news of the allied progress. Now, something seemed to be happening and they crouched tensely over the set.

Matt's French wasn't very good, but he sensed from the announcer's tone that there had been an exciting development. Raoul and his friends broke into excited chatter and began shaking hands, kissing each other's cheeks and hugging.

"What is it, Matt?" Ginger asked. "Are the allies here?"

"Didn't you hear, *mon ami?* Paris is liberated. We can all go home."

"Do you mean the war's over?" Matt asked.

Raoul sobered immediately. "No, I don't think it's quite over yet, *mon ami.*" He crouched by the wireless again. "We must wait for more news."

A knock came at the door and one of the Frenchmen opened it cautiously.

"Come in Pierre," Raoul said.

"You heard the news?" the man asked, holding his hand up for silence as they clamoured round him. "Paris may be liberated, but there is still fighting. There are German patrols nearby so you must keep these two hidden," he said, nodding towards Matt and Ginger.

The rest of the day passed almost in silence, no one wishing to speculate on what the news meant for them. Pierre and Raoul took turns to keep watch at the window while the others sat at the table and tried to concentrate on a game of cards.

It was time for the next news bulletin and they listened tensely, hoping that the allies were nearing Rouen. Suddenly Raoul switched the wireless off and stood up, holding up his hand for silence. Outside came the rumble of tanks. Matt crept to the window, pulling the curtain aside.

"Quiet," Raoul warned. "You'd better get down to the cellar — just in case."

"No." Matt's voice rose, high-pitched with excitement. "They're American."

Ginger rushed to the window, pushing him aside. "He's right. It's them — it really is. Thank God."

He grabbed Matt's arms and whirled him round in an impromptu dance, then followed Raoul and the others outside where doors were opening, voices raised in welcome. Behind the tanks marched a column of weary men who soon perked up when a group of young women appeared blowing kisses and throwing flowers.

A jeep carrying several officers appeared round the bend and Matt stepped into the road. It stopped and one of the officers got down. "What's the trouble, man?"

"No trouble, sir. I'm English and, by Jove, am I pleased to see you!"

"English you say — well now, let's see." He walked over to the group, holding his pistol loosely at his side. "Didn't think you fellers had made it this far." He peered at Matt suspiciously, gesturing with his gun. "ID? Discs? Papers?"

"Sorry, no papers," Matt said, shrugging off his coat, to reveal his RAF jacket.

The American relaxed somewhat. "Where did you spring from then?"

Their French friends had been swallowed up by the crowd, leaving Matt and Ginger to explain that they were escapees and had been on the run for several weeks.

"Hold it, buddy. Better get you to HQ, talk to my superiors." Still suspicious, the officer detailed two men to escort them to the half-ruined church on the other side of the town where the Americans had set up their headquarters.

After several hours of questioning by an intelligence officer, the American was satisfied with their story. He leaned back in his chair and grinned. "Sorry we had to put you through that," he said. "You wouldn't believe some of the tall stories we've heard in the past few weeks."

"What are our chances of getting back to England?" Matt asked.

"We'll get you boys home, don't worry. Might take some time to arrange. Meantime, why don't you go over to the mess and get some chow?"

"Sounds like a good idea. What do you say, Ginge?"

Ginger nodded enthusiastically and they followed their escort to the large tent behind the church which had been set up as a mess.

The smell of cooking had Matt's stomach rumbling and he grinned at Ginger. "We seem to have fallen on our feet at last," he said.

They sat down at the long table and dug into the best meal they'd eaten in a long time. After clearing his plate, Matt yawned and stretched.

The sergeant sitting opposite him stood up. "Come on, buddy. Looks like you're both ready for bed," he said.

They were taken to a partially-bombed house and left to get on with it. Ginger threw himself down on the bunk and said, "Better than the prison camp, eh, Matt?"

Matt nodded and lay down. He closed his eyes, revelling in the luxury of not having to stay alert for enemy patrols. But despite his exhaustion, he couldn't sleep. He took the now battered and creased snapshot of Celia from his pocket and gazed at it. In a few days at most he would be home, bowling along the country lanes on his motorbike on the way to High Trees Farm. His eyes closed and the photo slipped from his fingers. His last thought before he slept was the hope that the mechanics had kept the old bike running and that he'd be able to snaffle enough petrol for the journey to Sussex.

CHAPTER
TWENTY-FIVE

It was the middle of December, a year since Matt had been captured. After the first few letters, there had been no more word and Celia was now really worried. Bill the postman had just been bringing a handful of bills and a letter for Joyce. Celia looked on enviously as she ripped open the envelope from Ed, trying not to feel jealous as her friend avidly devoured the contents.

"You mustn't give up hope," Joyce said as Celia got her bicycle out of the shed. "Anything could have happened to stop him writing."

"That's what worries me," Celia replied. "What if he's been killed or injured trying to escape?"

Joyce took her hand. "Don't get yourself in a state. You listen to the news every night. Anything could be happening over there. I know we all thought it would be over soon, but the Nazis aren't giving in without a fight. Perhaps the POWs have been moved to another camp."

Celia acknowledged the truth of her friend's words, but if anything she was more worried. But she forced a smile and said, "What does Ed have to say?"

"Nothing much," Joyce said, but her flushed cheeks and sparkling eyes belied her casual remark.

"I'll leave you to it then. Don't want to be late for work." Celia wheeled her bicycle through the gate and set off into town accompanied by gloomy thoughts about the progress of the war and the chances of her ever being reunited with Matt.

Joyce was right, she thought. Things weren't going as well as everyone had hoped after the D-day landings. Spirits had been high at first. Surely the war would be over soon. But as the months wore on, despite the liberation of Paris and Brussels, there had been setbacks too and it seemed that there were still many battles ahead.

Celia could only be grateful that at least one of the men in her life was safe and seemed to be a lot happier these days. Joyce was the best thing that could have happened to him and Celia could picture them settling down at High Trees once Ed was discharged from the RAF.

She liked Joyce, who'd always made the best of things, cheering them all up with her mischievous laughter despite sometimes being exhausted from the long hours of farm work. She was the perfect antidote to Stella.

But, as Joyce had remarked earlier, the other girl seemed to have stopped sucking up to her father. At one time she had thought she might end up having a stepmother the same age as herself. She thought Stella's change of heart had been brought about since Ed's convalescent leave. Perhaps she realized that with him coming home after the war, especially if he and Joyce got together, there would be no place for her. The other day Celia had seen the annoyance on her face when she made a suggestion about the farm and Larry had replied, "We'll think about that when Ed comes home."

As she pedalled over the bridge and into the square, Celia stopped worrying about her family and their problems. She wasn't looking forward to work today. Mr Allen had been badgering her for her column, but she was completely out of ideas.

"Have you done it yet?" he asked, the moment she walked into the office.

She shook her head. "I'm sorry Mr Allen. I just can't think of anything new to say that I haven't said before."

"But we go to press tomorrow. Please, Celia, try. You know how popular your column is. I can't bring out the paper without it."

Despite being flattered by his faith in her, she thought he was exaggerating. Whatever she wrote would make no difference to the progress of the war and, besides, people had more to think about than silly stories and re-hashed recipes. She tried to convey her feelings to her boss, but he just smiled and said, "I know you can do it, Celia. Leave your other work and just put your thinking cap on."

"All right. I'll do my best," she said reluctantly, sitting at her desk and taking the cover off her typewriter.

"Have it on my desk by lunchtime," he said and returned to his own office.

She groaned and put her head in her hands. He really was expecting too much of her, she thought. How could she write cheerfully about Christmas when all her thoughts were with Matt?

After a few minutes she sighed, pulled a notepad towards her and began jotting down random thoughts. But it was no good. She just couldn't come up with anything original. Then she had an idea. It was a bit naughty, she thought, but it might get the boss off her back. She went to the cupboard under the stairs and began to rummage among the old newspapers stored there. "That's it," she said triumphantly, pulling last year's Christmas edition of the *Advertiser* from the pile.

Back in her office she turned to the page which featured the *Countrywoman* and read through it quickly. With a bit of creative editing she decided she would be able to re-write it and make it sound new. Surely Mr Allen wouldn't remember what she'd written a year ago. There was a recipe too which she could amend slightly. Smiling, she rolled a sheet of paper into the machine and began to type.

It was a few minutes before the lunch break by the time she had finished — just time for a quick read-through before she took it through to Mr Allen. He smiled and looked at her over his glasses. "There, I knew you could do it," he said.

Celia stood holding her breath as he read the typescript, only relaxing when he looked up and said, "Very good — quite up to your usual standard. I don't know what you were so worried about, my dear."

Thankful that he didn't seem to realize she had merely written a re-hash of the previous year's Christmas column, she said, "With rationing getting

307

worse than ever, I'm finding it hard to dream up tasty recipes. People want something special for Christmas and there's nothing in the shops." She sighed. "And how can I write these cheerful little stories with what's going on over there? We thought it would all be over by now and here we are — yet another Christmas at war."

Mr Allen nodded sombrely. "No news of your young man yet?"

"He wrote from the prison camp, but I haven't had a letter for ages."

"I'm sure there's an explanation. I heard that as our chaps are moving eastwards, prisoners are being moved to camps further away. Maybe that's it."

"Perhaps you're right. Joyce said something similar." She was about to return to her office when she realized that her boss wasn't his usual self. She had been so wrapped up in her own troubles that she hadn't noticed before. The strains of the long war were beginning to tell on everybody. "Are you all right, Mr Allen?" she asked.

He took his glasses off and rubbed his eyes. "I'm worried about my daughter-in-law — these new flying bombs in London — they're even worse than the doodlebugs." He shook his head. "Let's hope Russell can bring her home now."

Celia hadn't given a thought to the boss's son this morning. Since his reconciliation with Marion she was only relieved that he had stopped bothering her and she didn't miss his coming into the office for a so-called friendly chat. "Has he gone to London then?" she asked.

"After hearing about the latest big explosion on the news last night, he decided to drag her back by force if necessary." Mr Allen gave a tired smile. "You know how impulsive he is. He was all for jumping in the van and dashing off straight away. I persuaded him to wait until it was light at least and he left first thing this morning."

Celia couldn't help smiling at the thought of the glamorous Marion travelling in the grubby old works van. "Let's hope he's successful," she said.

The short winter afternoon was drawing to a close and Celia had left her desk to fix the blackout blind over the front window when she heard the van pull up outside. So Russell was back. But was his wife with him? She peered through the window into the gloom, a smile breaking over her face as Russell went round to open the passenger door. She called through to the back office, "Mr Allen — they're back."

Then she rushed outside and greeted her friends.

Marion gave her a hug. "It's good to see you, Cee. Still keeping the office afloat then?" They all went inside and there was a flurry of hugs and handshakes.

Relief had wiped the tiredness from Mr Allen's face and he beamed at his daughter-in-law. "Good to have you back, my dear," he said.

"Let's go over to the Swan. We need to celebrate," Russell cried.

Celia could tell that Marion didn't want to go and she said, "I think your wife wants you to herself for a while, Russ. Besides, I have to get home. It's my turn to cook and I don't like to let them down."

"Celia's right," Mr Allen said. "Take Marion home and spend some time together. I need to clear up here. Plenty of time for a celebration later."

Russell tried to insist. He was always up for a party. But Celia was pleased when Marion took his arm and said, "Let's go home, dear. We need to talk."

He didn't protest and they went off together leaving Celia to tidy the office and lock up. As she mounted her bicycle and began the long cold ride up the hill out of town her gloomy thoughts of the morning returned. Of course she was pleased that Mr Allen was satisfied with her work, which he had often told her was as important to the war effort as that of the land girls and munitions workers. And she was delighted to see Russell's obvious happiness at being reunited with his wife.

But the niggling thought persisted. What about me? What would happen to her if Matt didn't return? Would she have to carry on working at the Downland Press for ever, perhaps living in a lonely bedsit in town? She couldn't imagine staying at the farm if Ed and Joyce married. Although she would welcome her friend as a sister-in-law, she had been the home-maker at High Trees for so long that it would be hard to see another woman taking over.

She cycled along in the dark, peering down at the tiny glimmer of light from the shaded bicycle lamp reflected on the uneven lane. The front wheel caught a stone and made her wobble. She should snap out of it and concentrate on getting home in one piece, she told herself. She turned in at the farm gate and dismounted, leaning her bicycle against the barn wall. Hearing a murmur of voices coming from inside, she pushed the door open.

The land girls were forking hay down from the loft to feed the cows, which had been brought in from the milking shed. Celia was about to greet them when Stella threw down her pitchfork and put her hands on her hips, eyes blazing.

"You don't know what you're talking about. Anyway, it's all right for you, you've got your man. Fallen on your feet, haven't you?"

"Look, Stella. I didn't mean to upset you. I just asked what you were going to do when the war's over. You seem to have taken to farming — you could get a job anywhere on the land."

Celia shrank back. She didn't want to eavesdrop, but neither did she want to draw attention to her presence. To her surprise, Stella burst into tears and she peeped round the door to see Joyce putting her arms round the other girl and murmuring apologies.

After a moment, Stella wiped her eyes. "I don't know what came over me," she said in a shaky voice.

"Is it Mr Raines — Larry?" Joyce asked.

Celia held her breath.

Stella shook her head. "Not really. I'm fond of him and if things had been different I could see myself staying here after the war. But I see now it wouldn't have worked out. I was just kidding myself. I'll probably go back to my old job — they said they'd keep it open for me."

"But didn't you leave there because of — what's-his-name — your boss?"

"He's married — that's why I left. But I still love him. I thought Larry would help me forget him but . . ." She sniffed and pushed Joyce away, the moment of intimacy as if it had never been. "It's not your problem, is it? As I said, you'll be all right." With a brittle smile she picked up the fork and began pulling down the hay bales once more.

Celia crept away and entered the farmhouse. The little scene had explained a lot about Stella and she even felt a little sorry for her. But it wouldn't do to let the other girl know what she had overheard.

Matt was becoming increasingly frustrated. He was anxious to get back to Celia, to reassure her that he was all right and that he would soon be home. Not only that, he felt useless sitting around here while the Yanks were fighting on and pushing the Germans back. He wanted to be back with his squadron, doing his bit to end the war.

"I thought we'd be back by now. What exactly does ASAP mean?" he grumbled to Ginger.

"What it says, I suppose." Ginger sipped the mug of fragrant coffee and grinned. "I'm just as keen to get back, but I'm not looking forward to canteen grub and all the shortages at home. These yanks certainly know how to look after themselves."

These past few days of good food and rest had restored them to their previous fitness, but that only added to Matt's restlessness. He stood up, banging down his coffee mug. "I'm going to find that major — see if there's any news."

He went outside just as a jeep pulled up outside the mess tent.

"Ah, Dangerfield. I was just coming to find you. Fetch your buddy. You're to come along to HQ. They've laid on transport for you."

Matt's face split in a huge grin and he rushed back inside shouting to Ginger. "Come on, mate. We're going home."

As they scrambled into the back of the jeep and set off along the bumpy road north, the major turned and said, "Guess you fellas can't wait to get back to your girls, eh?"

Ginger punched Matt's arm. "Not me — him," he said. "I was doing all right with the ma'mselles."

Just at that moment there was a flash and a loud bang. Matt was thrown in the air and landed at the side of the road. Dazed, he raised his head and saw Ginger lying a few feet away. There was no sign of the major and his driver. Matt tried to stand but his legs gave way and he fell, his ears ringing from the explosion. Then the world went dark.

CHAPTER
TWENTY-SIX

Celia wiped a hand across her face leaving a smudge of flour on her forehead. She was trying to make mince pies, but the pastry wasn't turning out quite right. Not enough fat. Oh well, it would have to do, she thought with a sigh. They were lucky to get mince pies at all. At least the mince looked all right. She had made her own, using one of her mother's old recipes. She just hoped no one would ask her what she'd put in it.

She glanced round at the familiar old kitchen and smiled at the makeshift decorations. She and Joyce had spent the past few evenings making them out of old cut-up magazines. Sprigs of holly cut from the hedgerow were strewn along the mantelpiece and Celia had added a piece of red ribbon which she'd found in the sewing box. Stella had stayed aloof from the activity, saying she was far too busy for such nonsense but Celia and Joyce had wanted to make the place look as festive as possible for Ed. He had managed to get two days leave and would be home on Christmas Eve. Both girls were excited at the thought of him being here although he would have to leave early on Boxing Day to get back to camp on time.

If only Matt could be here too Celia's happiness would be complete. But there had still been no word. To try and dispel her gloomy thoughts, she switched on the wireless and twiddled the knobs, trying to find some music. But the relentlessly cheerful Christmas songs only fuelled her depression. She switched the wireless off and picked up her rolling pin once more.

She had put the pies in the oven and was clearing up the mess she'd made when a knock came at the door. Wiping her hands on a tea towel, she hurried to open it.

"Miss Raines?" said the young lad, holding out the instantly recognizable buff envelope. Her legs felt weak and she grasped the door frame while holding out her trembling other hand.

"Any reply, miss?"

She shook her head and went inside, sinking into her father's chair by the range and staring at the unopened envelope. It must be news of Matt — bad news. Her stomach churned and she felt cold all over.

She was still sitting there when the door opened and the girls came in.

"What's that smell? Something's burning," Stella said loudly. "Celia, what have you been up to?"

Celia came out of her reverie and looked up. "I've got a telegram," she said.

Joyce came over to her and grasped her hands. "Is it Matt?" she asked softly, taking the envelope from Celia's unresisting fingers. "Shall I see what it says?"

Stella pushed past her and opened the oven door letting out a cloud of smoke and steam. "Totally ruined," she said, taking the tin out and dumping it in the sink.

"What's all the commotion?" Larry asked, entering the kitchen behind them.

"Celia's burnt the pies," Stella said.

Joyce rounded on her. "Can't you see she's had a shock?" She waved the telegram under the other girl's nose.

"Is it Ed?" Larry asked. "Is my boy all right?"

"We don't know — she hasn't opened it yet," Joyce said. "Perhaps it's just to say Ed can't get here for Christmas Day." She patted Celia's shoulder. "You're probably worrying over nothing." She tore open the envelope, her face paling as she took in the contents.

"Is it Matt . . .?"

Joyce nodded. "He's been wounded."

"But he's in a prison camp — how could he be wounded?"

"Don't ask me. It just says he's been wounded and is in hospital in Dover."

Celia jumped up and snatched the telegram. "I must go to him," she said.

"Calm down, Cee," Larry said. "What's all the fuss about?"

"It's Matt. He's hurt."

"Oh, that chap you've been writing to. But, Cee, you can't go rushing off to Dover."

"I must, Dad. I told you. He's more than just a pen-friend."

Stella had been silent for a while but now she chipped in. "There's no dinner ready and we've got to see to the animals before it gets dark. And your father's right — you can't just rush off."

"Getting your dinner ready is the last thing on my mind right now. Why don't you do it?" Celia's voice choked. How could she be expected to think of food at a time like this?

Joyce said soothingly, "Let's try to find out more before you go? It's a long journey and you might not be allowed to see him when you do get there."

"You're probably right." Celia's shoulders slumped.

Joyce turned to Stella. "Come on, let's heat up some soup and do some sandwiches. That'll keep us going until this evening."

Reluctantly, Stella began to cut slices of bread while Joyce heated some soup.

Celia seemed frozen in place, clutching the telegram and scarcely noticing the activity around her. When the meal was ready Joyce persuaded her to sit at the table with them, but she couldn't eat. How had Matt ended up in an English hospital when the last she'd heard he had been a prisoner of war in Germany? And how badly was he hurt? She thought about her brother and what he had gone through. She couldn't bear the thought of something like that happening to Matt.

She stood up abruptly, pushing her chair back with a screech on the tiles. "I'm going to phone Mr Allen. He'll know who to get in touch with."

"He won't thank you for disturbing his Sunday dinner," Stella said.

"I don't care — I must do something," Celia replied.

"Why don't you wait till Ed gets here? Perhaps he'll have heard something," Joyce said. "I'm sure they would have let someone at Metworth know."

"I can't wait that long." Celia went over to the phone and dialled the *Advertiser* number. There was an extension which connected to her boss's flat above the office, but it just rang and rang.

Eventually she gave up and plonked herself down on a chair. She put her head in her hands. She just didn't know what to do next.

Stella finished eating and started noisily clearing the table. "Come on, Joyce," she said. "Some of us have work to do."

"Do you have to be so bossy?" Joyce snapped. She touched Celia's arm. "I'm sorry, but Stella's right. We must get on. It'll be dark soon. Why don't you try phoning Metworth? Even if they can't tell you anything, they might let you talk to Ed. He'll know what to do."

"It's worth a try, I suppose. Thanks, Joyce." She managed a smile.

Larry had hardly spoken a word while they ate and now he went to get his boots from the back porch before following the girls outside. He hesitated in the doorway and then came over to where Celia sat. "I'm sorry, lass. I didn't know this young man meant so much to you. I'm sure he'll be all right." He gave an embarrassed cough and continued, "At least you know now where he is."

"You do understand, Dad? If they'll let me visit, I'll go down to Dover like a shot. The girls will just have to manage Christmas dinner."

"Don't worry about that. You do what you think's best." He patted her shoulder awkwardly, the only gesture of affection he seemed capable of, and hurried outside.

Celia knew the number of the Metworth airbase by heart. How many times had she hesitated by the phone wanting to ask for news of Matt? But she knew that telephone calls from civilians, especially personal calls, were not welcome in wartime. This was different though, she told herself, picking up the phone.

It took nearly an hour to get through and then she was kept hanging on for several minutes before someone could be found who was willing to talk to her.

She explained whom she was enquiring about, but the reply was not very helpful. "Are you a relative?" she was asked. "I can only give information to a next of kin."

"Please, you must know something," she pleaded. "Look, my brother is on the staff at Metworth. Could I speak to him?"

The clerk, or whoever he was, kept her waiting so long that she thought she'd been cut off. She was about to put the phone down when another voice spoke.

"Ed — is that you? Oh, Ed, thank God." She was almost incoherent as she told him about the telegram and several times he had to ask her to slow down so that he could understand what she was saying.

"Don't get so excited, sis," he said. "I'll try to find out where he is and how bad it is. If they'll let you visit, I'll take you down there."

"Thanks, Ed. You will phone and tell me, won't you — whatever they say?"

He promised and rang off.

Celia couldn't settle to anything as the afternoon dragged on and there was no phone call from Ed. Should she try phoning again? And she ought to get in touch with Mr Allen and ask for the day off. There wouldn't be much to do in the office on Christmas Eve anyway, she thought.

She glanced at the clock, realizing that her father and the girls would soon be coming in for their supper. She still didn't feel like eating herself, but she ought to get a meal ready for them. Perhaps keeping busy would take her mind off things.

They had cleared away and settled down to listen to the wireless news before Joyce went back to the Robsons' for the night when the phone rang. Although she'd been listening for it, the shrill ring made Celia jump. She leapt out of her chair, letting her knitting trail on the floor, and grabbed the receiver.

"Ed, what have you found out?" There followed a lot of nodding and smiling before she said, "I'll be there." She thanked him and put the phone down.

"Well? Come on, tell us," Joyce said impatiently.

Celia sat down. "Ed couldn't tell me the whole story, but it seems Matt had escaped from the prison camp. I don't know how he got hurt, but the Americans helped him to get back to England. Not sure how bad it is, at least he's alive though."

"And they're going to let you see him?" Joyce asked.

"We hope so. Ed's going to meet me in London and we'll go down to Dover by train."

Celia got off the train the next day after a frustrating journey wondering how on earth she was going to find her brother. The concourse was crowded with men and women in uniform but, as she handed in her ticket, she heard her name called.

Ed was standing just the other side of the barrier and she would hardly have recognized him if it hadn't been for the fact that he was leaning heavily on a walking stick. He was looking so much better than when she'd seen him off after his convalescent leave. She had doubted then that he was fit for duty. But she had to admit she'd been wrong. Apart from a slight limp, he was his old self once more.

He gave her a hug and urged her to hurry. "We've got to get right over to the other side of the station. We don't want to miss the connection," he said.

She wanted to ask for news of Matt but he forged his way through the crowd so fast, despite the stick, that she had to run to keep up with him. Was there something he didn't want to tell her? But when they were on the train he smiled and apologized.

"Sorry I had to rush you. But if we'd missed this one we could have waited for hours."

Trying to catch her breath, she shook her head. "It's OK. It's just I've hardly slept for thinking . . ."

"They couldn't tell me much. It was hard enough to find out which hospital he was in." He reached forward and patted her knee. "We'll know soon enough."

There wasn't much else to say other than useless speculation and they were both silent for a few minutes. Celia gazed out of the window at the backs of the terraced houses which seemed to go on forever when Ed spoke.

"I thought Joyce might have come with you," he said.

"She wanted to, but Dad said she was needed on the farm. Anyway, you'll see her later — you are still coming back with me, aren't you?" Celia was suddenly worried that as they'd let him leave camp early, he might have to go back sooner.

"Don't worry — nothing will stop me," Ed said with a grin.

As the train pulled into Dover they became quiet again. Celia was lost in thought, excitement at seeing Matt again warring with concern at how bad his injuries were. She sighed, determined not to let her imagination run away with her.

Outside the station they asked for directions and were told they had to get a bus to the hospital which was on the outskirts of town.

As the grim grey building loomed up in front of them, Celia felt the butterflies start up again in her stomach. She couldn't speak without her voice trembling and she let Ed do the talking.

They followed an orderly down echoing corridors to the ward where Matt was. As he opened the door and pointed out Matt's bed in the far corner, Celia held her breath. Even from here she could see that his head was bandaged and that his right arm was in a sling.

Her feet seemed glued to the floor as memories of the last time they'd been together flooded her brain. They had parted on such bad terms and, although they had been reconciled through their letters, she still wasn't quite sure how to break the ice.

She felt Ed's hand on her back gently urging her forward and she took a few hesitant steps. Matt was sitting up in bed gazing out of the window and at first he didn't seem to realize they were there.

She was almost at his side when he turned and caught sight of her and the smile which lit up his face told her everything she needed to know.

Her own smile matched his and for a few seconds they just gazed at each other.

Ed broke the silence, grasping Matt's left hand. "It's so good to see you."

Matt tore his gaze away from Celia and said. "You too, mate. I can't believe you're alive. I thought you went down with the plane."

"It's a long story, but you don't want to hear it now. I'll leave you and my sister to catch up. I think you've quite a lot to say to each other."

"That we have," Matt said, gazing into Celia's eyes and reaching for her hand.

Ed fetched a chair and Celia sat down without letting go of Matt's hand. She still hadn't spoken, her voice too choked with emotion. Matt waved Ed away saying, "Go and talk to Ginger — he's over there." Then he turned to Celia and the pressure on her hand increased. "Come here. I want to kiss you," he whispered.

"And I want you too," she said, leaning over and touching her lips to his. His good hand came behind her head and pulled her closer and she closed her eyes, revelling in the storm of feelings he had evoked in her.

Suddenly he pushed her away and she blinked in confusion, then smiled as he muttered, "Damn this sling." He struggled to sit up and pulled the sling off.

"No, Matt, you'll hurt yourself," she protested.

"I don't care. I want to hold you properly." His arms came round her and his lips met hers once more. Above the pounding of her heart, she could feel his beating in unison.

As she gave herself up to his embrace she was oblivious to their surroundings until a voice interrupted them.

"What on earth is going on here? I will not have this sort of behaviour on my ward." The sister in charge bore down on them, her face livid. "Flight Lieutenant Dangerfield, replace that sling at once. As for you, miss, if you cannot control yourself, you will have to leave."

Celia's face was scarlet and her embarrassment increased when she saw her brother and his friend grinning at the other end of the ward.

Matt however did not seem at all abashed. "I'm sorry, sister," he said. "This is my fiancée, Miss Celia Raynes. We haven't seen each other for nearly two years so I'm sure you understand . . ." He flashed her a charming smile and she relented.

"Well, in that case she can stay — just for a little while." She leaned over and adjusted his sling. "But please try to behave with a little more restraint."

As she walked away, Matt pulled Celia towards him again. "That will be very difficult," he murmured, his lips against her hair. "Still, perhaps we'd better behave ourselves. We don't want to make the other chaps jealous."

Celia kissed him again and then reluctantly drew away. Mindful that the sister could return at any moment and shoo her out, she asked him what had happened.

A cloud crossed Matt's face. "I've spent the past few months on the run through France. I'll tell you all about it one day," he said. "But I hardly know how I ended up here myself. One minute we were bowling along in a yankee jeep, the next I knew I woke up on board a ship just coming in to Dover harbour." He touched the bandage round his head. "Concussion," he said.

"Oh, my poor Matt," she murmured and bent to kiss him again.

"I was lucky — Ginger too," Matt said. "But I don't want to talk about that." He smoothed her hair back from her face and ran his finger down her cheek. "I can't believe we're together again. It's all I thought about — in the camp, hiding out in the woods . . ." His voice trailed away.

Celia put a hand over his lips. "I'm here now and I'm going to stay. I'm not letting you go again." She sat up straight as she heard footsteps approaching. "I think I'm going to be thrown out, but don't worry, I'll be back."

"I won't be in here long anyway," Matt said. "They can't wait to get rid of me." He frowned. "I'll have to go back to Metworth. The war's not over yet and as soon as I'm fit it'll be back to duty."

As the ward sister approached, Celia stood up. She hesitated then her words came out in a rush. "Matt, you told the nurse I was your fiancée . . ."

"Sorry, jumping the gun a bit, wasn't I?" He grinned and squeezed her hand, then his expression grew solemn. "Celia, will you marry me?"

"Yes, oh yes." She sat on the edge of the bed and threw her arms around him. He struggled to free himself from the sling once more and pulled her more tightly towards him. The kiss seemed to go on forever and would have gone on even longer but for the discreet cough and the tapping of a shoe on the floor.

"When you've quite finished, this man needs his medicine," the ward sister said sternly. But when Celia looked round she discerned a distinct twinkle in the woman's eye and the vestige of a smile.

They left the hospital and Ed returned to Sullington to spend his Christmas at High Trees. But Celia insisted on staying. "Dad will understand," she said. "And I'll telephone Mr Allen and explain."

Ed couldn't dissuade her and she managed to find a room in a boarding house near the seafront. She remained in the town for the next few days, determined to stay with Matt until he was well again.

Visiting hours were restricted, but the sister in charge was sympathetic to the young couple. Using the excuse that the rules could be relaxed as it was Christmas, she allowed Celia to stay well beyond the allotted time.

When Matt was recovered sufficiently to be allowed out of bed, they would sit out on the covered balcony with its views over the town and out to sea, holding hands and talking about the future.

Matt recounted a little of his adventures on the run in occupied France and Celia told him what she had managed to prise out of Ed concerning his bravery and how he had lost his leg.

But mostly their talk was of the future and the phrase "after the war" recurred frequently. Strangely, Celia felt no sadness that High Trees farm, where she had always hoped to end her days, did not figure in those plans for the future.

"I know how you feel about the place, but we can farm anywhere," Matt said.

"What do you mean, 'we'?"

"How do you feel about a smallholding in Devon?" Matt gave a little laugh at her expression. "I don't think I could afford a proper farm."

For answer Celia kissed him, a kiss that went on for quite a long time. When they paused for breath she said, "I truly don't care where I live, as long as I'm with you."

★   ★   ★

The doctor hung his stethoscope around his neck and looked down at Matt. "Well, young man, I don't think we need to keep you here any longer. Your wounds have healed nicely and there seem to be no ill effects from the concussion. A week or so convalescing at home and you'll be fit to return to duty."

"I won't be going home, sir," Matt replied, doing up his pyjama jacket. "I'm going to get married."

"Congratulations." The doctor smiled. "The young lady who's been so devotedly visiting you, I take it?"

"It's all arranged. The hospital chaplain's going to do the honours and my mate Ginger is going to be best man. You're invited of course."

"Well, if I'm free I'd be delighted. When is it to be?"

"Right now," Matt said, gesturing towards the end of the ward.

The door opened and the chaplain entered, followed by Celia on the arm of her father with Ed and Joyce a little behind.

Ed looked smart in his RAF uniform and he had managed to discard his walking stick today. Joyce was wearing her land army uniform, spiced up with a sprig of holly in her hat.

But it was Celia his eyes feasted on. She could not have looked more beautiful if she had been wearing a conventional wedding dress and veil, he thought. Despite the cold she had on a pretty summer dress of sky blue, sprigged with white daisies — the one she had been wearing in the photograph he had carried with him throughout his captivity.

He swallowed the lump in his throat as they came towards him and reached out his hand for hers.

Celia trembled a little as she entered the ward. She knew she was doing the right thing but she still felt a little nervous. It was a big step, marrying someone who in some ways she scarcely knew. But they'd gone through a lot in the past few years and with the war still raging in the far east and Matt's imminent return to duty, who knew how much longer they had? They had to take their happiness while they could.

Her hand tightened on Dad's arm as they walked towards Matt. She was glad he had felt able to leave the farm for this special day.

Then Matt reached out for her hand and she went to him, smiling up at him with eyes full of love as the chaplain began the beautiful words of the marriage service.

Also available in ISIS Large Print:

Full Circle

Roberta Grieve

Although she believes nothing can really come of it, ladies' maid Daisy March is eagerly awaiting the return on leave of naval lieutenant Jack Davenport, the brother of her mistress Georgina. She hopes that this time he will defy his family and declare his love. But before he can do so, she is accused of stealing and summarily dismissed. Daisy takes up nursing, but, to her dismay, Georgina is also among the new recruits. When WWI breaks out, they are posted to Malta, where Daisy hopes to be reunited with Jack. When scandal threatens both girls, they renew their friendship. But tragedy strikes and it seems there will be no happy ending for either of them.

ISBN 978-0-7531-9072-2 (hb)
ISBN 978-0-7531-9073-9 (pb)

Love or Duty

Roberta Grieve

Louise Charlton sees herself as plain and uninteresting beside her vibrant sister Sarah, a talented singer. When she falls in love with young Doctor Andrew Tate she is convinced he is not interested in her. While Sarah sails to America to pursue her musical career, Louise stays at home, duty-bound to care for her selfish manipulative stepmother. Tricked into marrying James, the son of her father's business partner, she tries to forget Andrew and make the best of things. When James reveals his true nature, Louise throws herself into war work to take her mind off her situation. Her life becomes constrained by duty. Then she meets the young doctor again . . . will love win out over duty for Louise?

ISBN 978-0-7531-8940-5 (hb)
ISBN 978-0-7531-8941-2 (pb)